THE SWEETER THE JUICE

Edited By

MARCUS ANTHONY

I0526439

Herndon, VA

Published in the United States by STARbooks Press
PO Box 711612, Herndon, VA 20171

Many thanks to graphic artist John Nail for the cover design. Mr. Nail may be reached at: tojonail@bellsouth.net.

Printed in the United States

STAR books
P R E S S

Herndon, VA

CONTENTS

LUBE JOB
Logan Zachary

I was running late for my night class, and the day at work had dragged on and on. The last thing I needed was a flat tire, but there it was. Driver's side front.

"Fuck."

It wasn't completely flat, but it was almost there.

I was sure I could make it to the gas station and add some air. Time would tell, but I needed to hurry. It was rush hour and getting stuck in traffic would really suck, especially with a flat.

I pulled out of the parking lot and headed down the frontage road. Two blocks down the frontage road was a Quickie Lube.

I did need an oil change, but would they be able to fix my tire? Maybe it only needed air. Hopefully, that was all it needed. The clock on the dashboard clock read 5:10. Class was at 6:30.

I continued down the frontage road toward Quickie Lube. The wheel didn't flop as I picked up speed, but I wasn't going to hit twenty. My car moved forward and didn't pull to the side, so I slowly advanced.

No line of cars waited to get into the oil exchange garage, so I turned into the driveway. A large black man hosed off the parking lot. He looked like the convict in movie *The Green Mile*.

I pulled up to an open stall and waited. The man that stood there had an amazing round and tight ass. His dark blue pants hugged his butt like a second skin. He turned and faced me and smiled.

"Wow!" my heart skipped a beat. He was beautiful, an even smile and dimples, dark skin and a massive chest. His chiseled body sloped to narrow hips and that great ass. Bodybuilder legs held the whole package erect. His nametag read "Stanford."

Stanford dropped the hose and walked into the garage and rounded to the opposite side of the pit. He smiled again and waved me forward. He signaled for me to veer to the right, and I turned the wheel a little bit. He motioned for me to come forward and finally stopped me when he held up his hands.

I turned off the engine and opened the door.

Stanford closed the door in front of me and continued strolling down the line of doors, closing them as he moved down the row. He walked over to the entrance side and did the same for all three doors.

Seth, a tall buzz cut blond called me over to his computer. He asked, "What can we do for you today?"

"I noticed my tire looked pretty flat after work, and I need an oil change, so I figured I'd better stop."

"I saw that when you drove in. We should be able to look into that."

"I have class tonight, and I'm running late."

"We'll have you done in ten minutes," he promised.

"Great. I just put on new wiper blades, so those should be fine." I hoped saying that now would save me a few minutes later on, when they tried to sell me more services and products.

"We'll check your fluids and all the other things on our checklist, and we'll get you on your way as soon as possible. If you want to wait in there, we'll get started." He motioned through a wall of windows to the waiting area. A television played the local news, a coffee pot waited all day, and several mismatched chairs lined the walls.

All the doors were closed, as Stanford pulled out a thick vacuum hose and started cleaning the passenger's side.

I entered the waiting area and looked into the office. A young college boy worked behind the desk. He nodded and stood up. "Brandon" was embroidered in red on his shirt's tag. He wore gray slacks that clung to his body. I saw he wore no underwear and his cock's outline was easily seen, and it was huge. It hung to the left, and the thick mushroom head stood out prominently. The shaft was wide and his balls flopped down the right leg of his pants. The two orbs were bigger than a pair of plums.

I forced my eyes to look up into his eyes.

He brushed his brown hair back and smiled.

My face burned red with embarrassment.

"Hard day?"

"It was long, and it just got longer." My eyes darted down to his crotch, and I felt myself grow harder, too.

His dick seemed to swell also.

I bit my lower lip. "It was busy, but good. I didn't need a flat tire though."

"No one ever does, but we'll get you inflated and hard again."

"If there's a hole in it, are you able to fix it here?"

"We'll take good care of you and get you back on the road in no time."

I walked around the waiting area and checked my cell phone for the time. 5:20. There were no messages, and I flipped my phone shut and slipped it into my pocket.

I took a deep breath and headed over to the window that looked into the garage.

"Do you have big plans for tonight?" Brandon asked.

"I have class down at the U at 6:30."

"You should be out of here in ten minutes."

I wondered if that was their company motto. "I don't want to go to class tonight, but I only have a few left." I looked out at my car.

Seth's blond head looked under the hood, as he checked the fluids and air filter. Stanford finished vacuuming the back seat and moved to the driver's side. Another man worked underneath my car in the pit, but I couldn't see him clearly.

Seth finished under the hood and picked up the air hose. He inflated my front tire, which didn't explode and seemed to hold its air.

My body relaxed as he moved onto the next wheel and checked its pressure.

Brandon walked out into the garage with a clip board in hand and followed behind Seth, checking items on the list as he went. His gray slacks hugged his ass, and his bubble butt was AMAZING!

My cock started to itch and extended to its full length and strained against my underwear. I would love to see Brandon naked. I wondered where he worked out. Wouldn't it be great to shower next to him? I'm glad I didn't work here all day because parts of me would be raw by noon.

Stanford finished vacuuming and spoke with Brandon. He pointed at me and nodded. Stanford entered the waiting area and said, "Sir, could you step out here?"

Now what? A new air filter? A radiator flush? Money, money, money and time ticked by faster and faster. My class …

"Okay," I said, and followed him.

Stanford walked over to a yellow hand rail and started down the stairs. "Please hold onto the railing as you come down here. The steps can get slippery with all the oil around here."

I didn't have time for this, but I descended down the metal stairs and stepped under my car.

A handsome Latino man in coveralls wiped his hands on a rag. He stepped back as I approached. His zipper was halfway down, revealing his bare chest. A dark triangle of black hair poked out. A big bulge proudly protruded in front on him.

Stanford motioned for me to join him. "I'd like to show you something over here."

I couldn't take any more bad news. Moving over to him, I looked under my car. The whole area was flooded with bright lights.

"If you put your hand up here, you'll see what I have." Stanford pointed by my front tire.

I reached up and tried to see where he pointed.

Stanford pulled out a handcuff and slipped it around my wrist and hooked it to a chain.

The Latino man slipped another cuff on my other hand and handed it to Stanford. Diego was on his nametag.

Stanford pulled my arm up over my head and clamped it shut on the chain. "We'd like to offer you the full service today."

Diego pushed a button on a control panel, and I felt my body rise up slightly off the floor. The handcuffs were padded and didn't dig into my wrists, but they held me firmly. My feet swung free in the air.

"Hey, what are you doing?" I shouted.

The volume on the radio in the garage rose, drowning out my voice.

"You can yell, but no one will hear you, and you'll only hurt your throat." Stanford smiled. "Just relax and enjoy."

Diego wheeled a tray on casters to us. A towel covered the tray with various sized bumps lay underneath.

"I have class."

"You'll get there. You may be a little late, but if you help us, you'll be on your way sooner."

"Are you going to steal one of my kidneys?" Fear fell over my body as my legs kicked.

"You're safe, and you won't get hurt."

Seth and Brandon descended the stairs and surrounded me.

Diego pulled the towel off the table. Metal tools covered it, a grease gun, several pliers, and various other tools.

Stanford stepped behind me and wrapped his hands around my waist. He started to unbuckle my belt, and I kicked harder and flopped against him.

Seth grabbed one leg and Diego my other.

Stanford undid my belt and started on my zipper.

My aroused flesh burned under his touch.

He unbuttoned my pants and pulled them down. My captors slipped off my shoes, and they worked my slacks down my legs. My hairy legs kicked for release, but did little good.

Stanford unbuttoned my shirt and rubbed my chest.

My nipples rose into sharp peaks. I could feel precum wet the tip of my cock and soak into my briefs. "You don't want to do this."

"Yes, we do," Stanford said. He massaged my pecs and traced my six-pack with his fingers. He drew lower and lower, circling my belly button and proceeded south. His nails combed through the fine hair that thickened further down. His fingertips ran along the elastic of my underwear and explored.

My erection jumped in my briefs, and precum soaked into the white fabric making it see through. My face flushed with embarrassment.

"Oh, he's shy," Seth said. "We'll fix that." He moved behind me and ran his hand over my ass. He kneaded my glutes through the cotton and ran his hand along my crease.

My ass tightened under his touch.

"He's tight, a nice firm butt. I can't wait to get started." He pinched my cheeks hard and then wrapped his arms around me, giving me a reverse bear hug. His hard-on pressed between my cheeks, spreading them wide.

I could feel how big he was. My eyes darted back to Stanford and saw the huge bulge there, which was growing even bigger. "Help!"

Had they seen a *Lavender Magazine* in my car? Our local gay rag that told of life in the Twin Cities.

Diego unzipped his coveralls, and more of his hairy torso burst out. "Step one, clean." He picked up a hose and adjusted the water temperature. "Perfect."

Seth pulled my underwear down in the back as Diego joined him behind me. "Did you lube the tip?"

"Si," Diego said as he inserted the end between my butt cheeks. He carefully dug around and found my hole. With even pressure, his skillful hand glided the tube inside me. He pushed the release button and water started to fill me.

It was warm and entered with some force. I could feel myself fill and expand.

"We don't want to get his underwear wet, do we?" Stanford's finger dug under the front elastic of my briefs and pulled them lower.

My thick pubic bush emerged.

Stanford licked his fleshy lips and pulled them lower.

My hard cock sprang free and bounced in front of him.

Brandon's eyebrows shot up, and he smiled and nodded.

Stanford worked my underwear off my legs and tossed them onto the pile of my shoes and pants. He moved closer and took my cock into his mouth as my ass filled to bursting. Water started to escape from my butt as Diego stopped filling me. He removed the tube and all the water flooded out. It shot out, releasing the pressure and my body relaxed. The remaining water ran down my legs and swirled down the floor drain.

"One more time," Seth said. "Get him nice and clean."

Diego re-lubed the tip and slipped it in. Water surged in and flooded my bowels.

Stanford swallowed my eight inches. His nose poked into my bush. He inhaled deeply and slowly pulled back.

My cock popped out, and he said, "You taste so fine." He smacked his lips and sucked me back in. My balls swung back and forth, bouncing off his chin.

His stubble pricked at my shaved ball sack. I have low hanging nuts, and they swing like pendulums.

Stanford drew down on my cock like a straw, and I could feel the precum slip out, as water continued to fill my ass. The pressure rose and threatened to explode.

My arms started to hurt, but Brandon pulled a leather sling from under my car and unrolled it across my back. He worked around Diego and pulled one strap and handed it to Stanford. "Hook it up." He grabbed the other one and waited.

Stanford sucked hard on my dick and slowly let it withdraw. His lips pulled along my entire length, and it popped out of his mouth. He smacked his lips and said, "Ahhh." He stepped back with the leather strap and nodded to Brandon. "Ready."

Together, they pulled, and my ass moved forward and up.

Diego pulled the hose out of my ass as it rose up and water sprayed over everyone and flowed down the drain. "*Señor* is ready."

Stanford and Brandon finished hanging the sling, and Brandon's young body stepped between my legs. He pushed them apart. "It's my turn." He stuck out his tongue and waggled it at my butt. His tongue's tip licked across my hole.

I puckered under his rough tongue. My whole ass tightened as I struggled to free myself.

Brandon opened his mouth and covered my hole. He sucked hard as his tongue circled around and around. The tip explored my sphincter and sought entry. Warm and wet, I felt my muscles relax, the sensation felt so good, my ass relaxed, and his tongue slipped in. He tongued me and drove it in deeper and deeper, as the sensation intensified. My legs went weak and stopped fighting. My body accepted the wonderful stimulation.

Seth tapped him on the shoulder. "We all get to play, you know."

Brandon retracted his tongue, licked his lips, and kissed my butt.

Seth picked up the grease gun from the rolling table and approached me. He pulled the trigger, and thick oil oozed out of the tip.

Stanford and Diego pulled my legs apart, opening my wet target for Seth. He pulled the trigger again, and I felt lube cover my tight pucker. He used the pointed end to spread it around and then found my hole. He aimed and fired. Grease shot out as he plunged in to me. The lube filled me and allowed the gun's barrel to slide in easily. Seth inserted the barrel up to the canister and continued to pull the trigger.

I could feel the grease enter and fill me.

On my left, Diego took the vacuum cleaner hose and turned it on. He ran the opening up my leg and watched as the hair swirled up and into the hose. He brought it up my thigh and headed for one of my dangling balls.

I could feel the air being sucked across the smooth orb and intensify as it came closer and closer. A faint suction breezed over my nut.

"No," I prayed, as he held it closer.

My nut started to swing with the rush of air.

Diego held the hose just out of reach.

He wouldn't put it there crossed my mind, as he touched the smooth ball to the opening. The pressure sucked it in and slapped the tube to my leg. Air rushed in as my ball blocked the end, as the tube tried to pull it in.

Seth slid the grease gun out of my ass, and then he pulled another vacuum cleaner's hose down and slowly ran it up my opposite leg. He didn't tease my other nut as Diego did. He touched it to the sac and zip; it sucked it into the hose. He let go, and the tube slammed against my body. Each ball was pulled in opposite directions, and my cock stuck straight up. The sensation edged me closer to an orgasm.

Stanford stroked my dick, his big black fist circled my shaft and squeezed. A pearl of precum pooled at my tip. He bent over and ran his tongue along the underside of my shaft. He worked it up to the mushroom head and followed the groove to the hole. His tongue tasted the fluid and spread the clear drop around the end. His lips surrounded the head and sucked it clean. Licking his lips, he smiled. "Delicious."

Diego unzipped his coveralls and his raging erection sprang out of its constriction. His ten-inch cock's hooded head dripped. He stepped between my legs and pulled my cock down to his. He guided his foreskin over my tip. A warm wetness sucked my dick inside, and my glans rubbed against his. Precum mixed and formed a seal around the flesh tube.

Seth grabbed our cocks and rubbed up and down. Diego's foreskin swallowed my dick's head. The sensation was amazing.

Stanford applied lube on the thick handle of a wrench and moved underneath me.

Brandon pulled out his massive meat and moved to my face. He slapped my cheeks with it and ran its fat head over my mouth. His tip oozed, and my tongue licked into the huge hole.

Stanford pressed the handle between my cheeks. "Ready?"

Brandon agreed, "Ready," and both men entered me. The cold metal filled my ass as a hot thick cock filled my mouth. My balls were sucked in the vacuum's hose, as Seth guided my dick deep inside Diego's foreskin.

My whole body was stimulated from every end.

Stanford pushed the handle into me all the way up to the tool's head. He twisted it and twisted, making the nerves in my ass scream. He pulled it out, twisted, pushed it back in, and twisted. He removed it and picked up another tool. This time, he chose the air ratchet for removing lug nuts on the tires. He fastened a black dildo on and pulled the trigger. The rubber cock spun, faster and faster, the harder he pulled. The black cock whirled.

I wondered if Stanford's cock was as big and as black. I bit my lower lip and hoped I'd find out.

He dipped the dildo into a thick white cream and pulled the trigger. He pushed down and pulled out. The black tip was coated white and coming my way.

My butt cheeks tensed; unsure if they could handle the girth or the speed.

Stanford pressed the tip to my opening and pulled the trigger. A rotating dildo spun between my cheeks, and I took a deep breath. Slowly, the spinning end drilled into me, spreading me open wider and wider. It rotated faster as it dove in deeper.

The suction on my balls increased as did Seth's hand jacking my cock. Overwhelmed by my senses, I felt the pleasure rising higher and higher, as my cock banged into Diego's. Thick fluid bathed our cocks and escaped out of the skin sheath to lubricate both of our dicks. Seth's hand slid from Diego's pubic bush to mine.

Diego's balls exploded and filled his foreskin. He coated my cock with cum as another wave shot out of his dick.

Seth milked the semen out of his foreskin. As the sensation of his orgasm overtook Diego, he pulled back, unable to stand anymore stimulation. A wet pop sounded as he backed up. Another rope of cum streaked across my belly and iced my torso up to my chin.

Diego's cum flowed down my shaft and as Seth's hand hit my pubes, my cock exploded in his hand. Wave after wave of cum flowed from me as every nerve in my body screamed in pleasure and pain. "Stop, stop, STOP!"

But, they all continued working my body.

I thrashed around in the sling as their touch set my skin ablaze. My cock shot another load out of my balls despite the suction on them.

As the flow stopped, Seth turned the vacuum off, and the hose released one ball. Diego turned off the other one, and my balls were free as the tubes dropped to the floor.

Seth stepped between my legs and slipped a condom on his dick. Lube poured out of my butt as Stanford pulled the black dildo out. It continued to spin, sending a spray of lube over everyone.

Seth caught some lube and smeared it on his cock and slid into me to the hilt. He pounded my ass five strokes and pulled out. He ripped the condom off and shot his load across my six-pack. He stepped back as Brandon pulled his cock out of my mouth and raced around my body. He rubber-coated his dick and entered me. His huge cock filled me and stretched me wider.

Brandon's long, thick shaft slid in and out. His pelvis humped me as his balls swung back and forth bouncing off my butt. His hand grabbed my tender cock and started to jerk it off again.

I couldn't take the stimulation, still sensitive from my climax. My body started to thrash around, trying to escape from Brandon. His huge cock burrowed deeper in, and his hand clamped down harder.

His breathing came in quick, violent bursts, and I knew he was close.

I made my butt clamp down on his cock, and he screamed as he came.

He pulled out, and I watched as his condom filled and stretched. The tip ballooned, threatening to burst.

Brandon removed the condom as his cock shot two more times. Thick cum pooled on my belly.

But before I could move, Stanford whipped out his cock. I gasped as he approached. There was no way. He'd rip me in half.

Stanford came at me with what looked like a Louisville Slugger.

The three other men grabbed me and held me in place, as Stanford pulled on a camel size condom. He didn't wait. He plowed into me, and I saw stars. The world spun and threatened to go black.

My body was spent. I couldn't resist or fight anymore.

Stanford's ham of a hand grabbed my cock and stroked it time with his thrusts. My butt swallowed him whole.

I'd never walk again.

His hand worked my engorged flesh and slammed into me.

My head dropped back as my ass absorbed him.

My balls pulled up alongside of my shaft as his hand milked me.

"I'm ... gonna ... come ..." escaped from me, and I felt my balls release. More white hot cream flowed out of me like lava.

Stanford pulled out of my ass, and slapped his dick on my cock. He ripped off the condom and rubbed his length along mine. Another spasm shot out of me and hit his dick.

Stanford screamed, "Yes," as the fire hose sprayed us. No one was safe, as a tidal wave of cum spewed out of him and coated all of us.

I was coated and felt globs roll down my sides and splat on the floor.

All hands released me, and no one moved for a few minutes.

Diego found the hose he used to give me an enema and gently washed the cum from my body. Water and semen splashed across the floor and gurgled down the drain.

Seth threw a towel to Stanford, and together they dried and buffed my body. Rubbing up and down, the friction warmed me from the cold water, and my cock started to swell again.

Brandon gathered my clothes, and as soon as I was dried, he helped me slide into my briefs.

Stanford and Seth unhooked the sling and lower my bottom half to the wet floor.

Brandon smoothed my briefs across my ass as he walked me to a dry spot, where he bent forward with my slacks. I stepped into them, but he pulled them up to my waist. I worked the zipper and belt as he slipped my shirt back into place.

"I hope you enjoyed our full service today."

"Come back anytime."

They escorted me up the stairs and back to my car. "We really did change your oil."

I looked at them confused. My front tire was still inflated, and my cell phone read 6:30. Class was starting right now.

The business's phone rang, and Stanford stepped to the computer console and pressed a button. "Hello, Quickie Lube."

The speaker phone cracked to life. "Ah, yes, this is Trevor Smith. I'm the actor who will be filming the movie at your shop. I'm running a little late. I got lost due to the road construction, but I'm almost there."

"What?" Stanford said into the speaker.

"I'm sorry I'm running late, but I'll be there soon, and I can get into make-up. Then we can start filming."

Stanford turned to me. "Then, who the hell are you?"

"I'm Tyler Schmidt. I'm an accountant who's working on his MBA in night classes."

"You're not an actor?"

"No, I'm an accountant."

Brandon, Diego, and Seth surrounded me.

"But you knew the script," Brandon said to me.

Stanford looked down at the computer, but continued his conversation on the speaker phone. "We'll see you when you get here." He hung up and turned to the men. "I'm spent, and I can't shoot again today."

"What are we going to do?" Seth asked.

"You're all actors?" I asked.

They all nodded their heads.

"And you filmed all that," I pointed into the pit, "down there?"

"You had fun," Brandon said.

"Your oil was changed," Seth added.

"And your tired is fixed." Diego smiled.

"Have you ever wanted to be a porn star?" Stanford asked. "Here's your chance."

"I'll get a copy of it?" I asked.

"As many as you want," Stanford said. "And we'll even pay you for it, too." Then he quoted me an amazing amount.

14

"Let me sleep on it, and I'll get back to you, tomorrow." I slipped into my car and turned the key. The dashboard clock came on. "Open the door. I'm late for class."

"Will you let us use the movie?" Stanford asked.

"Sure."

He smiled and exhaled the breath he had been holding. He opened the door, and I pulled ahead.

"I'll stop by tomorrow, and we'll work something out."

A car horn beeped at the entrance.

Seth opened the entrance door and waited as it slowly rose. "How will we explain this one?"

"Tell him the truth." And I drove away, heading toward class, and kicking myself for not agreeing on a higher price.

But, maybe I could get more tomorrow …

LEBRAWN THE BARBARIAN
Evan Gilbert

In another world, in a dark and dangerous age, in a sprawling nation of misty plains and dense green forests, a mighty castle bestrode rolling hills. Its thick stone walls and imposing towers were redoubtable, visible for miles in any direction, the clear seat of the land's power. The master of both castle and country stood at the center of a vast, circular chamber atop the castle's loftiest pinnacle. A tall man, lean of build, he was dressed in full-body plate armor cast of highly polished steel, custom-fitted over finely woven mail. Beneath the eye and mouth openings of his deep, spiked metal helmet, only darkness could be seen. In gilded leather scabbard at his waist was a gold-handled, steel-bladed sword. His right fist, gloved in mail, held a war hammer, and on his left arm, he bore a kite shield emblazoned with the royal crest. The sword was honed to an edge sufficient to sever limb from limb in a single sweep. The war hammer could shatter bone even through armor. The shield could resist the sharpest blade. Indeed, His Magnificent and Mighty Majesty, Lord of the Western Lands and King of Great Bougier, was terrible to behold.

He was scared shitless.

"Would you please stop shaking?" The queen, seated on the higher of the two thrones atop a white marble dais at the rear of the chamber, rolled her eyes. "I can hear you rattling all the way back here."

Without, battle raged fiercely. The invaders were little more than disgruntled rabble from the outer regions of the Western Lands, but a Barbarian who hailed from the wilds of Afreek was leading them, and they had breached the walls of the castle. The Imperial Guard, the royal family's elite fighting unit, had met the invasion superbly when it reached the castle and immediately battled the treasonous interlopers to a standstill. That pissed off the Barbarian, who made his way to the forefront and single-handedly broke the Guard. Now the battle raged through the corridors and halls of the royal palace itself. The Guard still resisted bravely, but the strident sounds of fighting grew steadily nearer the throne room, evidence that the Guardsmen were falling one by one.

Outside the door of the throne room, there were outraged shouts from the four men posted there. That was followed by fleet footsteps, the loud clang of metal upon metal, horrendous screams, and the precise thud of four heavy bodies hitting the stone floor. Then there was only silence.

A squeak, not unlike that of a rodent, escaped the throat of King Dickless.

Her Highness, Queen Wottaho, smiled bitterly at the sound. She was a very comely woman only twenty-four years old, possessed of voluptuous hips and breasts with glossy blond hair tumbling down her back. Ladies of the aristocracy, regardless of age, dressed in velvet, floor-length gowns. Wottaho, however, was attired today in pale green silk veils that concealed only the naughtiest of her naughty bits, leaving much fine, porcelain skin on display. Ladies of the court were always attended by maidservants. In another break with tradition, Wottaho had, from puberty, selected only young, handsome, strapping men as her attendants.

The latest of these, Bigmounds, stood at her right side, slightly to the rear of her throne. He was a brown-skinned man of twenty-two, with a face more handsome than any the queen had yet seen. An Afreekian, he was taken at the age of fifteen in one of the periodic raids of that continent and placed on the auction blocks of the Western Lands. Wottaho had purchased him on sight and instantly made him her right hand. She hired tutors to educate him in the ways of the Bougiesh, which was necessary for him to handle the tasks of the position. She also put him through workouts with the country's best athletic trainers. The duties of an attendant did not require any particular athleticism, but the queen preferred her attendants to be fit. By her decree, Bigmounds' official uniform consisted of a white cotton loincloth that covered only his genitals. She wanted his ass out because it was firm and round and finely dimpled on either side, and she liked looking at it. She liked looking at his dick and balls, too, but that, much to her daily regret, could only be done in private.

"Bigmounds," the queen snapped.

The attendant stepped forward and bowed. He was tall, with the lean, muscular build of a warrior. "Yes, my queen?"

"Stand beside me and take note of all that follows." The queen's smile widened, and became positively wicked. "I'll expect you to make an official record and testify to these events as it pleases me."

Bigmounds bowed again. "Your Highness, your wish is my will."

The throne was Wottaho's by lineage. King Dickless came to the throne by matrimony. He had not been the queen's choice. The marriage had been arranged when she was but a toddler, a deal struck by her father – now in eternal kingly repose – to unite Great Bougier and the Western Lands. She was under pressure to produce an heir, but she wanted her sons and daughters to have spirit and strength, qualities in which the now middle-aged Dickless was sorely lacking. The prospect of his seeding her womb, it seemed, was something that would shortly no longer be of concern. If the Guard fell – as was likely already the case, given the sudden and alarming silence just beyond the throne room – King Dickless would be the queen's last line of defense.

The door of the throne room consisted of gold plating over wood beams that were a foot thick. Bigmounds had barred the door by hefting another foot-thick wooden beam into the great metal brackets securely anchored on either side of the jamb. No battering ram could take down that fortification.

There were three blows. The first shook the entire door in its frame, sending crumbs of broken masonry raining to the floor. On the second blow, the curved, rusted, bloody blade of an axe pierced the gold plating on the inside of the door, opening a slit that ran from top to bottom and so wide a man could have easily slipped through it. The third blow severed the crossbeam.

A leather-booted foot kicked the ruined door inward, sending the smashed pieces clattering across the floor.

Amid the swirling dust and crashing din, a figure stepped into the throne room. He was verging on seven feet in height. His skin was so dark it shone like finely polished ebony. From his neck to his feet, he was thick with muscle. His colossal shoulders and bulging chest tapered down to a narrow waist, from which draped a ragged leather breechcloth barely sufficient to conceal his hugely dangling dick and the tight hills of his ass. His body bore a glistening sheen of sweat and gore, but there was not so much as a scratch upon his skin. A contemptuous sneer rode on his thick, rough lips. The tattoo of a white lion glared from the top of his shaved, dusky head, and his fierce black eyes struck fear in friend and enemy alike. Thirty years old, his burly body was at the peak of its formidable power. He was LeBrawn the Barbarian, and there was not a soul in the seven great lands who had faced him in combat and lived.

His rugged face, as he gazed about the throne room, was flat with ennui. When he caught sight of the battle-suited king, his nostrils flared ever so slightly. He turned to the queen. "Seriously?" he growled in a deep, rumbling voice. "This is the best you have left to throw at me?"

Drawing herself up on her throne, Wottaho scowled at her husband. "Well? Are you going to just stand there and let this foul outlander insult you in your own palace?"

The trembling Dickless was inclined to do just that. Against his better judgment, however, he raised both shield and war hammer. He choked out a battle cry. He charged the Barbarian.

LeBrawn never took his eyes from the queen. With the most casual of shrugs, he backhanded the onrushing king across the face. The helmet flew from His Majesty's copper-haired head, while hammer and shield went skidding in opposite directions across the chamber. The man spun full around and dropped, unconscious before he even clanged to the floor.

The queen smiled, wickedly. "It seems, O' Barbarian, that I am at your mercy."

The Barbarian sneered. "And, we all know things aren't always what they seem, don't we?" Resting the axe across his shoulder, he began to walk toward the dais. "I'll have the throne now, in the name of the Westlanders, who paid me handsomely to take it from you."

Her Majesty leaned back in her seat and raised her legs. Slowly, she draped her knees over the armrests of the throne, and then she pulled aside her veils, revealing the royal pudenda, red and wet. Her smile became downright evil. "Isn't there, perhaps, something you'd rather taste first?"

The Barbarian's eyes riveted themselves between Wottaho's legs. He licked his lips and smiled, hungrily. "Aye. Perhaps there is, O' Queen."

As LeBrawn strode purposefully toward her, Wottaho leaned toward Bigmounds, who stood stoutly at her right side. She whispered, "Take heed. You will write in the official records that the king died battling the Barbarian, and that the Barbarian, in attempting to ravish me, fell beneath my blade."

"But, His Majesty isn't dead," Bigmounds whispered back.

"A minor detail, soon to be addressed. Now pay attention to the Barbarian. Your servicing of my pussy has been laughable at best. Watch and learn how to pleasure a woman." Her perfumed hand shifted beside her left leg, subtly lifting a pearl-handled dagger from her veils. "Then you'll see how a queen defends her throne."

Seconds later, the dais shook as the hulking LeBrawn mounted it in two solid steps. He tossed his bloody axe aside. Wottaho reached out invitingly with her right hand. "It's yours, O' Biggest of Men," she purred, waving at the moist juncture between her legs.

In turn, LeBrawn reached out. He grabbed the queen by her right arm, snatched her from the throne, tied her arms and legs tightly with her veils, and tossed her aside. He grabbed the dagger she left on the seat and flicked it across the chamber to bury its point solidly in the stone wall. This was all done in such swiftness that the seductive, iniquitous grin was still upon the queen's face as she fell flat to the floor.

"What is the meaning of this?" she gasped finally, rolling over to gaze up at the Barbarian.

"You have a nice, tender pussy, woman, and I've plugged more than my fair share of them," answered LeBrawn. "But you mean me no good, and what I want to taste now is right here." He grabbed the muscled shoulder of Bigmounds and turned him roughly around so that he could ogle the young man's tight, exposed butt. "Daaaaaaaaamn!" he drawled lustily. "Fuck me blind, Bigmounds. You are aptly named!"

The queen turned a confused and furious gaze upon her fine, handsome attendant. "How does he know your name?"

The smiling look Bigmounds turned upon the queen made her shiver, for it was filled not only with sudden contempt, but also a fierce cunning she now realized had been in him from the day she bought him at auction. "Because I gave it to him in the letter I secretly sent, telling him that you were the one who actually hired him to lead the Westlanders in revolt, that the entire invasion was just a ploy to rid yourself of the king. You thought LeBrawn would easily slay King Dickless, and you intended to kill LeBrawn in turn. With LeBrawn dead, the remaining palace guard would be able to put down the rebellion, leaving you a widowed queen free to choose another mate. And, you did promise the Duke of Dodge that he would be your choice once all the dust settled, didn't you, Highness?"

Wottaho, wide-eyed, began to sputter. "But ... how did ... how could you ...?"

"My head may have been under the table and pressed between your sluttish thighs whilst you were at dinner with the duke last month, but I heard everything," Bigmounds snapped. "You conveniently forgot to share with the good duke your intention of getting yourself some Barbarian dick before you stabbed LeBrawn in the back. But, I heard you mumble that part of the plan in your sleep, so I passed it along to LeBrawn as well. He promised me my freedom, and I promised him a ride he'll never forget."

"That you did, buttboi," LeBrawn growled. He gave Bigmounds' ass a resounding slap. "And I'm ready to collect my payment."

Bigmounds ripped away his loincloth, releasing a dick and balls that were almost as impressive as his rump. "Watch and learn how to pleasure a man," he sneered at the queen.

Bigmounds knelt on the dais before LeBrawn, then reached out and undid the towering Barbarian's breechcloth, which he tossed aside. "Gods preserve me," the young man whispered as he took in the sight of the Barbarian's equipment. LeBrawn's cock curved downward by a good thirteen inches ... and it wasn't even fully hard yet. Bigmounds' overwhelmed brain whipped back and forth between delighted anticipation and sheer terror.

"Time to get busy," LeBrawn announced. Wrapping one big palm around the back of the youth's head, he smashed Bigmounds' face to his crotch. The Barbarian's cock slipped between Bigmounds' lips and plunged right down his throat.

The queen gasped, expecting her attendant to choke at the gargantuan intrusion. And, choke Bigmounds did, gagging forcefully against the thick tube of meat in his gullet. But, he rallied quickly, determined to take every inch of the Barbarian's cock, and he opened his mouth even wider, relaxing the muscles in his throat. Seconds later, he was easily swallowing the long, smooth, raunchy strokes LeBrawn fed him.

"That's it, boy. That's it," the Barbarian grunted. "I fucking feel your fucking tonsils!"

Bigmounds swallowed repeatedly, his cheeks dimpling as the huge cock shoved into his mouth and puffing outward as it pulled back. Obscene, wet slurps bubbled around his lips, and the Barbarian's heavy, hairy nut-sac slapped against the underside of Bigmounds' chin. On and on it went, raw, impassioned groans coming from both men, the mouth-pounding stretching on for some fifteen minutes before LeBrawn finally shoved Bigmounds violently away, grabbing his dick in his fist and squeezing desperately. "Shit!" he hissed.

A look of alarm flared on Bigmounds' face. "LeBrawn, what's wrong? Did I hurt you?"

"Hell, no, boy," LeBrawn snarled in reply, hunched over his groin and still clutching his swollen member. He gave a deep growl of a laugh. "You were about to make me come, and there is still much damage I intend to do you, so I backed off. Fuck! You suck cock like the great whirlpool of the Necrolium Sea sucks down ships."

The queen gave her attendant an admiring stare. "I've seen the great whirlpool swallow the biggest galleons whole," she remarked, fully impressed and equally jealous. "You have a talented throat indeed, Bigmounds."

"Aye," the Barbarian agreed. The heat in his groin having dropped to a manageable level, he reached out again and took Bigmounds firmly by the shoulder. "And now, I want to find out how talented that big pretty ass of yours is."

LeBrawn turned Bigmounds so forcefully that the young man lost his balance, falling forward and planting his hands against the plush seat of the queen's throne to catch himself. This left him bent over at the waist, his luscious butt poked out in the Barbarian's face. LeBrawn grabbed a thick brown dome in each hand, massive fingers crushing down as if testing overripe melons. Bigmounds groaned, thrilling to the mixture of pain and pleasure as the thick hands massaged his ample ass. He was completely shocked when, abruptly, he felt those powerful hands spread his cheeks, and next moment the crack of his ass was filled with the Barbarian's entire face. The big lips nibbled and kissed while the long, hot, wet tongue speared again and again into his very eager little pucker. Bigmounds' groans grew louder, and he began to roll his hips, grinding his ass against LeBrawn's face. LeBrawn's hungry, muffled growls and steel-hard, leaking prick bespoke his own steadily rising desire.

But, Bigmounds and LeBrawn were not the only ones getting turned on. Wottaho could not take her eyes off the writhing men. The royal pudenda was heating up and getting exceptionally succulent. Her arms were bound together at the wrists, but that did not stop her from slipping her hands between her legs. "Eat him, O' Big Cock," she goaded. "Eat my attendant's fine brown ass!"

LeBrawn licked, kissed and slurped for several long minutes, barely coming up for air. Soon Bigmounds' butt was dripping with spit, and his tiny hole had been substantially loosened by the vigor of the Barbarian's tongue. To prepare the young man for what was coming next, LeBrawn formed a wedge with his fingers and thumb.

Bigmounds gasped when those digits went up his ass. "Ye gods!"

"Yes, yes!" the queen cheered. She began wriggling sideways across the floor, trying to get closer to the action. Though bound at the wrists and ankles, she maneuvered her body until she was able to crawl forward on her elbows and knees. It was painful and undignified, but by the Gods, she would not be denied.

LeBrawn poked his tightly clutched fingers into Bigmounds' butthole like a tanner working an awl through a stubborn piece of leather. With each shove, Bigmounds' head jerked upward, his ass grew looser, and the fingers went deeper. When the Barbarian's hand sank to the palm inside the young man, when Bigmounds began whispering "Fuck me, fuck me" in an urgent, demanding chant, LeBrawn knew that beautiful ass was ready to accommodate something more substantial.

He straightened his back. He grabbed Bigmounds' waist with his right hand. He seized his dick with his left hand. He put the head of his rigid cock, big as a boy's fist, against the gaping, anxiously flexing, spit-wet hole.

And, he plunged up Bigmounds' ass in a single, deep lunge.

Bigmounds was indeed hot for a good reaming, but as open as he was, LeBrawn's cock was still too much for him. "GODS!" he bellowed. He was lifted off his feet by the powerful thrust, and it felt as if the monstrous dick had gone up into his chest. His eyes bulged as the pressure filled his gut. Arms snapping backward, he dug his fingers into the Barbarian's waist, trying to push himself off the appendage that plugged him so thoroughly. Held aloft as he was, he could not get any leverage. "It's too much, too much!" he protested, wild eyes roving in panic. "I can't take it!"

"Yes, you can, boy." LeBrawn kept the young attendant's ass crushed to his groin, all but the very last inch of his dick sheathed in that trembling body. He pressed his lips to Bigmounds' ear, whispering soothingly to him. "Hang on. Take your time. Let yourself adjust. It will get better."

It did. In only seconds, it seemed, the pain and anxiety were gone. Now there was just the incredible urge to be plundered.

Bigmounds arched his back, pushing his butt into LeBrawn's crotch, trying to absorb that last inch. "Come on," he urged. "Give it to me."

The Barbarian obliged. He set Bigmounds down on the dais. Standing on tiptoe, the attendant leaned forward once more, hands braced on the armrests of the queen's throne. LeBrawn began pounding into Bigmounds' ass, making the fleshy mounds quiver. A loud, steady SLAP SLAP SLAP filled the chamber as Bigmounds pushed back to meet each thrust.

"Yes!" yelled the queen. She had reached the edge of the dais, and gazing up, she could see the tight, raw, shockingly stretched ring of flesh that was Bigmounds' asshole, twisting itself inside out as the immense Barbarian dick sawed back and forth through it. "Tear him open, O' Biggest of Cocks! Damn it, FUCK HIM!"

Bigmounds, on the other hand, could not utter a sound just now. He was stunned – eyes and mouth gaping with disbelief – at the sensation of the huge organ filling his perfectly round butt. In all his years at court, he had never strayed far from the queen (who kept him near for her own pleasure), but he had managed to sneak in a romp or two with one of the king's menservants. He had been fucked before, but never so deeply, never so forcefully. The fat, meaty knob of LeBrawn's dick massaged Bigmounds' prostate deliciously each time it plunged in and slid out, and that sent wave after wave of libidinal pleasure racing through the attendant's groin. Bigmounds' own cock swelled in response, jutting straight out like an axe handle. It began to drip shiny, viscous little pearls, sexual fluid forced out of the young man's body by the unrelenting action in his rump.

The queen's eyes, locked on Bigmounds' jumping, leaking cock, swiftly glazed over with desire. Though nowhere near the size of LeBrawn's piece, the attendant's dick was still larger than average, a very desirable eight inches. She had never seen it so hard and had certainly never been able to bring it to such a state in her chambers, despite her persistent and very talented efforts. She couldn't just watch anymore. "Loose me, Barbarian!" she cried. "Loose me and let me have my pleasure!"

Initially, LeBrawn ignored her plea, intent on literally tearing Bigmounds a new one. The notion that the queen might fight or flee if freed didn't trouble him at all. He could easily subdue her again if it came to that. Moreover, he could tell at a glance exactly what was on Her Majesty's mind – and it wasn't fight or flight. The woman was adept at deception, but not even she could fake the crazed lust that burned in her face. Freeing her, however, would require him to stop fucking. Lost in the succulent tightness of Bigmounds' ass, LeBrawn wasn't inclined to pause even for a moment.

Still, there were some very freaky, very nasty possibilities here. It might be interesting to see what developed. He yanked his cock out of Bigmounds, drawing a startled and outraged gasp from the young man. "Put that back in me!" the attendant demanded, reaching behind him, grabbing for the Barbarian's dick.

"Patience, boy," the Barbarian said, smacking the flat of his hand across the youth's hungry butt. He reached down and ripped away the veils binding the queen's hands and feet. With an almost desperate, animal squeal, she scrambled up on the dais and lay herself before Bigmounds, legs and arms thrown wide.

"Ravish me!" she screamed at both men, not caring which rose to the task.

"Fill her up, boy," LeBrawn ordered.

The sight of the queen's gaping, undulating pussy – she was spreading the wet, red lips of it apart with her fingers while grinding her hips in an obscene circular motion – had the same effect it always had on Bigmounds. His dick shriveled to half-mast in a single heartbeat, and the look on his face was that of a seasick sailor on a hurricane-tossed boat. He swallowed hard to keep from throwing up and turned to flee.

LeBrawn would have none of that. He grabbed the gagging attendant and turned him back. He put his lips against the youth's right ear and whispered in a rush of hot breath, "Here's the deal, boy. The only way my dick's going back up your tunnel is if your cock goes in her cunt." He fisted his own cock, letting the head of it glide oh-so-slowly along the crack of Bigmounds' ass. "So, what will it be?"

Bigmounds' dick gave his answer, springing back to full, throbbing attention at the teasing motion of the fist-sized knob against his backside. He was on the queen in the next instant, blindly plunging

his dick into her wetness while glaring over his shoulder at the Barbarian's hard monster piece.

"Ahhhhhhhhyessssssss!" Wottaho screamed, thrilled and filled to her very womb with Bigmounds' manly meat. Her arms and legs wrapped around his body like a springing trap, and she clutched him tightly to her.

Bigmounds barely noticed the slick, juicy warmth that enveloped him. His eyes were on the Barbarian's dick. His asshole clenched repeatedly, eager to take the monster in again. He pushed his butt up, pulling his piece out until just the head remained inside the queen. The motion drew a hissing gasp from her. He shook his ass at the Barbarian. "Take it, LeBrawn. Take my ass!"

Dick in hand, LeBrawn was already climbing over Bigmounds. Peeling the queen's legs from around the younger man's waist with his free hand, he rammed down into the boyishly fine rump again, and that sent Bigmounds' dick sinking back into Wottaho's pussy. Queen and attendant screamed in unison.

A rhythm quickly developed, with Bigmounds pushing into Her Highness as LeBrawn pulled back from him, then shoving his ass upward to meet LeBrawn's down stroke. The three of them fucked in rapturous frenzy, LeBrawn pounding Bigmounds so furiously that, to the queen, it was as if the Barbarian were plundering her right through her attendant. She raked at both men with her fingernails, head tossing from side to side, gasps of pleasure huffing again and again from her throat. Grunts of "Oh, shit!" and shouts of "Oh, Gods!" issued from Bigmounds as the sensations shooting through his groin from his dick melded with the ache-ecstasy burning in his thoroughly abused asshole. Only the Barbarian was silent, intent as he was on crushing the three of them through the dais into the chamber below.

Their passions built for nearly twenty minutes. Wottaho reached the peak first and went flying over, her legs flapping like a bellows, her arms pounding the dais, a piercing yell erupting from her throat as she came. Seconds later, Bigmounds smashed his ass upward so violently that he actually lifted the Barbarian off his knees, if only for a moment. That pulled Bigmounds' dick out of the queen just as his raging orgasm sent stringy gobs of man-juice spurting forcefully from his cock. The spasms in his asshole sent the Barbarian plummeting over. With one final shove into Bigmounds, LeBrawn came.

And came.

And came.

He shot so much hot sperm up the young man's overworked butt that the stuff squirted out around his cock, dribbling down in big white gobs over Bigmounds' balls.

"Eeeeeeeeeeeeeeeaaaaah!" squealed a sudden voice from the front of the throne room.

LeBrawn, Bigmounds and Wottaho turned their heads upon the king. Dickless had apparently wakened some time ago. He stood near the shattered main entry, the breastplate of his armor removed, right hand shoved beneath mail and metal, stroking out his own orgasm. "Gods of a pig's arse," he said, wild-eyed and breathless. "That was the hottest fuck ever!"

"Fuck me blind," LeBrawn growled. "That it was." He jerked back, his still-stiff dick pulling out of Bigmounds with a thick, wet sound. "In fact, I enjoyed the sex so much, good king, that I'm going to leave you and your wife with your lives. Take your woman and never let me see either of you on this continent again."

"Barbarian, please," begged the king, "let the queen and me stay here with you."

LeBrawn stood up and laughed. His body drenched with blood-streaked sweat, his dick wet with the juices from Bigmounds' ass and trailing a thin, shiny string of cum down to his shin, he folded his massive arms across his even more massive chest. "Hell, I'm not staying here. You're off the throne, which I'll have the Westlanders place now in Bigmounds' hands. My job is done, and I'm eager to sail the seven seas for fresh booty, and booties, to plunder."

"Then take us with you," said Dickless, "so I can watch you fuck my wife again and again."

"Aye, O' Biggest of Men," Wottaho said, rubbing a finger over her sex. "I, too, can give you rides you'll never forget."

"And I'd rather sit on you, LeBrawn, than on the throne," added Bigmounds, standing unsteadily beside the reclining queen. His ass was dripping cum down the inner sides of his thighs, and his legs were delightfully weak from the fucking he'd taken. "Let me come with you as well."

"Tempting offers, all," said the Barbarian. "But where LeBrawn walks, he walks alone." Naked but for his boots, LeBrawn picked up his axe and strode for the main entry, his flexing muscular buttocks drawing ravenous stares from the three pairs of eyes behind him.

He stopped in the doorway. He looked back over his shoulder. "Which is not to say that we will not fuck again someday," he said with a nasty smile.

Then he was gone.

THE COLOR OF TRUST
Don Mika

"Don't worry about me; I'm doing fine," Michael Patterson breathed into the payphone. He wasn't sure whether he lied for the sake of his overprotective mother or to talk himself out of taking her up on her offer to send him a plane ticket home to Delaware. Either way, he wouldn't tell her that he had been robbed twice since he arrived in Norfolk, Virginia. He wouldn't tell her that he was afraid to leave his rundown, roach infested apartment unless his only friend, Nyeem, accompanied him, nor that he was the only resident of the housing complex that wasn't African-American or Latino, which made him a prime target for abuse. "No!" he sighed, struggling to hide his homesickness, "I moved out here to make my own way. Tell Dad that I don't need him to send me anything. Okay, Mom. I can get by on my own. Don't cry! I love you, too."

As he hung the phone up and turned to address his waiting bodyguard, he could tell from Nyeem's expression that they shared similar thoughts: Michael was dumb as hell to have turned down any offer of money, especially when he had been robbed of his last week's pay and had spent days sulking and wondering what he was going to do for groceries and utilities. Thankfully, he was smart enough before the move to have set aside some emergency money, which would take him through to the next month's rent.

"I don't need their help," he shrugged, answering the confused look in Nyeem's probing brown eyes. "What's the point of moving away from home if you're only going to run back every time something bad happens?"

"I wouldn't know," Nyeem retaliated. "I've been wanting to get away from home for over twenty-two years. Every time I think about leaving, I think about all my little brothers and sisters that are going to be left here to fend for themselves. I feel you on wanting to make your own way, but why here? What's here for you … for anybody?"

They began to walk, Nyeem not looking back to acknowledge Michael, whom he knew was sure to be close behind. Michael tried his best to mimic his leader's carefree posture and match each "fuck the world" stride, which held the declaration that the streets belonged to their creator. Michael's steps were clumsy and offbeat in comparison, keeping beat with his own heart instead, which kept telling him that he was out of his element.

"Do you know what they'll do if they knew that I live around all black people?" Michael chuckled, hoping that his revelation wouldn't turn his one friend against him. "They'd come down here and physically drag me home. All they know about blacks are the images they see on television, the nightly news and such. To them, all blacks are criminals."

"Getting your ass whipped twice since you been here, having all your money stolen, and having to walk to a payphone because you got stuck for your cellular hasn't made you think that they might be right about that?" Nyeem teased.

"Bad people come in all colors. So do good people. You're black, and you're one of the coolest people I ever met!"

Nyeem shrugged and tried not to show how delighted he was with Michael's brilliant reply to his rhetorical question. He wasn't the type to ever get sentimental, especially not before someone he had known as briefly as Michael. "Fall back," he instructed as they came upon two of his waiting clients. "I got to handle this business. Nobody's going to fuck with you; that's my word!"

"Alright," Michael swallowed, knowing that if he followed his friend across the street, the fiends would assume he was an undercover, and that assumption could be dangerous for the both of them.

He tried to not look panicked as he stood alone and watched Nyeem's meticulous maneuvering, the way he pretended to dap the junkies up as he slipped their purchases into their palms, stepping on the money they dropped on the ground to keep the wind from taking it until they had walked away and it was safe to bend over and scoop it up without drawing attention. All the while, Nyeem never stopped talking and smiling, as if the illegal exchange were as natural to him as breathing.

Michael, flushed red on the other side of the street, a million thoughts racing through his mind about what would happen if the cops rolled through at that moment. He was sure he wouldn't be arrested, but even if they only took Nyeem away, that would mean that he would be left to journey home alone, and even that simple task of six blocks scared him shitless, while Nyeem, who had everything to lose, remained composed. Even the way Nyeem did things that Michael considered beneath him made Michael envious of the raw machismo that seemed to ooze, sexily, from every pour of the guy.

Michael drew in a deep breath and pretended not to notice how low his companions baggy shorts were riding, revealing a trail of curly, black pubes. His throat grew dry as he thought of what thick delight waited at the end of that trail. He also wondered how, by simply playing basketball, Nyeem had managed to achieve such a great body, when he, who had access to the most high-tech gym equipment prior to his move, just barely had any muscle definition in his own flat stomach.

"That didn't take too long, did it?" Nyeem teased, completely removing the sweat-soaked T-shirt that had previously been pulled back so that it only remained on his body due to both arms still being in their rightful holes. All else of the shirt had been stretched behind his back, blowing carefree in the wind, a makeshift vest that accented his well-chiseled body.

Michael was too busy watching the same T-shirt become fashioned around Nyeem's head to reply. The vest was now a makeshift turban, tying back his shoulder-length dreadlocks. Michael marveled, thinking how he would have only thought to tie his discarded shirt around his waist, or tote it around in his hand. He never stopped being amazed by the innovative nature of the people who surrounded him, and even when he feared his for his life, there was always some part of him that ached to be one with them, to belong, and to know their secret of being so fearless, effortlessly sensual, and in control.

Growing up with strict, prudish, Baptist parents, he had to hide his deep-rooted love for anything hip-hop influenced. He especially had to hide his desire for the black male physique, and that was the one secret that he hadn't been allowed to unleash, even after moving out on his own. If there was one thing he was certain of, it was that being openly gay would only increase his potential for being prey to violence.

He hadn't even told Nyeem about his curiosity, not even on the night when Nyeem had walked him home from work, and they had spent the night getting drunk and smoking weed, talking about their upbringings. That night, the part of him that he hated, the part that remained skeptical of Nyeem, whom had looked out for him since his arrival, fending off his attackers, and even loaning him money for groceries, told him that he would be a fool to sleep and leave the strange, black man with access to his laptop and the few possessions that hadn't been stolen from him the first night in the building. The weed and the liquor helped him to override those thought, and when he woke, Nyeem was long gone, but everything remained in place. Nyeem had even walked to the corner store and had left him a breakfast burrito in the microwave before departing. Money for his bus commute had even been left behind, along with a note to be safe.

As he ate and verbally punished himself for giving into the ignorant ways he had been raised, he noticed that his computer had been left on, and when he traced Nyeem's cyber footprints, each page took him to homoerotic content, mostly white guys being brutally fucked by black cocks that seemed surreal in length. He bookmarked the sites for later masturbatory purposes, but his mind was too cluttered with thoughts of how knowing what he now knew about Nyeem may somehow complicate their friendship to allow him to give in to his current arousal.

Nyeem was smart. He had fixed the laptop just days earlier and bragged that his uncle had taught him everything about computers. Why hadn't he thought to erase the browser history? Had it been left behind for Michael to purposely find? Was Michael supposed to make the first move, and if he did, what would Nyeem's retaliation be? What if Nyeem had picked up on Michael's lustful, hungry stares, and was only baiting him, waiting for the boy to be foolish and attempt to act on his desire, only for Michael to have the shit kicked out of him and to lose his only friend? Michael decided to keep the discovery to himself, no matter what the case.

The subject remained avoided, for three weeks, until the next time Nyeem invited himself to stay over. The two had gone almost completely through a twelve-pack of extra dry Coronas, and Nyeem, who had just finished rolling their sixth marijuana blunt, turned to Michael and unapologetically asked, "When you going to stop acting all shy and get you some of this good dick?"

"What the hell?" Michael struggled to sound as if the words were outrageous to him, even though he had been asking himself the exact same question in his mind, only the words lacked the sexy confidence in his head that they held when they rolled from Nyeem's tongue.

"You know you want to," Nyeem insisted, crawling from his reclining chair, the marijuana blunt tucked behind his ear as he made his way over to Michael, who lay sprawled on the shaggy, blue rug. "You really going to lay there and act like you're not aching to feel me on top of you ... inside of you?" He ran his fingers through Michael's shaggy brown curls, staring into his brown eyes the entire time, daring him to deny the mutual attraction that had them drawn to one another like the opposite poles of two magnets.

"Is this real?" Michael laughed, reaching out to caress the bare torso that was now less than two inches from his own naked chest. The humidity from the stuffy room had Nyeem's skin glowing with a translucent film of sweat that seemed to define every muscle and ripple of his god-like body. "Are you being for real with me, man? You really want to fuck me?"

"No," Nyeem corrected. "Animals fuck. I want to make love to you."

"So, you love me now?" Michael slurred. Drunk from the surplus of beer and high from the shit-load of weed they had just consumed, his mind was still clear enough for him to compute the possibility that a guy as street-wise as Nyeem had genuine feelings, beyond sex, for him. The answer was slim and none.

Nyeem's eyes narrowed with a hint of anger as he watched Michael sway with drunken laughter. "Why the hell is that funny? I can't love you?"

"You can," Michael smiled. "But, I just don't think you do. Not yet anyway."

"Look at me!" Nyeem ordered, palming the sides of Michael's head. "I've been looking out for you since you got here, Michael. It ain't because I want nothing from you in return. In fact, if you tell me you don't ever want to have sex with me, I'll be cool with just being your friend. What I don't want you to ever do again is tell me you don't believe I care about you; you got that? We've been through too much shit together, and I deserve better than that."

Michael struggled to free the sides of his face from Nyeem's grip, but then something he saw in his friend's eyes made him give up struggling. It was sincerity. Instead of pulling away, he leaned forward and gently pressed his mouth against Nyeem's. His hands roamed Nyeem's torso, and he could feel that his companion's heart was beating just as fast as his.

He told himself that a guy as suave as Nyeem couldn't be nervous about what was going to happen. That emotion was reserved only for Michael, a church boy, who had only experienced sex through what the boys that his parents forbid him to hang with had told him in the locker room, and recently, through following the links that Nyeem had left on his computer.

"You know I'm going to make it feel good for both of us; don't you?" Nyeem promised, pulling at Michael's basketball shorts. Michael raised his hips to aid in the removal of the stubborn fabric from his sweaty body, but his nerves wouldn't allow him to answer his friend.

When they were both stripped completely to their bare flesh, and Michael could feel Nyeem's sweat mixing with his own, he closed his eyes and clenched his teeth, awaiting the pain of the entry. He had felt the length and girth of Nyeem's cock sliding up and down his stomach and probing between his thighs as they kissed, and he was certain that he was in for a large degree of pain.

"You ever sucked dick?" Nyeem asked, trying to make the question sound as respectful as it possibly could.

"No, but I want to try."

"Follow my lead," Nyeem instructed, positioning himself so that his crotch was level with Michael's face, and Michael's with his. "Wow, I guess what they say about white guys isn't true," he laughed, marveling at the girth of Michael's thick, nine inches.

Michael thought about giving a retort, something like what he had heard about blacks certainly being true, as he lifted Nyeem's pulsing eleven inches to his mouth, but he was afraid his nerves would make it come out more offensive than funny. He let go of the thought and ran his tongue across the purplish head of Nyeem's cock, and then he opened his mouth to accept Nyeem's demanding thrust. His body shuttered as his friend reciprocated with all the gusto of a seasoned veteran.

He would have never pegged a guy with as much machismo as Nyeem to be a champion cocksucker. Yet, there they were, tangled together, fucking each other's faces with a rhythm that seemed to come so naturally. Michael was also surprised by the fact that he didn't need to follow Nyeem's lead. He was returning every tingle and erotic sensation that Nyeem offered him with so much finesse that Nyeem began to question if this was really Michael's first sexual experience.

Michael's back stiffened as he felt Nyeem lean over and spit into his exposed, twitching asshole. He was so repulsed by that sensation that he gave up trying to reciprocate the pleasure he was getting, now from the vigorous hand job that Nyeem was giving him. He was about to question why his partner would do something so cheapening to him, when he felt Nyeem's tongue darting across his rim, massaging the saliva in. That feeling was even better than the blowjob he had just been blessed with. He stopped trying to orally please Nyeem and bit his own tongue to hold in his moans. Nyeem would have to settle for a hand job, too.

"You ready for the real thing?" Nyeem questioned, when he was able to get two fingers inside his friend's pouting hole with only a slight moan of discomfort as a retort.

"Do you have any protection?" Michael asked, his eyes nailed shut, still awaiting Nyeem's painful entry, regardless of the answer. He had come too far to turn back.

"I told you I was going to take care of you." Nyeem whispered, and gave Michael's closed eyelids a kiss. "I got you."

Michael remained still, and tried to stifle his trembling as he heard the rip of a condom packet and felt something slicker and more heavy than saliva being rubbed across his waiting rim.

"I'm going to put it in now," Nyeem warned, lining his mushroom shaped head up with his tight target. "Just breathe in real deep, and it'll be over."

Michael screamed out in pain as Nyeem pushed inside, inch by inch, until his scrotum was all that remained outside. Nyeem's deep thrusts made him question if even that would remain outside, scraping against his spread cheeks. He reached down to feel himself for tearing, but his hand was pushed away and Nyeem's hungry mouth devoured his lips, forcing his tongue inside Michael's mouth, much like his penis had just invaded the opposite end. Their fingers locked together as if Nyeem was offering his hand to aid Michael in coping with the pain. That idea of subtle intimacy turned Michael on, and his meek erection began to fill out to its capacity again, scraping the ridges of Nyeem's chiseled stomach.

"Jesus!" Michael screamed out when his mouth was free, and he wondered if it was from pain of pleasure. He certainly didn't want whatever Nyeem was doing to him to stop. He could feel the pressure of each thrust course through every erogenous zone of his body. His cock made pools of precum as it smashed between their stomachs. He didn't know if Nyeem would ever reach his climax or feel a need to slow down, but he knew that he was seconds away from erupting himself.

He wandered if it would be proper to announce his approaching orgasm, like the guys he had watched perform this act on the Websites, but he thought that screaming, "I'm going to come," would cheapen the ordeal, so he lay there, tangling his fist in the sheets as his convulsions took Nyeem by surprise. His fluids landed just below Nyeem's sweaty neck and oozed down his flexing chest.

"Yeah!" Nyeem moaned, evidently turned on by the mess of it all. "Give me every drop! I won't pull out 'til you give me every drop!"

"OOOOW!" Michael howled as he felt Nyeem dive deeper. Suddenly he was exploding for a second time. His hands hugged the sofa pillow to his face to keep the noise down.

Nyeem stayed inside of him, not moving, but in as deep as he could go. He held the quaking boy to his body and whispered, "Good boy. Let it all go, baby!"

It seemed to Michael that Nyeem was also unloading into the condom. He thought he felt it swell inside of him. He was sure when Nyeem fell flat against him and began to pant like a dog in the summer's heat.

Nyeem withdrew without saying a word, and walked to the bathroom to discard of the rubber. Michael's eyes drank in the wonderment of his friend's glory, and his heart sped again as he contemplated releasing the questions that formed in his mind: Did what just happened between them make them officially lovers? Was this a one-time thing, and if so, would Nyeem treat him the same now that they shared this secret?

"Ready to get some sleep now?" Nyeem asked, crawling behind Michael's spun body. He cradled the boy with such a sensitivity that all of Mike's concerns subsided. All that mattered was that moment in time, and the only two people in the universe were he and Nyeem. There was no place safer nor more comfortable than Nyeem's broad chest and arms.

The next morning Michael awoke to find that Nyeem had long abandoned him. His head pounded from last night's beers, and his bladder screamed for a release of pressure, his asshole was throbbing with a sensation that was a little less than what he could describe as pain, but all he could focus on was his heart. It beat a mile a minute as thoughts raced through his head. Had Nyeem gotten what he was after all along? Would he ever hear from the man again?

He told himself that he was being foolish; Nyeem wasn't that kind of guy. Nobody who had made love to someone as passionately as Nyeem had made it to him the night before would just pick up and leave the person without so much as a goodbye. Just when those words began to win out, he noticed that Nyeem hadn't left empty-handed. The eighty bucks that he had tucked under a book on the living room table was gone, and so was his beloved laptop.

Michael had been played. The thought made him nauseous because Nyeem was just starting to make him rethink what his parent's had taught him about black people all of his life. Admitting that Nyeem, who he trusted with all of his heart, was capable of such an act, meant that there was no end to the evil that blacks he didn't know as well as he thought he knew Nyeem could do to him, if he allowed himself to be taken again.

He thought about calling his parents, but as he held the spare phone that Nyeem had given him for emergencies and began to dial the number, the thought occurred to him that he would have to give them an explanation for his change of heart. He felt bad enough hiding the truth of his living situation from them for so long that there was no telling what parts of it he would let spill from his mouth in his time of panic. He had just gotten over the brutality of the robberies himself, and hearing his mother cry, let alone his father's "I told you so" would just be rubbing salt in a closing wound. He certainly couldn't tell them about Nyeem. What would they think of their precious son if they knew he had committed the soul-damning acts that his father preached against nearly every Sunday, and with a black, street hooligan, no less?

He felt bad for that thought, and tried to make himself think of a good explanation for it all, some reason why Nyeem, who had befriended him, been a shoulder to cry on, and even loaned him money in his time of need, would steal his last penny and leave him alone, afraid to venture outside for the fresh air he needed to clear his head. Why did Nyeem pick the night after he had surrendered his heart and his virginity to show his true colors?

Nyeem simply wouldn't do anything that heinous, he told himself, and tried to remind himself of all the times he had left Nyeem with access to all of his valuables. Of course, he had yet to give the fucker the most valuable thing of all at those times, possibly what Nyeem had been baiting him with kindness to get all along. How could he be so stupid?

He realized that the thoughts going through his head belonged more to his parents than him and tried to calm himself. There had to be an explanation beyond the conclusion he had jumped to. When he couldn't find the answer, he tried calling Nyeem's cellular phone, but all he got was the voicemail message and a beep. This cycle was repeated every thirty minutes over a period of countless hours, until Michael had given up all hope that he was wrong and cried himself back to sleep, ignoring his hunger and choosing to focus on his broken heart.

He awoke again hours later, blanketed by the dark and scared out of his mind as he heard footsteps in the living room. He wished Nyeem was there to protect him from whoever it was, and then reality set in. For all he knew, it may have been Nyeem, sneaking in again to get what he couldn't tote away in the broad daylight. Michael's hands nervously gripped the metal baseball bat that he kept beside his bed, and he tiptoed into the living room, not even thinking to step into his pajama bottoms.

He could make out two figures, but it was too dark to see their faces. The light switch was on the other side of the room. To get to it, he would have to dodge pass them. His throat grew dry, and his knees buckled together as he realized that he had never committed an act of violence a day of his life. Even with the bat in his hands, he was fucked.

"What are you doing, up?" he recognized Nyeem's voice as the leaner of the two figures came towards him. "Give me that before somebody gets hurt!" Nyeem laughed, snatching the bat out of his hands. "Michael, this is my homeboy, Little James. I did him a favor today, and he's helping move this furniture in here for you in return. I wanted you to just wake up and see it, but I guess you spoiled that plan, huh?"

"Surprise, fucking surprise!" Mike breathed angrily. "I've been calling your phone all damn day. Why didn't you answer? I didn't know what to think!"

"Like I said, I was doing my boy a favor." Nyeem's posture seemed to beg Michael's forgiveness.

Michael's heart sped, and his body tensed in discomfort, but he knew that if he was to ever trust Nyeem again, he had to get answers to all of his questions. "I locked the door; how the hell did you get back in here? And what happened to my computer and the money I left on the table? Do you know that that's what I had to eat with today? I've been hungry all day and worried to death!"

"I'm sorry," Nyeem cooed. "I should have thought about that, but you was sleep when I left and I didn't want to wake you up. I couldn't lock your door, so I didn't want to leave nothing valuable just lying around." He walked across the room and flicked on the light. "I put the money inside your laptop and I put the laptop in this closet. I figured you would get the laptop when you went for your clothes, and then you would have the money. As for the door, man, that piece of shit lock was too easy to pick. I'm going to have that shit changed tomorrow."

Nyeem seemed to have thought of everything, but what he didn't count on was Michael being so hurt and afraid that he didn't feel like getting dressed, making a trip to the closet obsolete. As Nyeem stood, watching Michael's anger turn to embarrassment, for the first time, the thought occurred to him that he should be the angry one. After all they had gone through together, especially the night before, Michael still didn't trust him.

"I'll be back tomorrow to hook the cable up. I think I should just get out of yawl's way," his friend said, shifting nervously.

Finally, Michael was able to focus on more than just Nyeem, and remembered that they weren't alone. He stared at Nyeem's friend, who was much taller, with a portly belly and cornrows. His face was handsome, but it lacked the drop-dead appeal that Nyeem's boyish face offered. The rough sex appeal didn't seem to balance out with the softness as well as Nyeem's, and the green contacts he wore did nothing for him.

"I'm sorry. I don't mean to be rude. My name is Michael." His hand was extended and accepted by the potbelly intruder. "Call me Michael."

"They call me Little James."

"Little James lives right across the street from you," Nyeem informed. "I'm going to be getting him to keep an eye on you and your place when I can't be around. He's good people."

There was an awkward silence, as Michael remembered that he was stark naked, and apologized a dozen times. Finally, Little James excused himself, and Michael and Nyeem were left alone to arrange the new furniture. Michael ached to ask where it had come from, but he knew he had already upset Nyeem with his lack of trust, and he hoped that the rest of the night would go smoothly. Possibly, they could pick up where they had left off the night before. Any questions could wait for the next morning.

"It looks damn good in here, don't you think?" Nyeem asked, walking behind his lover and engulfing him in his python arms.

"You think the sofa can stand up to our lovemaking?" Michael smiled devilishly.

"We'll have to test it out," Nyeem laughed, lifting the boy into his arms and toting him over to the couch, like a groom taking his bride over the threshold.

"Promise me that you won't ever do what you did today," Michael begged as Nyeem kissed around his neck. "Never just leave me alone like you did!"

"You wasn't alone. I told you, Little James watches out for me when I can't be here." Nyeem laughed. "As long as I'm alive, you ain't going to ever be alone. That's my word."

"That's all I wanted to hear," Michael smiled, pulling Nyeem's T-shirt over his head.

"Uh-uh!" Nyeem chided as Michael leaned in for a kiss. "Before I put everything into this, you got to promise me something, too. Promise me that you won't just pick up one day and move back to Delaware. Not after you already got me for my heart." Nyeem demanded, nibbling Michael's earlobe. "Promise me that!"

"You don't have to worry about that, baby." Michael smiled.

Nyeem turned to Michael with a serious look on his face and said, "I love you, boy. I swear to God, I won't ever do nothing to hurt you."

"I know," Michael answered with full sincerity. "I feel the same way about you, and it feels good to finally have that."

43

ROMEO
AT NIGHT
R. Talent

Romeo spends the better part of his days asleep, either over here or over there. Over here being with me and over there can be one of three places: his sister's house, his girl's apartment, or at his baby momma's crib.

He tells me he loves it over here with me the most. He feels the need to say that, I know. It's part of the game. But, from his full sexy lips, I believe he is quite honest and very sincere about that. Romeo doesn't have to say anything he doesn't mean, you know. All he has to do is flash that sinister grin of his (the one with the crooked tooth) wrapped around in that straggly beard, and he knows he is in. That he's got me. Plus, I don't give him much grief about the way he lives his perilous life or his lack of a real nine-to-five, with the added bonus that he can get laid without running the risk of leaving another bitch pregnant.

Romeo and I are cool like that. We have a simple but beautiful understanding. He loves to lay pipe and as an undercover bottom brotha, my walls enjoy being custom-fitted for that piece of steel with each and every stroke: Anytime, anyplace, and any damn where. No fuss. No unnecessary melodrama.

I can't stress that enough.

In this city that is absolutely crucial with so many hungry asses out here constantly on the hunt for their next dick feeding. Too many faggot-bitches go out of their way to play themselves, trying to build these pseudo-relationships in their minds. If the dick pops up more than once, then they try so hard to make it more than what it is. Going to the extremes of propping it up like a ghetto king, stuffing him gourmet takeout and designer clothing just for him being as good as the last nutt he busted. Unlike them, I'm not so into getting dicked by Romeo that I will part with my senses or my wallet just to get him to stay – at least, that was my thought.

My thinking before was that if he comes, he comes. If he goes, so be it. But after losing my job a few weeks ago, Romeo surprised me. He has really come through, above and beyond, shoring me up with the dollars to take care of the bills and whatnot. I am not hurting or anything, and he knows this. I have always been good with the money. He wants to feel like my man, and for him, this is how.

I use to feel bad about it in the beginning, thinking I was taking away from his families. Then, one day, after he got tired of me refusing, he showed me the several large wads of cash he had laying about, telling me he was good at doing what he does. Because he is dick and I am ass, I never gave it much thought, thinking with his stocky build and macho-mean good looks and his abilities to put it down, I thought he found some silly ho to fund his ways.

He is an entrepreneur. His way of making money is pretty sweet – illegal, but sweet.

At night, he hustles. He grinds to make that paper, slinging dope or taking on petty hits, hurting or even murdering those that don't pay on their respective tabs. He even goes so far to funnel the life in his lyrics for the artists that are signed to his start-up independent label.

He needs help, he tells me, something on the line of doing a bunch of tedious paperwork. Something I am good at, something I know. I ask him, how much does it pay? He runs his finger against the print running along his left thigh and with his smile framed by his straggly beard he says about a good ten inches. I wink back turning away from the television showing a rapper swiping a credit card between some butt checks and say something smart like that it is only as good as the teller that accepts it.

My job starts with typing up menial document and making copies and running errands for the office before I am propelled to the level of executive secretary to the higher ups. It feels like a real job after a few weeks. It pays and comes with benefits like a real job. And, I forget about Romeo, the man I sometimes share a bed with since he is all about business in this environment the more he gets into it. He tries to make a serious effort at professionalism. He cares more about his paper than smoking blunts and getting it between my ass cheeks, at least, here at work. He gets mad respect from me, more than ever. He is proving that he is much more than another worthless gang banger packing a nice piece.

I know for certain that I am in trouble when I walk through the building sporting a broad smile, proud of my man, no morning sex, just because. I want to sing it aloud. I want to shout it from the rooftop, and then it hits me he is no such thing to me. He is a piece. I am a piece. I regain my focus. I try to use my free time, lunch and breaks, to pull away from him. I don't want to wake up one day and find that this job is my career, and I am bound to it or him because of him or the job. As much as I try, or as much as I want to believe, I go about my search half-baked. Doing just enough to know that I can leave if I want to but hold back just enough so that it doesn't have to happen.

Romeo begins to change slowly but steadily, going from a jovial thug earning a legitimate keep to a typical moody and irritable businessman that has a foreign shish-iness in his eyes. So, it came as no surprise one otherwise beautiful morning when he whizzes pass me, instructing me not to let anyone disturb him. I oblige in the parameters of superior and subordinate.

I go about my business playing with the papers when three guys approach my desk. They bypass the receptionist and the rent-a-cops, demanding to see Romeo. I lie and tell them that he is gone. And when that lie obviously doesn't work, I try to maintain my professionalism and tell them that he doesn't want to be disturbed. They show me their gun hoisters and go right in, closing the door behind them.

The men reappear, heading off to the elevator. Their meeting is brief. There is no bloodshed, fights or gunshots. There is a smudge of relief in the air to find that Romeo is not distraught. I want to ask him a thousand questions in one. I can see that he isn't in the mood. It isn't the right time. And, of course, it isn't any of my business even though I feel that I am in too deep. He may want to feel like my man, but he isn't. I cannot settle for him, I think, resisting the consideration that he has been there for me.

"What was that all about?" I ask, my mouth betraying my thoughts.

"Don't worry about it, folk." He brushes off.

"When folks start pulling a gun to my head, I ain't got much choice in the matter but to worry." I say as calmly as I can.

"They … huh … they …"

"How do you think they got back here?"

He becomes unnerved at this news, distraught. He doesn't know what to say, and it puts me in the mind of our first night together, at a loss for words after we lost ourselves in the passionate moment. For me, it was the afterglow of getting my ass pounded out, and for him, he was in a jam since it was too late to board the train of the night.

"You wanna suck my dick?" He asks waving me back from my trip down memory lane.

He asks in such a fashion as if he is going out of his way to do me a favor with his fine-looking meat just hanging between his zipper.

I try to be strong. He has proven that he is more than his dick to me. So I know that I am more than a watering mouth and a dampened hole.

"Look," he says, disappointed in my reaction. "Come here. You need to chill … I need to relaxation … let's chillax together."

He pulls me close. I swallow hard.

The many complications of working together and sex in the office place is at the top of the list. The exciting danger of homophobic hip-hop and two down low brothas play into mind. But since Romeo was so serious about being so serious, I squashed any such ideas.

And here it is.

I go down in front of him.

It is strange, this time, or maybe it is just being here, as a cool heat rolls off of that thing, and I kiss it like I would kiss him on the mouth. I wrap my fingers firmly on the base, and slowly put my lips around his dick. His drug-hardened hands grabs at the back of my head.

He isn't forceful with it as much as he wants me to know how much he needs me now. He keeps one hand on my head. He cups the other under my chin. I feel the wire whiskers that are his long dong ball hairs. He quivers as my tongue is slow to dive deep in his slot. I listen to him mumble. I take more of him into my mouth, brushing my nose against his hairs and pull back, and come in again.

Romeo groans and thrusts his hips forward. My mouth is full of him. My throat is to act as his prisoner, yet I feel like it in imprisoned gulping for air. He takes the other hand, the one on my chin, and puts it on the back of my head trying to find his breath. He pumps violently, forgetting my face is my face, and I soon feel the familiar throbbing of a ramrod that is ready to explode. He locks my face in place with his hands. He grunts deeply. About a few seconds later, I feel the spurts of fluid oozing down my windpipe and down into my belly.

He is satisfied, catching his breath. It has been a long time coming, read his eyes. I am reaching that plateau myself, cleaning his dick tip with my mouth, squeezing out every pearl of cum with one hand and jacking off with the other hand.

There are no other office rendezvous after that. It is business as usual, no lingering smile or quick glances. Romeo starts to pull away, not only from me, but from the office as well. His business is always elsewhere, and people are looking to me to find him. It is almost comes off as a veiled attempt to try and confirm our romance. I try to put the thought out of my mind, going about business as usual. But, I can't. Too many things still linger in my head to the point that he is no longer there for me to be concern.

When he ceases to show up for work, there is a peace around the building, a sigh of relief. It is obviously something is going on that someone isn't telling me. Everybody is cordial, but distant. And maybe, it's just me, but it feels like it is only directly towards me. Because of the nature business, I feel comfortable coming in later than I want to and staying even later than I need to, just to avoid the glares and phoniness of the masses.

I try to seek new employment again, and I am going to be for real about it this time, whatever comes my way. The market is on lock. I can't leave without a safety net, unemployment or severance like I could have from my old job. I am stuck. My job becomes a stress, and my booty call becomes my absentee man. I curse the day we ever met.

I am well worked up over my recent tirade over Romeo when I find a man sitting on my doorstep. I am all man, so there isn't a fear of scared in my face or in my eyes returning home. He seems thrown, confused. He wants to ask me a question. I beat him to the punch and throw them out at him since he is at my door invading my privacy. He leaves eventually, telling me to tell Romeo that he needs to get in contact with him.

I am fed up. I call Romeo, and tell him that I quit. I want out of this shit. I tell him that if one of his fucking goons comes by my house again, I'm taking him out and then gunning for him. I say everything so quickly that Romeo needs me to repeat it. I tell him again. He tells me to stay still. He is coming over. He looks like the Romeo I use to fuck, not like the dressed up creature from the office. He is true street again, in thug apparel, looking like he sleeps all day and fucks all night. He looks like he has girlfriend trouble, baby mama drama, and still thinking with his dick when he sees me.

I am too upset to fall into his trap. Everything would have been fine if he remained my dick and I remained his piece of ass, and stopped stepping up to be my man. It didn't help that I am standing at the window watching this hooptie pass by my apartment several times before it rattles gunshots at my window. We duck and we cover, and crawl out on the floor out the front door. It goes without saying that it isn't safe for me to stay there, so Romeo takes me in my car elsewhere to be safe.

He orders his girlfriend to fix us a plate and asks his sister to spare a bed. I am cooped up in her house for days on end, waiting on Romeo to tell me the rest of his plan. He is slow to come up with one, so those men that are after him come up with one, breaking into the house where me and his sister are in. They don't hurt us, but scare us enough that we both no longer feel safe there either. I am angered that he feels comfortable enough to send her back home, somewhere back in the Caribbean, Martinique or Guadeloupe or The Turks and Caicos, somewhere like that, but insists on keeping me here with him.

I am not happy with him, as we check into a motel room. He spends most of the days and nights sitting at the window with his pistol in his hand, waiting on some invisible bad man to burst through the door. We wait and wait and wait some more. And, instead of gunmen bursting through the door, the phone rings from the office that someone left a message. He instructs me to hide under the bed until he comes back, making his way over the door. He comes back a few moments later. He gives me the keys to my car, and I drive him to this random spot downtown. He tells me he wants to go hang out somewhere, the mall or park, and afterwards a nightclub and an after-hours spot. But whatever I do, "Don't return to the motel until morning." His final words to me are to be careful and to watch my back and to make sure that no one is following me. I do everything he says. I return to the motel to find him in a wifebeater and a pair of blue boxers with his pistol in tow. Only this time, he looks like he is contemplating about using it on himself, the way his body slumps over and the gun just hangs in his spread lap. I try to snap him out of it, but he cries that he is in too deep and he owes too much money. I try to take his mind off of his problems with other things. He is too stubborn to respond. I kiss him and his lips are limp. I take hold of the mighty dick that is always eager to greet me, and it is dead on arrival. This shit is serious, I think. I tell him to tell me everything, holding nothing back. He does, and I see how everything started and is bound to end.

We come up with a plan, spending most of the day and into the night pounding out the details. I see his spirit rise. By dusk, the next night, he becomes the hustler I fell in lust with at the train station that time. He is confident with swagger, and his dick is drooling through is saggy jeans. He gets a package on consignment and flips it for profit threefold. He takes his portion of his bread and split it in four letting me sit on half while he tries to double in a crap game. He barely breaks even. The good thing is that he didn't lose too much. He more than makes up for what he lost when some of the debts he calls in pay off, and it starts to count even more so when the favors he calls in come through. It is not enough to pay off what he owes, but still it was better than he had, better than taking his own life. That is where the backup plan comes in hand. He didn't want to do it; it is a last resort next to robbing his company, but he has to. He knows the ins and outs of the liquor store that his ex-girlfriend used to work too well not to try and get the money from them. He hates it because the owner was cool with her old man, but he knew that the owner fronted about having the place well guarded with burglar bars and shit. He knew that the old man was too cheap to put in surveillance or a security system, and his safe key code was 7-4-1. Like magic, Romeo is in and out in five minutes with several thousand dollars in tow. It is around the time the clubs lets out, so there is a bit of traffic to pick up something to eat at some of the 24/7 drive-thru eateries, but we make the call to his creditor letting him know we made the note and we are on our way to make the payment, but not before we pig out over a feast like old times or when he caught a case of the munchies. As we are on our way, we stop back at my place and pick up his car. He gets in his car and rolls out without me. He tells me to stay still, as he rides out into his creditor's rival territory, shooting blindly at the drug house, and speeding off. That is the plan, I worry, trying to reconcile why home no longer feels like such a place.

He returns safely. I breathe a sigh of relief. He tells me to call "them" up, and "try" to warn them that Creditor is going to take a hit out on them tonight because business is low and "before sunrise" there will be only one dealer left. He bites, but has many of questions, and I answer all of them the way Romeo and I rehearsed. I am nervous, too, if he is really sinking his teeth into our story. He almost comes off doubtful before he flips the script and digests everything we give him as gospel, telling him where he can find his enemy.

We jump in my car to get a front row seat to the show that will go down. It becomes crystal clear when he pulls up that everything is about to go down the way we plan, and we have the money only as insurance if it doesn't. Meaning that with the exception of the robbery, most of the money is ours, given that he is without word going to give me a cut for aggravation and compensation. We sit and wait, wait and sit, sit and wait and sit some more. I am bored and nervous and a bit scared that one of the stray bullets is bound to hit me or Romeo or both in this car. Romeo looks over and thanks me. He smiles widely, with no mischievousness laced in. In all the time I have known him, I've never known him like this. He leans forward and kisses me, and I am taken aback. There is nothing around but the building and streetlights, but I feel that an embrace like that is too open, especially out here. My refusal it seems turns him on. He kisses me some more, but it is more than a kiss. He wants something more.

"Not in here," I say, with my seat somehow reclined and he somehow on top of me.

"Why not?" He asks.

"Because," I say, hoping that it is enough.

"Because of what? Ain't nobody out here. If there was, they might learn something." He says with that familiar sinister grin hovering over me.

I want to stop him, but my dick betrays me demanding to be free from its fabric prison.

"I want to but ... but ... but we ain't got any rubbers." I say hoping this is my out.

I always gave in whenever he wanted it, but never without a rubber.

He surprises me with his readiness, showing me a gold wrapper and one of those fat clear packs of individual lube.

The next thing I know, my pants are down and so are his. I can't see them, but I know they are down because can feel his hard dripping dick thumping against my stomach, grinding even hard as he kisses me. He does this so seductively in the small space we have, with him trying to pull off my shirt. I am in the moment going for his coat, yet I am fighting it every step of the way, afraid about what is going to happen if we are caught out here. And before I could come back to any kind of sense, my legs are spread and my hips are raised greeting the bloated head of his penis with my hole.

My body tenses as he pushes it in. The dick that I once received on the regulars seems so much foreign and bigger than I remember. I am gritting my teeth realizing that I was crazy to ever take this kind of dick even though I am the kind of man that loves it inside of me.

"Relax, babe," he sooths.

I do what he says. Everything comes back to me on how to master his monster, sinking it in ever so slow. Because of our confined space, he needs time to build the crescendo that I love so much. I begin to tremble from the heaven-like numb my hole feels from his balls nuzzling against my ass as he plows deeper and faster with every soulful stroke.

I try ever so hard to hold in the grunts that I am so use to letting out. The vehicle offers no sound barriers. A mist of joy starts to seep out of the crease of my eyes. I don't want him to see this, for him to see what he does to me. I try hard to keep my lips locked with his or somewhere on his face. He warms up a fire deep inside of me, forcing me to arch my back and let out a whimper. He knows this is his finest hour. He wants to shout it out, tell me how good this ass is to his jabbing slings, but he knows he can't. Not the way he gets loud when he gets it in. Not the way I get loud the way he gets loud getting it.

"Ah," is all Romeo can mumble freely, and he says it distinctly three times before he warns me he is coming, slowing his strides, and then like a madman he pounds into a war cry that is snuffed out by the rounds of gunshots blazing nearby.

My body shakes, I shoot a cannon-fire load that paints our abdomens with gleaming white.

He falls on top of me, not for a rest as he waits for the smoke to clear.

It is done.

The next day, I awake in my bed with Romeo snuggled next to me, thinking of all the money that is going to sustain his label. So I am surprised when he pulls a gun out on me, and says I know too much. I try to reason with him, telling him I am in just as deep as he is.

And then …

NEW YORK
R. Talent

Black. White. Latino.

Blatino. Biracial, black and white. White and Latino. Puerto Rican (*Boricua*). *Dominicano. Mexicano.* Part Puerto Rican and half Dominican. Black Mex. Black and Puerto Rican. Black and Dominican.

Half Mexican and part Dominican.

Puerto Rican and Mexican.

Cuban. Jamaican. Panamanian. Columbian. Venezuelan. Brazilian.

Chinese. Japanese. Filipino. Mongolian. Italian. Greek.

Live in x-borough; want to fuck in all the boroughs.

Passport, visiting from overseas.

Plan on staying for just a little while.

For business, for pleasure.

Corporate. Thug. Corporate Thug. Average. Slim. Stocky. Thick. Muscled-up. Pay for play. Masc. Fem. In-between. Hell, if I know. Don't have a fucking clue!

Top. Bottom. Versatile, everything.

Oral top. Oral bottom. Just want to suck and get sucked.

It sounds like a freaking buffet! But no, not at all.

It is New York – the land of the five freaking boroughs.

It is the land of overfed pythons and violently spitting anacondas, tight tolling tunnels and bottomless pits all at my convenient disposal. 24 hours a day. 7 days a week. 52 weeks and 365 days a year.

Every time I leave the house, I find that the New York air washes over me with a horniness that causes my pipe to leak and my ass to get slippery at the thought I can get my dick wet and my man-pussy pounded out at any second just by standing at the front door.

I try to play it cool. Have my clothes blending in with theirs. The usual street soldier uniform: baggy, saggy jeans, a pair of Timbs, and something that allows me to show off my defined muscled-out torso at the drop of a dime to the highest quarter bidder.

I even took to smoking trees in the don't-dare-smoke-anywhere-city. Actually, shit, I just hold a burning blunt out of my mouth and try not to inhale just to show that I can be down with whatever, only to end up making a fool of myself behind closed doors.

Inhaling and coughing. Inhaling and coughing. Damn near nauseous.

They laugh. The all laugh, from the handsomest of inglorious bastards to the gnarled shit-faces of angry gangsters. They like that I'm different and that my cornbread brown skin is fresh and clean and sun-kissed bright. They love that I am from the foreign land of South Carolina, that I talk with a deep southern twang, calling me Country Boy at every bend.

They don't hold back. They want to fuck some of this good country ass. The way it teases them the way it sticks out like a sturdy bar for a drink, teasing their hard-ons like some sort unusually cruel joke. They want to suck some big country dick feeling good that the myth is true (at least in my case it is). That a country boy with big country hands and big country feet, size seventeen to be exact, has a big country prick that can stretch out any available hole.

Digging deep and swimming long at nearly every turn in this concrete jungle paved of gold is sweet. But what gets me off though is being a big dick bottom for some swinging dick top that knows how to calm an insatiable hungry hole like mine the fuck down. I think everybody gets off on the hard heavy thwacks of a hefty penis hitting a six pack, or a flailing magnum bobbing up and down like a carriage ride in Central Park.

I spend some time introducing my sex to New York by having a different man every night in a different borough and outskirt. Manhattan. Queens. Brooklyn. Staten Island. The Bronx. Yonkers. Jersey City. Mt. Vernon. New Rochelle. Paterson. Newark. Elizabeth. Long Island. My ship comes in at a very popular sex party in The Bronx. It is too wild for me. Either it is too fast for my bumpkin ass or I am a snail in this jackrabbit world. One guy bends over to suck off another guy, and a line twenty deep seems to grow out of his asshole. I go to the roof to get some fresh air from the pollution of rowdy sex below to find other men doing the same thing. Most seem to know the other and vice versa, leaving me to feel solo on this run. There is no non-sexual Meet & Greet sex party etiquette – just Meat & Grind with your hidden parts. But I still try. Not too hard, though. Most choose to ignore me. A handful of others try to play me, trying to run some lame-ass game stealing lines from the late Big Poppa, like 'what's my name, what's my sign,' directly chucking from my behind.

I coyly flip them off, look and make out the river to the city and the lights and dark in between.

"Not as dumb as those asses, I see." He says rolling up beside me.

He is no walking Adonis, a descendant from the great heavens above. He is no Greek God or Zulu Warrior. He is however an ugly motherfucker in a sexy thuggish sort of way.

He has this low-cut almost shaved bald head with these small-ass ears and these big-ass lips. He has this raggedly beard that makes him look like a subway prophet. He has these fiery eyes that look as if they are fueled by a 150 proof elixir.

He sounds New Yorker. He tells me he is a chocolate Nuyorican by way of Brick City. I smile and inquire about what that all means. He grins devilishly and says in due time, ba-be. He also says that his name is Ralo. I tell him mine is David. He says from now on he was going to call me Reno 'cause I look like that black cop from the show.

To go back in and seduce him to do the wild thing with me seems sort of awkward, unkind to our pleasant conversation. I leave quite satisfied like I had to empty a thousand loads after one hundred years celibate. My regret comes immediately after I am spit out into the abandoned streets with nothing more than the impression of his scent and swag.

Our paths were destined to cross again on the local subway train home. He dons his finest chains, his flyest gear and his most expensive leather do-rag. He is on his way to the studio to lay down some tracks. He tells me he is a rapper and invites me to join him. I tell him to spit some rhyme, give me some kind of reason to go off with him. He breaks into laughter in mid-verse, telling me that he is only a producer but that the rest of his story is true. Against other judgments, I play follow the leader to this spot down in the Lower East Side. I watch Ralo do what he do, and pay close attention to everything he shows me.

I fall asleep on the couch. I wake up next to him, appreciating his nice sturdy build keeping me warm throughout the cold night. He kisses me on the forehead good morning. He takes me out to breakfast at Mickie D's. Once we put the last crumbs in our mouths, he slips me a card with all his contact info. Call him anytime, he says. I am hesitant to use it over the next couple of days. I don't want to come off too eager, too hopeful, too clingy. And how we met does not lay the greatest foundation for something more, something real, which often dances through my head when I think of him and rubbing up against his straggly beard.

We eventually hang out. We chill, and he kisses me but nothing more. With the exception of the pecks here and there, I sometimes think his mind is on building a good friendship and nothing more.

He surprises me one night over the phone after one of our casual movie nights. He starts talking real low and sexy-like, asking me what I had on. Not catching on, I told him the truth. The same thing he just saw me in. When I reverse the question, he laughs, only a pair of socks and a smile. He tells me about how he likes roaming around his bedroom in the projects butt-ass naked jacking off to the beat of the busy city below. He thinks about me, tugging at his crotch. He tells me that he thinks he is in love with me every time he is with me. He falls into lust every time he is without me, thinking about oiling up that phat booty of mine and going at it like a Hungry Man dinner. He says that if this was a perfect world we could have a picnic lunch in Marcus Garvey Park, stroll under the streetlamps of the Brooklyn Bridge, and share overnighters at some fancy B&B further up the Hudson. He gestures of romance turns into adrenaline-rushing sex with freaky ideas of oral-to-genital fixation in the dirty alleyways near his building or having me grunt in crescendo as he takes my ass on the rooftop of some anonymous unguarded tenement. He playfully asks me to come over. There is an abandoned spot in his building where we can 'make love.' I don't mind being with him in that way, but I am somewhat paranoid about the underworld that is his projects where I figure the seediest of activities transpire. He senses my hesitance through the phone. He confesses he wouldn't do me like that. Not me. Not the first time, at least. He needs time and space, a spot for our groove to be long, nasty and really, really slow. He wants to kiss me there and there and everywhere and enjoy everything. I need for him to be my man.

He says all the right things. And I help him screech his way to a milky end laced with vulgar breathing and heavy tones. I let him recover. He thanks me. I hang up, busting my own nutt with my legs spread to some porno later on.

Over the next few weeks, he no longer talks about studio stuff. Not with the passion that once sung in his heart. Instead, his business is about running errands. Errands this, errands that. He doesn't have time for me anymore because he is always running some fucking errand. I simply figure it is somebody else somewhere else out there in the world. I considering giving him the sex I crave just to keep him around, if for nothing more than booty calls. In going through my back and forth on what to do, I catch Ralo browbeat on the train. He doesn't see me. I don't make myself known. I stay to the side, follow my instincts and follow him on the ride out. His errand runs are consumed with small brown packages, handing them off to unscrupulous men and hoodrats on the sly, sometimes even collecting these packages showing off his gun tucked into his waistband and taking them to the other end of the alphabet and numerical lines.

I say absolutely nothing. I go about my business.

See no evil. Hear no evil.

I try to go through detox, detoxing him from my life. He is a drug and I continue to follow him to make sure he stays okay. My life is now a contradiction. My trailing of this man is an obsession, yet my contact with him is passé, almost none now.

I find solace on the quiet end of a platform, away from the chatter of the mobile world. I try finding my peace in a chaotic book that I am on my way to the library to return. Ralo is no longer on my mind, finally, and then there he appears standing in front of me.

"What're you doing?" He asks abruptly.

He looks different. More refined, more confident, yet that glow that initially made him attractive soon disappears.

"Reading a ..."

"You know what I mean, David." He cuts me off. I know he is serious because he puts David where Reno usually is, "following me around the city like some kind of stray mutt."

"Fuck you, motherfucker." I spit back. "I've been worried about you. I've got a very good reason to be."

"Look ..."

"No, you look!" I jump up in his face, casting my book to the bench below. "For some dag-on reason, I caught feelings for you. I don't want to see my hopes and dreams for us somewhere out there in the middle of the damn East River!"

He looks at me. His eyes try to shy away from mine. He can't help but to see that I am sincere. It is never his intention to hurt me, but he sees for the first time he is.

"This is something I got to do." He says mournfully.

"This is something you want to do. You're good at what you do in the studio. Do that." I say.

"But it ain't paying the bills."

"Fuck the bills! At least fuck this!" I gesture at this precise time a train roars by.

"Babe, I can't bring you home because I'm still with my moms and them. I can't take you away because I don't have much ends because I try and hustle legit. Can't you see I'm doing this for us?"

"Don't use me as an excuse for this." I say. "If you do this, you're doing it for you not me."

"Babe ... David ... Reno ..."

"You know what the sexiest thing you've ever done for me in your life has been?"

"That little freak session over the phone?" He laughs.

"For me," I correct him. "Let me use your chest as a pillow that night in the Lower East Side. Kissing me on the forehead with your funky morning breath, that bought you more with me than you could with the bread you make from doing this."

He looks at me and kisses me and holds me like he should have, tight and firm like he is never letting me go. It is like we are in that perfect world on that flawless day in that park we always talked about, under free and clear skies. It feels so real that I can feel the sunshine kissing our noses under the crisp snap of autumn. I quickly snap back into reality remembering that we are two men kissing in the cloaking darkness of an MTA subway station. I remember the hypothetical tragedies that happened to these kinds of boys back in Spartanburg, South Carolina, and cringe at the fate of us here in the Big Apple.

The danger must excite him because his need to grab at my ass is urgent. His dick is on brick through his jeans. But, the rise in my own causes me to pull away, fall back on the bench. I look up at him. Yes? No? Maybe? Before I decide in my head, my hands decide for me, pulling Ralo to me by his drooping waistband.

"What are you doing, man?" Ralo asks surprised.

He always takes lead in kissing. Though, this isn't kissing.

"Oh, you'll see."

Removing layer upon layer of zipped and buckled jeans and standard boxer briefs, I peel out a smooth and thick caramel-chocolate decadent brown uncut candy cane hanging there like some ridiculously big handlebar. I sniff the designer knock-off cologne and his musk before wrapping my lips around his fat dick. It feels warm and full in my mouth. Even I am startled that I want more of it. Damn it! Just it being in my mouth and all I want to do is taste him. My eagerness outranks my logic. I have to restore balance, pushing him back enough just to work the tip. He moans as I work my tongue around the head, under that small hood of foreskin in the back, and over into the cavernous piss slit.

"Ah, damn, Dave, ba-be." He murmurs.

His dick tastes even better leaking with its sweet pineapple juice flavor.

He is lost on what to do with his hands, so he rests them on the top of my head like it is a buzzer on a game show.

"Suck my dick, man, ohh," Ralo breaths softly.

I give his shaft a good once over. I pull off choosing to work over his meaty one-eighth Italian meatballs and trying to get to that spot between them.

Ohh and Ahh.

I go back to taking care of the rest of his dick with my mouth, lost in the safety that Ralo is my man, and he needs me to take care of him in this way. I am shaken back to where I am with the rick-rack of another passing train.

"There you go. That's my ba-be!"

I try going for the gold, getting his pubes to tickle my nose. But he is too big and too long. He grunts and groans, nevertheless, and begs me to pull off. He has held back too long. He doesn't want to first load we share together to come out like this.

So I oblige.

"You're right." I say. "You got a rubber?"

"Yeah," he says, and then, "here?" after finally catching on.

"Makes for a great first time story," I say, feeling more than confident that it won't be the last time.

I gently remind him of our circumstances. He lives in the projects with four generations of woman, and I live on the down low in a hand over fist situation with my five roommates in a small two bedroom apartment. Even though the space is quite public, it is also quite private like that rooftop he has always dreamt of for us.

"You fo' real?" He asks, attempting not to grin too wide.

"I'm fo' real with it. You?" I say with a twinge of second doubt.

He grabs my hand encouraging me to stand again. He kisses me again and tastes himself on my tongue. He enjoys his flavor – so I believe. This, though sweet, is an elaborate rouse to check his pockets for a condom.

"There are cameras around you know?" He says guiding my hand to his firm exposed sex.

"How many do you think are actually working? Are actually being watched by rent-a-cops?"

"You got me there." He smiles going in for one more kiss and pulling away briefly to show me a small black square with the word MAGNUM written in gold.

I ain't mad 'cause it is true.

Being a prepared boy from the Deep South, I can give as good as I get, which is why I carry four packs of lube just to be on the safe side.

We begin this dance that sort of plays like a romantic comedy twirling around as a Hollywood montage plays in the foreground as we get our bearings, making sure we are out of eyeshot of anyone that might give a damn.

I plop my ass on a small rise above the bench where he stands and leans back a little as we both try to undo my pants. He wants to shuck them off. I insist that I keep one leg on, around my ankle, around my boot.

"I never fucked a dude in his Timbs before."

"First time for everything, ain't it." I huff in the fear of my lust.

He uses one pack of lube on his dick. He then puts on the tailor-made rubber and slathers on another lube pillow. He slathers a third one in and around my hole, and split the fourth pack between the second and third options.

"Ah, GOT DAMMIT!"

I wince at the head thudding against my entire back hole and then some on both ends. It damn sure isn't going to fit, I think. I brace myself. I try to relax. I try not to scream again and hope to God that I don't damage my pleather jacket too bad as it is tested to protect my butt-nakedness.

Ralo pushes in.

I breathe out, listening to the crackling of condom and lube. I squirm. This invader is the best of the worst. Most guys like to just ram it in, thinking it's the best way to open up some ass – it ain't. But this motherfucker here wants to take the scenic route. He wants to go nice and slow. I love it because it means he cares. I hate it because it's forever big, forever hurts, splitting me apart like a rusty can opener.

I feel his balls crush against my sweaty buns. I would make a crude joke about a meatball sub, but with him inside me like this I feel full, complete, and laboring through the searing pain. He pulls back and I begin to help wiggle him out of my trembling hole. He drives in again, only this time it is sort of sluggish. The best way to describe it is like the beginning of a roller coaster ride. It drags with something more to come. It takes a moment to settle into his rhythm, and I understand patiently and pleasurably. None of us has ever done this like this before, and we were driven by the excitement of where we were and the fear of getting caught. It probably doesn't help much that I cannot react like I should, or normally would. And it doesn't help that what separates my bare ass from raw concrete is some thin, awkward and squeaky fabric.

The pain slowly floods into pleasure with the ache of ecstasy bumping against my prostate. I let out a few murmurs of delight with each passing train car. I reach for my own hard big dick. I thump it against his hard clothed stomach shaking down the boiling magma ready to erupt into scorching white-hot lava.

Ralo catches my eye. We exchange simpers. This here is unplanned, but still our first time. He sinks it in deeper, more control. He peaks at another level, and I give in completely. He owns my guts, and he knows it, putting me to the screws.

"Fuck. Oh, fuck! Dammit!" Ralo gasps.

He grabs the top of my thigh right at the bend. He slams it back in each stroke, harder than the last. I feel that my body is a sturdy tree and his enormous dick is like a chainsaw sawing into me with each brutal thrust.

He comes back from the place in his mind. That place behind his closed eyelids. He looks down at me. He lets my legs go, go as they may around his standing body.

"Damn, baby, you got a nice piece, too!" He says matching my shaft in strokes.

I scream, not knowing my own voice, and shoot all over everything. My shirt and my jacket; his shirt and his jacket, and even some on his pants, I believe.

For the first time, I feel the tears that fill in my eyes … those that were already there for some time. There is so much I cannot do, so much that I want to. I feel my hole close tightly around him, engulfing him, enveloping him, and suffocating it, as he tries to keep his strong moments going. He is grinding to an end. His face tightens and that row of sweat on his forehead begins to show.

"I'm on my way, ba-be!" Ralo announces. "I'm on my fucking way!"

We hear a train pull up to the platform. He works harder than ever before. He bucks. He shouts. He bucks again roughly just seconds before the train rolls by and after he comes – hard.

I am feeling a mix of emotion as he pants his way down from Cloud 99. Happy. Elated. Glad. Mad. Had. Fucked. Sore. But the thing I feel most in the moment is empty and disappointment as he shrinks and pulls out of me.

He unrolls his condom from his dick.

I feel like a mother giving up my child for adoption as I never get to see the nutt that I help milk with this tight willing hole. I am left to grieve the seeds he tosses into the train track to be a feast for the rats and them.

The two of us take deep breaths as if we beat our criminal rap. We each pull up our pants. He helps me stand up. He lingers around looking at me before making the move to kiss me once more. We stay frozen in the minute and begin running towards the new train as it approaches the platform.

I believe that he will stay with me on the ride to the library. He has other plans, though. He has an errand to run.

When I return to the brownstone later on that evening, Ralo sits outside of my building with a bag of candy and a money clip that is calculator-thick with fifties and twenties. He wants me to join him on another train ride elsewhere. I am reluctant to go because I will not go down as the subway freak. We ride out to this spot in Manhattan to this little bitty-ass apartment not far from his studio. He grins showing me around every nook and cranny. I don't know what to say or make of the situation. He hems me up against the wall affectionate and says that he wants to make this our new home.

BROTHA-IN-LAW
R. Talent

Michelle wasn't really my sister. She was just part of the all-expense package deal that came when my mom married her father when we were both still teenagers. So when she came strolling through the door at the end of her sophomore year at FAMU with an engagement ring courtesy of her newly-signed pro-football playing boyfriend, Chauncey, the family wasn't the least bit surprised.

Michelle was the head cheerleader at our high school, so it was only befitting that she was on the arm of the star quarterback. At the time, I held that title with my big glorious dreams of making it to the NFL before my do-good school decided to put me on academic probation. As far as I was concerned, it wasn't a real biggie. It wasn't as if I was one of those dumb jocks that couldn't read or write like some of my other teammates. I was probably one of the smartest people in my class. It was just that after I got my nose opened for the very first time with my substitute teacher, I figured that a warm fresh pair of soft butt cheeks felt far better in my grown-man hands than some old sissy school books. Besides, I knew that my simpleton school wasn't dumb enough to ice my career with as many record-shattering stats I had under my belt. Even with all the fair warning, I was still dumbfounded when they pulled the plug on my playing career. And with that, I went from being the star of the show with one of the phynest girls on my rounded bicep to a sub-zero scrub that got less play than a bucktoothed geek monster sporting some bright yellow high-water pants. But in the end though, it turned out to be a totally good thing, considering that after I got my grades back up, I did my thing on the wrestling mat bringing home all-state titles galore and my third-tier road dawg

Chauncey got a taste of the spotlight and went on to do bigger and better things.

He was about seven years into his football career, happily married to my stepsister and was continuously showering the family with cash and luxurious gifts, when he got bowled over with a career-ending injury. I think it was well understood by everyone that the good times as we knew it had come to an end. No longer were we going to spend the holidays in Jamaica or Barbados or vacation in St. Tropez partying it up with the faux-trendy celebrities. We simply chucked up everything as being good while it lasted. In saying that though, just because his career on the field was over with, it didn't mean that his livelihood in the game was. Thanks to a great publicist, his sparkling good looks and his smooth sexy pseudo-educated voice, he was a shoe in for one of those flashy television jobs for one of the sport shows. So, even though his days of spoiling us silly had ended, we weren't worried about him not finding his sea legs during this difficult transition.

What we did not know at the time was that without that big payday ol' boy didn't have a pot to piss in. He was so sure that he was going to get back on the gridiron that he wasted his money on the most expensive specialists and physical therapists to tell him what everybody else already knew what wasn't going to happen. As a result, he hired more people to confirm the very thing that the first group of people had already told him to begin with. Soon, the bank foreclosed on his larger-than-baller mansion and repossessed his unreal custom-made cars. He spent so much money flossin' and glossin' that the little he was smart enough to save went into a couple of failing businesses that needed more money that he didn't have to keep them afloat. And as for those promising job interviews, he didn't even have the money for airfare to fly out and meet all his prospective new employers.

Without question, Michelle, who had made a career of being an arrogant bitch by then, was livid when she had to climb off her high horse and beg our parents to come back home. I had already been back weeks earlier when my baby momma kicked me out for the umpteenth time after she found out that I was moonlighting as a wrestler with the hopes of making into the WWE.

For the first couple of months, we stayed clear of each other given my work and wrestling schedules along with training wherever I could squeeze it in. But after Michelle got laid off from her job, she was eager to greet me with her newfound frigidness every time I stepped through the door, trying to put me down about my life even though I was floating a smidge higher than she was in that cesspool. As soon as Chauncey got a whiff of his wife's misdirected wrath, he tried making a concerted effort to apologize for her behavior. It was sweet of him, but I joked it off saying that regardless of who she would've ended up with, it was obviously her destiny to end up back home.

He had to laugh at that one. We became really quick friends after that.

When Michelle was off looking for a job and I had some time off from mine, I hung out with Chauncey in the sitting room playing video games. He still had a nice little penny to his name to lounge around the house debating what his next move was going to be. Michelle wanted him to look at going back to school to get his master's degree. But with me talking about my love for my job as a satellite installer, he sort of romanticized about working with his hands again, wanting to go back to school to become an electrician. Of course, that meant that his stuck-up wife could no longer bank on a life in the lap of luxury again. So he kept his hands busy on the gaming controllers as I steadily kicked his butt in any game he threw in my face.

The tide of our budding friendship changed one morning when I was getting ready to go to work. Michelle was already gone, and Chauncey was knocked out sleep in his bed with his hard muscled ass up in the air passing some loud odorless gas. I thought the shit was funny and was about to make my way downstairs when I decided to rescue my laptop that he held hostage from the night before. Since he was the one that bought it for me in his pecuniary heyday, it was no big deal that I let him borrow it for his internet searches. So I crept on in there, grabbed my computer, and headed down stairs. I wouldn't have never even thought about it if it wasn't for this wrestling website I stumbled on right before he asked to borrow it. I couldn't remember the address, and when I pulled down the little scroll thing most of the websites I was used to browsing were cleared. I was just about to go upstairs and cuss him out when I remembered that I could go back into the history. Thus I do so when I start coming across these websites that I had never seen or heard off. Then, I came across this one site that I thought looked familiar by name, only for this naked black dude side-fucking this light-skinned Brazilian dude that I seen around the way on various other websites. And as I clicked onto more websites to find more man-on-man scenes like this, I walked away knowing that my brother-in-law Chauncey was a freak.

I was tempted to laugh it up in his face when he came down and joined me for breakfast. But before I could question him on his viewing pleasures, he asked me if he could join me on my truck for the day. He said he was getting a real bad case of cabin fever and needed to break free from the house. Since the company that I work for really didn't give a shit just as long as he didn't touch anything, didn't ask to be compensated for his time, and could fit into our one-size-fits-all uniformed coveralls, he was good to ride shotgun in the van. We make a few house calls. He's talking a bunch of bullshit as I install the satellites and get the customers to sign off on the order form.

And as I'm driving about town, I can't help but look over at Chauncey from time to time. Chauncey was just too good-looking of a dude to be fucking with those kinds of websites. Brotha-in-law was six-four, two hundred and forty solid, muscled up and golden brown, clean-shaven except for this thick-ass chin badger he insisted on keeping. I say that to say this, all he had to do was step outside, take off his shirt and flash his million dollar smile, and he could have had anybody on the block at the mere flex of his heavenly pecs. And that was besides the fact that he was starting to look like some bodybuilder that fell slightly off point. Don't get me wrong, buddy row was still fine as fuck. But knowing where he was when he was playing ball to where he was slipping down to be was slightly annoying at the most. But, still.

It wasn't like I didn't get around, too. There was always some queer fiendish for this cherry brown black Haitian pipe. I may not have been blessed with the accent, but I know how to fake it for the right folks, especially when I know I can give my balls some much needed relief when they become a bit too cum-swollen. I wasn't even above blackening out a few brown eyes when I was going through a serious booty drought. However, I didn't fuck around with those websites like I got off on that shit or was I planning on fucking some man-ass on the regular since I wasn't ugly nor desperate.

While I was pondering what made Chauncey willing to get off that way other than his wife being a professional bitch, I wasn't paying attention in the least of the ritzy million-dollar neighborhood I was driving into. If I had known that it was in Chauncey's old gated community, I would have skipped out on the call altogether or rescheduled it for another time. Chauncey was good at being accepting of everything of his new station in life except giving up that big ol' house. The six-bedroom, eight and a half bathroom home was his pride and joy. And being that the call house was directly behind it, where he could see the top of his roof crystal clear over the tree line, even brought a teardrop to my eyes, and I had no hope of ever living that large.

I was tempted to make a quick turnaround out of there, but the owner was already outside waving away the moving truck and guiding us in. I went to work, feeling bad that I had to leave him in the van to stare at his old house just a few feet away. As I'm steadily trying to get the nameless fuck to sign off on my work order, desperately trying to get my boy out of there, I find Chauncey passing me by ringing the doorbell about to ask the homeowner if he could take a piss. I was about to tell him to hold on a minute, let me take him to the gas station down the street, but the homeowner let him in before I could open my mouth to the contrary.

I went back to the van. I waited and waited and waited some more before I got the sinking feeling that Chauncey wasn't coming back anytime soon.

"Please don't tell me this dude is taking a dump inside this man's house!" I mouthed under my breath, wondering what kind of complaint this customer was going to unleash on my supervisor.

Eventually, I got up the nerve to go back up to the door. I didn't know what I was planning on doing, but I had to do or say something. I was tempted to ring the doorbell, though I thought better to turn the knob, knowing from previous experience that people who lived in gated communities often had a nasty habit of leaving their doors unlocked like country bumpkins that thought they were immune to crime.

Just like I suspected, the door was unlocked. What I wasn't expecting was to find Chauncey shoving his dick through the homeowner's mouth in the middle of his living room pit.

71

"You like having some big dick down your throat, don't you?" Chauncey announced, with the homeowner sucking loudly as if he was getting the last bit of slushy out of the cup on the hottest summer's day, "Shit, breath through your mouth. I don't want to hear all that gurgling … just straw-slurping."

I always knew that Chauncey was working with a nice piece the way he used to bounce around the house in his briefs, but the length that was coming out of the poor homeowner's mouth was ridiculously unreal. It was like his dick kept growing and growing and growing. Where his mouth was at the hilt to where it ended up at the tip, the homeowner gave a new definition to deep throat. One would assume that if Michelle had something like that inside of her for the past six years she might be a lot laxer about life. Then, again, that was to assume that he gave her a stroke of it every now and then.

The homeowner was too busy doing his thing bobbing up and down to even notice my presence in the large sunken great room. I thought Chauncey was too busy gripping the homeowner's head, feeding him his snipped dick, as he silently waived me over. I was so shocked that the only thing I could do was just look.

"You want a dick in your mouth and a dick up your ass, don't you punk?" Chauncey asked the homeowner slowly face-fucking him, slapping his low-hanging balls underneath his wide rounded chin.

The homeowner agreed a muffled groaned.

"What are you doing?" I asked nervously.

"What does it look like motherfucker? I'm getting my dick sucked. I'm about to tag this ass while my boy takes care of you with this decent throat."

"Man, I don't get down like that." I stated trying to sound disgusted with my dick throbbing inside my coveralls at the sight. The only thing I can say was that my mind reverted back to my high school days, and I was deathly afraid that he could tell my mom about this.

"Get your ass over here," Chauncey demanded. "I know you're the one that man train on Toilet Mike."

I laughed nervously. I had totally forgotten about that back in the day, holding his head down in the toilet as me and my boys took turns dog-fucking the whining little sissy when his voluptuous sister with the ridiculous booty wouldn't give us any play. What can I say? Being a star athlete had its privileges.

"Three way, man? I won't lie. It sounds kind of hot. But I don't want 5-0 chasing me because he screamed rape."

"Please, this is his ultimate fucking fantasy: Two well-built black men accosting him in the middle of the afternoon to be their fat fair-skinned bitch." Chauncey laughed.

I looked over at the blissful homeowner cocksucker, pulling his pants down below his fat hairy bubble butt cheeks trying to show me he was down.

I unzipped my fly, letting some of the must and sweat from the day dissipate from my hot coveralls as I slowly made my way over to where the two of them were. Even from way off, the way the natural sunlight was coming into the room, I could spot the long dick dripping with spit dribbling over his hairy balls. As I got behind the cocksucker, Chauncey pulled out his dick and start slapping the guy across his face with it. The outside of his mouth was covered in his thick saliva, looking like he had been eating some sort of clear barbecue sauce. It was obvious he was loving every hard thump and crackling thud.

"You got some equipment, man?" Chauncey asked.

I somehow knew what he meant as I often kept condoms and lube on my person just in case I saw somebody that I wanted to fuck while I was out and about.

I handed him a couple of each.

"You see what I see?" Chauncey asked, nodding over to the low-lying white leather sofa.

I could just see the white Latino chub kneeing the sofa with some dick in his mouth and some dick up his ass.

It took less than a minute to get the homeowner into position plugging his mouth with my dick while Chauncey grabbed him by his waist and was teasing the lubed butthole with his sheathed dick. Now I will admit that I wasn't blessed with Chauncey's length, but I held my own in being extremely thick and uncut. I got the kind of dick that needs before and after shots as I work them over taking a tight hole and stretching it out to look like a bottomless abyss.

"Lick my balls, punk," I commanded in a loud whisper.

The homeowner got right to it, lapping up my balls with these long licks before popping in his mouth one by one in the same spirit he was sucking Chauncey off just moments earlier.

I was feeling it. The way he was licking and sucking and then followed by the coolness that just seemed to breeze over my sensitive balls was just like being in paradise. It was feeling so good that I thought I was just going to give him my nutt just like that.

"You need to get back to that head game, son." I mouthed, letting him lick my dick all the way up before coming back down on it with an open mouth. "Watch your teeth, motherfucker. You got it, boy, just keep your mouth open like that. Oh fuck, your mouth feels like some pussy. Damn, you know how to smoke the pipe, don't you?"

I was just riding his mouth without a care in the world, letting him use his tongue like he was going in on an ice cream cone. It felt like I could have ridden his mouth like that forever. But as I looked across the cocksucker's pale back, I saw that Chauncey was tired of teasing that hole and was ready to get down to it.

"Suck my dick, my bitch," I said forcing my dick down his mouth. "Get under that fucking foreskin."

Chauncey took his cue and stuffed his long beautiful dick into that waiting ass. The homeowner spasm through the roughness of it all and let his screams vibrate through my dick. Either the cocksucker was just that good or I was just that easy, but I was about ten second from just unloading in his mouth before Chauncey hit his rock bottom and the homeowner stopped using his wonderful mouth so diligently.

If he could have, he would have clenched his teeth, obvious from the pain swelling in his eyes. But just so that he didn't forget, I made sure he saw my closed fist if he ever forgot.

It took us a minute or so, but eventually we got into this sick rhythm where Chauncey was pounding him hard and smacking his rounded booty as I grabbed his ears and made good use of the homeowner's mouth as he yelped between breaths.

"Starting to put some of those ass muscles back to work I see?" Chauncey growled with sweat pouring off of his head, killing that hole.

The homeowner let out a few exhausted groans that vibrated back on my dick again before brazenly throwing his ass back on Chauncey like he was mad at him or something. It was as if the homeowner had gotten his second wind and was meeting Chauncey stroke for stroke.

"Damn, you're going to make me break a nutt off in this ass, punk! Oh, damn ... shit ... ah shit! Yeahhhhhh!" Chauncey hissed, pulling out of the weathered asshole, snatching off the condom, and sprayed his long shot load across wide pasty back in front of him.

This sent me into overdrive as I felt an uncontrollable throb build in my hefty dick.

"I can't hold it in, damn. I'm about to bust this nutt in your mouth!" I said grabbing the back of his head, holding it steady, getting my aim solid.

I let loose one of those forever groaning, ball-draining nutts that started off shooting down his throat with just enough to still squirt a healthy bit across his oval mustached face.

It took me and Chauncey about a good five minutes after that to catch our breaths before straightened up and heading out, leaving the homeowner to whack himself off to a satisfying conclusion with the curded dick milk we left on his face and back.

# # # # #

"So you get down." I laughed aloud, closing the front door shortly after we made our way back to our empty house for the day.

I thought it was best that I broke the ice seeing that neither one of us said a thing about fucking that dude after we left him on the sofa.

"Yeah," Chauncey smiled cupping his dick. "I started back in college. Whenever me and teammates or frat brothers couldn't snatch up some pussy or either found some chick on her period, we had a couple of flamers up the road that would always ready to suck and fuck at the sight of a stiff pipe."

"I imagine that you got some action on the road, too."

"Shit, you ain't lying. Thank God for an entourage! They can scoop up some dude for one-on-one or some straight-up homie fun."

"Gang bang?" I questioned, getting hard at the thought of some gaping hole being used by my dick in company with several others.

Chauncey nodded. "If you thought folks would do some shit for a Klondike bar, you ain't seen what they'll do just to get their crack stretched out. So what about you? When did you start to get down?"

"Probably about fourth or fifth time out," I said confidently, give or take a couple of more number. "For every phyne firecracker cock-teasing bitch there is a willing brother or cousin nearby that'll get down to it."

"Like Toilet Mike." Chauncey added.

"Yeah," I laughed. "He was just hungry. You hungry?"

"Yeah," Chauncey said, meeting my eyes.

"I was talking about making a sandwich," I said throwing back my thumb to kitchen, but I was already done with my statement when I saw the glint in his eyes that he thought I was offering him something more.

"Oh," Chauncey said with his face cracked.

"But if you're hungry like that, then that's cool with me." I said licking my lips, and pulling him in for a kiss.

Even though Chauncey was the pro-football player with the well-worked out body, his stature paled in comparison to mine in my arms. I felt like the quarterback again, and he somehow morphed into this male cheerleader that would do anything to make sure that I was good for the next game, and was more than glad to be of that personal service. I kissed him again, only this time he kissed back. I might say quite clumsily for a man that was married and had a multitude of girlfriends in his past.

"Shit, I've wanted you since high school, man." Chauncey blubbered in a falsetto between gasps, letting me know I was hitting some of his hidden hotspots.

"You can have me, son … damn," I said, reacting to my dick in full force.

The rush of ecstasy catapulted us upstairs and in my bedroom, which was situated a good ways off from the rest of the house. In short, meaning that nobody was bound to walk in on us easily without some timely notice.

I barely had the door locked when I found Chauncey already sprawled across my bed shucking off his clothes. I was still coming out of my coveralls when he went for the dick like he had papers on it. I thought the homeowner we left had some serious head game, but it was nothing in comparison to the things Chauncey was doing with his mouth. It was like he could unhinge his jaw without hurting himself to get me in his mouth. Not only that he took me down to the hilt several times not gagging, I was tempted to just bust one in his mouth and work him up to inviting me up his hole some other day. But with the house usually being quite busy and this was our only time to do something major before everyone came back home, I decided to join him on the bed.

He was still nursing my dick in his mouth as I got between his legs and started fingering his asshole. That shit was tight, yet it felt tender just like some regular pussy and even got wet like it, too.

"Man, this shit is soft like Charmin!" I mouthed, getting in a couple of tongue strokes and tasting the saltiness of his twitching hole. "If I known about this back then, I would've got your ass in the back of the locker room after every game and then some."

He agreed mumbling over a mouthful of dick.

"But right now, I'm going to give you the pipe that was the first stretched out your wife's smart aleck cunt meaning you've been getting sloppy seconds all these years. But that is okay, the first will be last and the last will be first this time." I said, mumbling off some shit that I thought would sound cool.

"Go on ahead and do what you have to do, Daddy." Chauncey said freely.

I knew that he wasn't a virgin by the way he sucked dick, and I knew he wasn't a virgin on the backside either by the ease he allowed me to play with his ass, but the way he said it was like he got pounded out like every other day.

"Cool," I said, reaching into my nightstand for this slick cream that I concocted for smooth stroking and chicken choking.

I got back into the bed, back into position, going back and forth palming the buttery stuff on my dick and fingering in his hole before posting up behind him. I swore up and down that Chauncey was going to nutt all over the place the way my dick thumped loudly against his sensitive crack. But I won't even lie, though, I was about to lose my own nutt just getting it past his ultra-tight opening. The friction – even with the incredible working lubricant – had us both moaning up a firestorm. Right up to the point that I was balls deep inside of him and was slowly stretching him out.

"Damn, baby boy, I knew you were a tight end but this shit is ridiculous!" I said between clenched teeth, panting, clawing his thirty-inch waist and spanking his rock hard ass, trying not to put my babies up in him out so soon.

And so, not to do so, we went from going at it doggie-style to putting him on his back and then rolling him onto his side. By then, I had stretched him out good, and he was letting me do my job blowing his back out.

"That's it, baby boy. Take that dick!" I shouted within reason, tearing him a new asshole. "Let brotha-in-law up in this sick-ass bitch! There you go!"

Chauncey was up there mumbling something incoherently. Whatever it was it was definitely more in the vein of pleasure than it was pain, though some was obviously present in his face.

"Get it in Daddy. Flood me out!"

It wasn't what he said it but the masculine way he said it that that sent me running towards the proverbial edge. It wasn't like I was about to bust a nutt as much it was that I was about to give birth to my brain through my urethra and swamp his bitch-ass out. So I fucked harder, ramming my hips against his ass, and as if something beyond me kicked out of my body and filled up his. I was so lost in a daze that I wasn't even aware that he had spewed a pool of cum on my mattress.

Michelle wasn't my sister. So there was no way I should feel bad about fucking her man. If anything, she should consider this payback for leaving me when I was down – but don't worry her man can get it every time I get it up.

THE
MOON HOUSE
Mark James

Do you think sometimes the future's right in front of you, only you don't see it? I do.

I saw him around noon. The sign said, "Beat Samson, Win a Prize." I didn't know they still had carnivals with a Strong Man act.

He was wearing faded jeans, no shirt. In the warm autumn sun, the sweat dripping off him gleamed like dark rivers in a forbidden dream. I watched him raise the hammer over his head, saw muscles in his chest bulge. He spread his legs, and for just an instant, I saw myself there, between his thick legs and ...

"You're smiling like you seen something you wanna try, boy," Samson said.

He was heading for the crowd. I didn't know he was talking to me until the people nearby edged away. Up close, I saw see his eyes. Something lurked behind the smile he put on for the crowd, a shadow, a ghost he kept back from the sunlight.

Close like that, he was bigger than life. All muscle, ebony black skin, dark eyes. A shudder ran through me, and I'd broken out in a light sweat. I was – God – there's no other way to say it. I was in heat. I wanted him. Bad. He could have had me right there.

He looked into my eyes, and I was sure he'd seen what I was thinking, seen how I'd get on my knees for him in a heartbeat. I felt heat in my cheeks; I was blushing the deepest shade of red I'd ever been.

"You ever get anything from a strong man, boy?"

To the crowd it sounded like carnival banter, just hooking another mark into the game. But I knew better. His eyes weren't playing.

"No." I looked down, and of course I was staring right at his crotch. "It looks hard."

I wanted to shoot myself. How could I say something so stupid?

My hands were shoved deep in my pockets. He grabbed my right arm, held it up over my head. "Here's our next champion ladies and gents. What do you say?"

His hand was big and beefy on my arm. Felt like he could lift me up without blinking an eye. For the first time in my life, I thought about taking a man inside me; thought how it would feel, Samson lifting me up, putting me on him, and just letting me ride.

Good natured applause came from the crowd as he pulled me forward to the hammer on the platform.

"It's easier than it looks, kid," he said, still talking to me and the audience. "All you gotta do is hit it harder than me."

The crowd laughed. I barely reached up to his broad shoulders.

"Think you can do that?"

Before I could stammer an answer, he grabbed the hammer – it was a tool on steroids up close – and hit home. The bell went all the way to the top with a big "Bling!"

The crowd laughed and clapped.

"Your turn," some wiseass shouted.

"Take off your shirt," Samson said. "Don't want anything on for this. Carny superstition."

He smiled for the crowd, all white teeth in a dark face. I wondered how different his face would look if I looked up at him from between his legs, with him in my mouth.

I tugged my T-shirt up over my head and flung it down. For a second, his eyes fell on my soft skin, pink and almost baby smooth, my arms, so much smaller than his.

"Come here." He grabbed the hammer. "Samson's gonna show you how."

He got behind me, the hammer in front of both of us. He slipped it into my hands. I nearly broke my wrists trying to hold on to it.

He grabbed my hands, so his big, dark hands were over mine, both our hands gripping the hammer handle. He was pressed right up against me. His sweaty chest slid against my back; his crotch pressed up against my ass, and oh God – he was rock hard.

Was this a dream, or what?

"Hold it like this," he said, pulling me even closer.

Then he raised the hammer up, and brought it down hard and fast, bending over to do it, and I thought, I want it to be you. When I get it up my ass the first time, I want it to be your cock stretching me wide open.

I barely heard the "Bling!" the little bell made, or the wild applause and laughter from the crowd.

Samson laughed for the crowd, then whispered in my ear. "I'm off at nine. Be here, boy."

He let go, held up my arm like I was some kind of champ and said, "He wins!" He shoved a rubber hammer at me with "State Fair" in gold letters on the head. "Who's next?"

He eyed the crowd. "Come on. If he can do it, which one of you men can't beat me?"

# # # # #

At eight thirty, I was standing in the shadows, watching Samson pack up the Strong Man booth, his hard body sculpted by the bright lights behind him. For a wild moment, I fought the urge to leap over the counter, land at his feet and claw his zipper open.

I know it sounds crazy, but it was how Samson made me feel –
like I'd do anything to take his dark cock in my mouth, up my virgin
ass. It was like I had a fever, and Samson was heating me to boiling.

"Come out the dark, boy." His deep voice went right through
me; made my balls thrum. "Let me see you."

I slipped out of the shadows.

He hauled up a box full of prizes and pushed them into a corner
on a crammed shelf. "You ain't a townie, boy. Where you from?"

The way he kept calling me boy should have bothered me, but
it didn't. With him it was okay. I'd be his boy any day of the week; hell
– any second of any hour of any day.

"I'm from around. I travel a lot."

Grunting, he hauled another box up onto his shoulder, before
he looked back at me. "Boy like you, traveling a whole lot don't mean
but two things."

Him walking like that, holding up the box on his shoulder,
made all the muscles in his thick arm bulge; made my cock so hard, I
ached. "What's it mean?"

"Running or hiding. Which one is it?"

I thought about telling him it was neither one; that I wanted to
see the country, visit places I read about. But then, I remembered that
dark thing in his eyes; he'd know if I lied to him. "Running. Got tired
of being my stepdad's punching bag."

He looked me up and down again. "You old enough to be out
on your own?"

"Turned nineteen two days ago."

"That's alright, then. I ain't trying to get caught up with no jail
bait."

"What do you do when there's no carnival?"

"Always a carnival some place, boy." He glanced at me,
smiled. "We travel a lot."

I swallowed. It was hard making small talk, keeping my eyes from wandering down below his waist. "You been a Strong Man a long time?"

He shoved the last box in place, leaned against the wall, arms crossed over his amazing chest. "Long enough."

Behind him a rollercoaster dropped, people screamed into the night. The sweet scents of the carnival blew over me in a cool autumn breeze – popcorn, doughboys, cotton candy.

I felt his eyes on me and between one pounding heartbeat and the next, I lost my nerve. I didn't think I could give him my ass, and I knew a man like Samson, he wouldn't settle for just a blow job. If he took me some place where nobody could see, nobody could hear me scream, I'd be ...

He laughed, deep and slow. "I seen a boy what lost his nerve, just slipped right on outta him like piss running down hill."

"I'm sorry." I retreated into the shadows, tried to keep my feet from tangling. "Wasted your time. I shouldn't have come."

He ducked behind the shelves for a second, then he was back, wearing a denim jacket that had enough buttons pinned on it to be a walking carnival. Between the buttons, it was faded blue, all the way up to the sky.

I looked at the buttons – blue, yellow, round, big, little, square. After a while, when it got real crowded, it had to be like working a jigsaw puzzle to get them to fit right. I didn't know what it meant, except that there was more to Samson than I was seeing.

"Come on. Let's get something to eat. Banging that hammer all day makes a man hungry."

"I got no money," I said.

"I know."

# # # # #

We walked down the midway, the rides all around us lit up like mini worlds, whirling, rolling, spinning.

"You like working in a carnival?"

"When you got a past, carnival's the best work there is. Nobody asks questions. You work. You get paid."

"What's in your past?"

"Nothing I'm gonna tell you about."

He took the sting out of his words by passing his thick fingers over my cheek. It was just a second, but I felt how soft his touch could be.

"I shouldn't have asked. Not my business."

"No big deal. You got a name?"

A soft breeze coaxed a low sound from the buttons on his jacket, like far off tiny bells, a sound that stopped me thinking about what could go wrong.

I was out on a cool autumn night, next to a man built like a dream, with a voice that made me melt; and he wanted me as much as I wanted him.

"Maybe I got a name." I shrugged, smiling. "Maybe I don't."

He glanced at me sideways. "You sure you want it like that, boy?"

I was still smiling. "Like what?"

Without me seeing him move, Samson grabbed me, hauled me up over his shoulder and shook me, like you'd shake a piggy bank to get money out. "Let me see if any names fall out."

A little kid came running up and said, "Me next, mister. Me next."

His dad grabbed him, shoved a purple cotton candy cone the size of Texas into his small hands, and dragged him off.

"Oh, shit." I laughed harder than I'd laughed in a long time. "Put me down."

"That's a funny kind of name," he said. "You want me to call you Oh or Down?"

"Litton."

He set me down, let me slide down his body, and I felt the hard muscle in his arms, his chest.

"You got a nice feel to you, boy."

Not as good you feel, I thought. "No one ever picked me up like that."

"I can do a whole lot of things no one never done to you," he said.

"I know." And suddenly, that strange shyness was back. I felt like the Whipsaw ride – up one second, down, sideways – didn't know which way was up.

He glanced at me, must have seen that every muscle in my body was suddenly tense, like a first time runner at the start line. "I ain't gonna take nothing you don't give me. Understand?"

I looked up at him, a million questions trembling on my lips. Was he sure he wanted a virgin? Could he do it slow enough not to make me scream or cry or beg him to stop? And the question I couldn't bring myself to think about, not now, not here with all these dazzling fantasy lights where everything felt so right – could I spend the night?

I nodded, and that seemed to be enough for him.

After that we walked in the kind of silence you fall into when you see a good friend after years, and you both start talking at the same time, then you laugh, and maybe take a quiet walk some place, and in the silence, you feel each other again, and it's all you need because the rest will come. It'll come, and you know it will, and that's enough.

I realized we weren't on the main midway anymore. The sounds of the carnival were fainter, the shadows deeper. "Where are we?"

"We call it out back," Samson said. "Behind the main show."

He reached out in the dark and took my hand. I loved the feel of his rough palm, his strong fingers through mine. "Going to see a friend – Straggles. Tells the future, cooks up a mean gumbo, and he kicks ass at chess."

If I looked back, I could still see the lights and hear people, but here, it was almost silent. We were in an alley formed by trailers. Samson pulled me between two trailers that were so close together, we were squeezed tight against each other.

He ran his hands over my face. When he leaned down and kissed me, and his hands cupped my ass and squeezed gently, every question flew out of my head, except the most important one – when?

I slid my hands under his denim jacket, feeling his hard muscle. I started to get down on my knees, but he took my arm, pulled me up. "Not like this."

"Why not?" I realized I'd been wrong before. I didn't have a fever – Samson was the fever – and it made my balls ache, made my cock press against my jeans. "I want to. Real bad."

He kissed me again, bit my lower lip, his big hand going down between my legs, pressing, feeling, rubbing. "And what happens when that hot little mouth ain't enough, and I wanna empty my balls in your ass?"

Even though there was no place to go, I pressed back into the trailer behind me. Samson laughed, tugged me out into the alley and got walking. "Easy, boy. I know you ain't had it like that before."

"No," I said. "Sorry. I don't wanna be wasting your time. You can have anyone you want."

He gave me that sidelong look again. "Maybe. But I want you."

# # # # #

A long shadow fell over both of us. "You making trouble with that boy, Samson? If he's giving you shit, kid, let me know. I'll sort him right the fuck out."

I turned to see a dwarf standing in the doorway of a trailer. It was painted the color of a midnight sky, spangled with silver half moons and gold stars.

"How many times I gotta tell you to stay out my business, Straggles?" Samson said.

For a second, as impossible as it seemed, I thought they were serious. Even with him standing on the steps, I could tell the dwarf didn't hardly go past Samson's knees.

"You come around with company and don't even call ahead and let me get out my good China?"

"You make gumbo? I don't want no carnival crap tonight."

"Out of luck." Straggles glanced at me. "At least with me you are. But I got soup and fresh bread."

"Sounds good."

"What sounds good?" Straggles came down the steps, and looked up at Samson. "I didn't offer you nothing." His sharp black eyes shifted to me. "You hungry, kid?"

Looking from the dwarf, to his trailer, I had to ask. "You really tell fortunes?"

"Depends." Straggles eyed me up and down. "You got any three dollar bills?"

I couldn't help laughing.

Straggles turned back toward his trailer. "Soup's still hot," he said over his shoulder. "Ain't no good China, though."

# # # # #

Inside the trailer, a string of bubbles in different colors hung from black beads draped along the wall. The bubbles gave off a strange light, made the trailer like a different time or place.

Straggles or somebody had painted every astrological sign in just about every language I knew of. Symbols trailed across the walls like strange sheet music.

A giant sun took up one wall. It had a face like the man in the moon – not friendly, not unfriendly – with rays coming out of it, and every ray had an astrology symbol on it.

"You like the Strong Man's work?" Straggles said.

My eyes slid to Samson, who was shucking out of his denim jacket, making his buttons jingle softly, revealing his gloriously muscled chest and thick arms. "You did this?"

"Life gets dull on the road, boy. It ain't nothing like you think."

I looked at the walls again. It was like the buttons on his jacket, a different, hidden side of him.

"Soup's up," Straggles said.

He set a bowl roughly the size of a basketball cut in half in front of Samson. My soup was in a chipped stone bowl that could have been carved out of black rock.

I saw bits of sausage and potato in the soup. He put two loaves of bread between us, and it all smelled so good, my mouth watered. I didn't realize how hungry I was 'til I grabbed the spoon in my bowl and tasted it. Suddenly I was ravenous.

Samson ate deliberately, like a man getting down to serious work, maybe laying bricks or setting stones on that famous Roman road that's still around. First he ate the soup, then he broke a loaf of bread in half – it looked so small in his big hands – and I swear, it was gone in about three bites.

"You want more?" Straggles said.

I looked down and saw my bowl was empty.

Now that I wasn't hungry anymore, my thoughts slid back to the alley, kissing Samson, feeling him pressed up against me, his hand between my legs.

I looked at his half naked body across from me and wondered if he painted in the nude. Maybe he'd like to try painting with me between his legs, and his cock buried in my throat.

Food was the last thing on my mind. "It was really good, but no thanks."

"I see you ain't been scraping the gutter," Straggles said. "Boy's mama taught him manners."

"Fuck off," Samson said between mouths full. He didn't even look up. The half a basketball was almost empty, and a loaf of bread was gone.

"Oh shit. Don't get all romantic on me," Straggles said. "You two lovebirds want I should leave you alone?"

Samson's eyes fell on me, and oh my God, I was so lost. Yeah, I wanted to say. Thanks for the soup, but could you get gone?

"You mind if I use the Moon House?" Samson pushed his bowl away. "The Pit's all ..." He shrugged his big shoulders.

Straggles picked up the bowls, stacked them neatly in a little sink. "You leave your dirty drawers lying around again?"

"Maid's day off," Samson said.

Straggles came up to me. With me sitting down, we were on eye level. "You wanna know what I see in your future, kid?"

"Don't even start," Samson said.

"I'd tell you," Straggles said. "But Samson here, he don't like me telling nobody he's a virgin. So I can't tell you you're gonna taste something that ain't never been tasted before."

Samson moved incredibly fast. He was on his feet and swiping at Straggles almost before the dwarf finished talking.

But Straggles hauled ass across the trailer and threw the door open. "You want witnesses, big guy?"

"You got the key?" Samson said, getting to the door seconds after it flew open.

"Yeah, I got it." Straggles went down the steps, waving over his shoulder. "Later."

#

Samson turned around and caught me staring at him, almost licking my lips.

That dark thing I'd seen in his eyes sprang out at me. "You know how I said I wouldn't take nothing you didn't give me?"

I nodded, wondering if he was gonna take me right then and there.

"That was before I felt that tight ass. You ain't been sure all night. Make up your mind, boy." His big hand was on the door knob, almost swallowing it whole. "'Cause after I close this door, you ain't leaving here a virgin."

Every instinct told me to run into the night.

Instinct can be wrong.

I took off my shirt let it fall from my trembling fingers.

"Alright, then." He pulled the door shut, locked it.

He held his big arms out to me, made little "come here" waves with his big fingers.

I was across the trailer in zero steps, then I was in his arms and he was kissing me, undressing me, unzipping my jeans, pushing them down.

He spun me around and both his big hands were on my naked ass, pulling me real close, grinding his rock hard cock into me. His rough jeans made a harsh friction on my ass, and it all felt so good; I was out of breath and wanting him so bad, I didn't even know my own name.

I turned in his arms, kissed his chest, slid down his body, trailed my fingers over his hard muscle, licked his dark skin along the waist of his jeans.

When my hands went to his zipper, he didn't stop me this time. I undid his jeans impatiently and almost ripped his drawers off him. I had time to notice that Strongmen wear Hanes.

His hands were in my hair, pulling me close. His scent – sweat, precum, and just his man smell – just about drove me crazy.

I slid my tongue over his cock head, licked up his precum, but he was even more impatient than I.

He tugged at my hair, pressed his fat, veined cock against my lips. "Open your mouth, boy. Just open it."

I opened wide and he slid past my lips, his dark cock sliding over my tongue, hard and smooth. He moaned and pushed a little deeper, 'til I gagged.

"Shit," he said, breathing hard. "Sorry. I been thinking about you all day."

Gagging didn't matter; the locked door behind him didn't matter. All I cared about was having his fat black cock between my lips, in my mouth, and oh God, I wanted to feel his cum filling my throat.

He took up an easy rhythm, holding onto my hair, fucking my face nice and easy. I looked up at him. In the dim light, he looked like a God, all dark, sculpted muscle.

"Nice hot mouth," he said. "Just how I knew it would be."

He wound his fingers deeper into my hair, held me tight while he drove his cock in and out of my mouth harder and faster, and fucked my mouth good. Fast and hard, but not deep enough to make me gag. And he was so thick. I couldn't get enough.

He moaned, deep and low. "Fuck, boy, here it comes."

He pumped hard into my mouth, then again, then he grunted, his cock swelled, twitched, and hot cum flooded my throat.

I swallowed, tried not to choke, felt it leaking out my lips, around his dark cock.

He pulled back, breathing hard.

I stroked his thighs, licked his big dark balls, kissing and sucking. "Oh my God," I whispered.

"Fucking right," he said.

He looked down at me, caressed my face, pulled me to my feet, kissed the side of my neck gently. I felt one thick finger trailing down between the cheeks of my ass, up and down, real slow, going deeper each time 'til he was rubbing my hole. "You want me to be your first?" he whispered in my ear.

I wrapped my arms around his neck, pushed back against his finger, felt my ass throbbing; for the first time in my life, I wanted a hard cock filling my empty, aching hole. "Can't think of anything I want more."

"Shit boy, boy. You could drive a man crazy." He picked me up in his arms, carried me across the trailer, through a door painted the color of silvery moonlight, kicked it shut behind us.

# # # # #

With a surprising gentleness that made me ache for him, he rolled me onto the soft bed, and lay down beside me. Kissing my neck, hooking one of his big legs between mine, pulling them apart, he took my cock in his big hand and stroked – long agonizing pulls.

Looking up into his dark face, feeling his muscled body so close, I couldn't stand it anymore. My balls were gonna bust if I didn't come.

He laughed quietly. "That's just how I want you, boy."

He rolled back, turned over, and turned back to me with a bottle of lotion in his hand. When he started lubing his cock, I saw he was already hard again.

I didn't say anything, but I felt my asshole pucker at the thought of all that dick sliding into me.

He must have seen the look on my face.

"You gonna give it to me?" he said, rolling over on top of me, pinning my arms to the bed. "Or I'm gonna have to take it?"

His thick cock was between my legs. I could feel him pressing his hard body against me, with a kind of savage aching that I knew he couldn't stop even if he wanted to. Whatever that darkness was in his eyes, he was riding the edge of it, and if I taunted him, teased him, he'd slip over into the dark.

If I said no, he'd just hold me down and take what he wanted. "You don't have to take it," I said, breathing hard.

He eased up off me. "On your belly. Spread your legs."

I turned over, and he lay on top me. I could feel him all along my body. Both his arms were on either side of my head, like thick dark tree trunks. He kissed the back of my neck, kissed down the center of my back, his lips brushing my spine, sending shock waves of need all through me.

He rubbed his cock against my ass, spreading my cheeks 'til he was rubbing between them. I felt him throbbing, felt his balls, big and heavy and smooth.

"You want it, boy?" he whispered in my ear.

He let himself slide down on his arms, until his body was pressing me into the bed, covering me like a living blanket of hard muscle, and all I could think was how bad I wanted to feel him sinking into me, taking my virgin ass, filling me with his dark cock.

I tried to push back against him, but I couldn't. I was pinned under him. "Yeah. I want it to be you."

He pushed himself up. "Turn over."

I had just enough room to wiggle until I was on my back. He kissed me, then pulled back, looking down at me, breathing hard through his nose, not moving, clenching his jaw. I thought something was wrong.

"What is it?"

"Just holding myself back, boy. I wanna bend that fine ass over and drill you deep."

I panicked. If he did that, there was no way I could stop him.

"Easy. Don't tense up like that." He let himself down again and kissed me, rubbing into me, humping me like he was fucking me slow and deep. "I shouldn't of said nothing. I ain't gonna make it bad for you."

I swallowed, spread my legs wide.

He knelt between my legs, put my legs up on his shoulders, guided his cock to my ass. I clenched tight, couldn't help it. He was so big. It felt impossible. No way he could fit inside me.

"Let it happen, boy. Nice and easy." He stroked inside my thighs, running the back of his dark fingers over my skin, while he kissed my legs over his shoulders.

He pushed a little, 'til his cock head was inside me.

I bit my lips, groaned at the pain of him stretching my hole, threw my head back, and closed my eyes.

"Look at me, Litton."

I met his dark eyes, watched his hands on my body, stroking me, caressing my balls.

"You wanna come with me, boy?"

My hips rose and fell to the rhythm of his hand on me. "Yeah, when you're in my ass."

He pushed a little, slid into me another inch. "I ain't talking about that." He grabbed my ass, squeezed. "I mean on the road with me."

"Do I get to ride the Strong Man?" I lifted my hips, taking him a little deeper.

He pushed into me, groaning low in his chest. "As much as you want, boy."

His hands slid up my chest to my mouth, and he ran his fingers over my lips, sliding his cock deeper into me.

I moaned. I was so hard, and I wanted him so bad. "Please. Just do it. Take me."

He laughed, rubbed up and down my chest. "And rip up the ass that's gonna be mine? Not a chance."

He slid into me inch by inch, 'til I felt his balls against my ass. He leaned close, kissed me, his tongue in my mouth. I wrapped my arms around his thick neck. Looking into his eyes, I traced the muscles in his back, feeling his hard cock filling me where no man had ever been before.

"Your ass is fucking hot, boy." He pulled back, stroked into me, holding my ass.

I squirmed and moaned. "You feel so good."

Then he wrapped his big hand around my cock and stroked, matching his thrusts to the same rhythm.

I arched my back and moaned. "Oh my God." My hips bucked. I was gonna come hard.

He stroked faster into me, short little thrusts that made my ass quiver around his cock.

"Oh God, please." I thrust my hips up at him. "I want it deeper. I wanna feel your cock filling my ass when I come."

Samson groaned, let go of my cock, and leaned over me, fucking me in longer deeper strokes. "I been waiting a long time for a boy like you."

I don't know how I held out with him fucking me long and deep like that. I started stroking my cock, but he pulled my hand away, pinned both my arms over my head, and rode my ass deep and hard, looking into my eyes.

"Come on, boy. Come for me. You don't need your hand. A hot thing like you, all you need is a thick hard cock to ride. Come on. Come for me."

He was driving me crazy, drilling into me, pinning me helplessly under him, his dark body towering over me. I felt the load building up in my balls, felt him stroking deep in me.

He kissed me hard, bit my lips, thrusting in me, not missing a beat.

My hips bucked against him harder and harder.

"That's it, boy. Give me that virgin ass. Come on my cock."

I thrashed, my head whipping side to side, his cock driving me over the edge. I cried out and blew the biggest load I'd blown in my life, moaning, thrusting my hips so hard, the whole bed shook.

Samson's rhythm didn't break. He was looking down into my eyes, watching me, fucking me. He let out a low animal growl, clenched his teeth, and I saw every cord in his neck when he threw his head back and grunted while his cock jetted hot cum up my ass.

He stroked into me, smiling, kissed my lips softly, ran his fingers through my hair.

"Fucking hell." He rolled off me, breathing hard, and lay on his back, his big arms wrapped around his head.

I wasn't a virgin anymore, not with Samson's warm cum dripping out my ass. I reached out, touched his chest lightly.

He lifted my hand to his mouth, kissed my palm, drew me into the shelter of his strong arms, and kissed the top of my head. "You ain't gotta run no more, boy."

I rested my head on his chest, tangled my legs in his, and let out the breath it seemed I'd been holding nearly all my life.

STACKED
IN BACK
Landon Dixon

I like to go to the library. Not so much to read any of the material on-hand, as their selection of porn is rather limited; more so to check out the literary guys, who may be available for check-out.

The counter personnel are usually as homely as a Louisa May Alcott novel, and the security guards as chunky as the latest Stephen King bestseller. But, a lot of the customers are nice to look at, and even some of the young men they get restacking the shelves make pleasant browsing for this horny patron.

So, a couple of Saturdays ago, when it was as hot as hell in my hole of a downtown apartment, I wandered on over to the main branch to cool down, and get all hot and bothered. I picked up the dog-eared copy of Robert Mapplethorpe's greatest works and pulled up a chair at a table with good sight lines, then started flipping pages and flicking glances.

The nude men erotically and provocatively posed in the pictures in the book had me throbbing down below in no time. And, a blond guy in a tight pair of black jeans and a white tank-top had me fantasizing about how I could erotically pose and plug him. Until some big-titted slut with way too much make-up and attitude walked up to the blond and kissed him on the cheek, slipped a covetous hand onto his lower cheek.

I grunted my disgust at the public, heterosexual display of affection and took my softening hard-on on over to the paperback section, where I knew there were some reprinted old gay pulp stories available for reading and wishful thinking.

I was just scanning through *Twilight Boys* between two towering rows of tomes, rubbing the semi-swollen front of my jeans every now and then, when fiction became fact; in the form of a studly shelver – a young, sleek, black guy with a lean, lithe body, gleaming ebony skin, and the roundest, ripest ass I'd seen in a month of *Buttmans*.

He was wearing a white T-shirt and faded blue jeans, and his ass bulged the thin material almost as wickedly as my cock was now bulging my panted material. His butt strained the seams of his jeans and my sense of self-control, when he walked right past me pushing his cartful of books.

He gave me a brief, brilliant-white grin, and I smiled back, ogling that obscene rump of his. He parked the cart not too far up the row, then plucked a book off the trolley and bent down to burrow it back into its rightful place in the stacks, displaying his ultra-peachy bottom for my gaping eyes, as he reached low, while his ass stood tall, and out.

The dirty paperback in my hand gathered even more sweat, as I watched those lush cheeks push out almost right in front of me. I lowered the pulp fiction, tented it over my engorged cock, slipping a hand underneath and rubbing the now-raging erection.

The ebony eye candy stood straight again, then picked another book off his cart and squatted down to the absolute bottom shelf. This display of flexibility and awesome ass-itude was even more impressive, if possible, the guy's butt cheeks splaying out on the back of his heels, thick flesh spilling out on either side.

I rubbed my cock harder with my hidden hand. I'd need a trade paperback or a hardcover book if this kept up because the small mass market paperback was barely containing my ever-swelling excitement. The young man stood up again, looked back at me and smiled again. Then he pushed his cart further down the line.

I had to do something. I had flaming questions; he had bouncy answers. I sauntered up behind him and croaked, "You got any books on Robert Mapplethorpe? I'm, uh, doing some research."

He turned and looked me straight in the eyes, his own liquid brown peepers making me weak in the knees, even stronger in the cock. "Just the one you were looking at, sir," he responded cheekily.

"Jeff," I gargled. "Call me Jeff ... Roy." His nametag said Roy. Nice touch by the city – get to know your library personnel on a first-name basis. They say the library is the city's living room, and I wanted to make myself right at home with Roy.

"Sure, Jeff. I saw you looking at the Mapplethorpe book a little while ago," he explained pleasantly.

His hair was cut short, his face almost delicately-featured; nice straight nose, somewhat thin lips, strong chin. His skin looked velvety smooth.

"Uh, what about Ralph Ellison? You got any, you know, literary criticism and stuff regarding his work?"

He grinned and nodded. "Follow me."

I followed right behind his behind, watching every twitch and tremor and sway and swish of his gorgeous buttocks. Fuck, those jeans of his had it lucky!

We passed row after row until we were right up against the far wall on the fourth floor, all by ourselves. I didn't really give a damn about literary criticism. But I knew that the '840' Dewey decimal section was nice and secluded, usually deserted, like it was now. Here was an area of the busy library where a man, or two, could get some real hard thinking and research done.

"There are a couple of books on Ralph Ellison's work," Roy said, pointing helpfully at a middle shelf.

I just stared at him, lost in his eyes and body, my inflamed thoughts all over his body and butt. He reached down and touched the paperback I still held shielding my groin. I jumped like the fire alarm had gone off, his long fingers pressing the pulpy pages against my erection.

Roy licked his lips with a neon-pink tongue, said, "I like that one, too. There are a lot of hot scenes in there."

He rubbed his fingers against the book, rubbing the book against my cock. Literacy never felt so good. My dick was a tingling length of raw, rock-solid emotion, Roy stroking me through the paper.

"Y-yeah!" I gulped. "It's really well-written!"

His fingers rubbed faster, pressing harder, carrying the book up and down my straining cock. I groaned, shimmering with delight, and lust.

This bookworm stuff had gone far enough. It was time to put theory into practice. I dropped the paperback, and Roy's slim, dark fingers landed square on my jeaned erection. "Yeah!" I moaned, leaning back against the stack, Roy's warm, pale palm now spreading over my spear, sensuously caressing it.

Fuck, it felt wonderful! His hand slid slowly along my surging dong, stroking me, stoking me. His other hand touched my chest, fingers finding a nipple almost piercing my T-shirt and gently pinching and rolling it.

I full-body shuddered, my dick leaping under his hand. I could barely control myself, knew I had to get back some control, or I was going to climax way before this erotic story should rightfully come to an end.

I grabbed onto Roy's head and mashed my mouth against his mouth.

He moaned, as I pressed my needful lips into his soft, warm, slightly moist lips. His hands left my chest and cock and his arms slipped around my body, bringing me in tight against him. He was hot and hard, my cock finding his cock in a semi-aroused condition, and pushing into it.

We kissed hungrily, wantonly, or lust exploding all over the pages of the books. My addled mind recalled what had first attracted me to the accommodating library employee, and I slid my hands down his curved back and onto his curved buttocks. He groaned in my mouth, as I clutched, squeezed, kneaded his mounded cheeks.

The pair were even richer and more pliable than they appeared. Still chewing on his lips, I lifted my hands up and then plunged them down the back of his jeans, searching for bare buttocks to grip and grope. And, the combined pressure I was exerting on the rear of his pants and the pressure his swollen snake was exerting on the front, caused his jeans to burst open, opening up his ass to my searching hands.

I dove into his underwear and grasped the smooth, heated hills of his butt cheeks. He groaned again, his tongue finding my tongue and speaking volumes of eroticism, as I massaged, mauled his buttocks, working the thick, swollen flesh with a wicked intensity, just about lifting the guy off the floor with my ardor.

He pulled my T-shirt out of my jeans, pushed it up, bent his long neck down and lashed one of my nipples with his electric pink tongue. I shivered, plying his back humps. He licked my other rigorously stiffened bud, swirling his tongue all around the jutting protuberance, painting my deeper-pink areolas with his hot spit. I trembled from tip to toes, but never lost my grasp on his wonder ass.

Until he dropped all the way down. And then, I almost lost consciousness.

This book learner was hungry for the knowledge of my dong. He popped my jeans open and pulled them down. My dick sprang out into his eager, beaming face, turgid as purple prose. He laced the noir fingers of his right hand around my pink, veined shaft, and I was jolted down to my fuzzy balls.

I stared down at him staring up at me. His hand wrapped my prick, sliding up and down, pulling me longer, harder, stretching me out beyond the realms of reality. The tip of his tongue peeked out from between his lips and touched the tip of my cock.

"Pulp friction!" I gasped.

Roy rotated his soft, wet sticker around my bulbous hood, spiraling me crazy. My body shook, my dick surging. He flapped his tongue back and forth across my slit, pumping me with his hand.

I clutched at the books behind me for support but only succeeded in clawing hard-covers off the shelves and raining them down onto the carpet. So I grabbed onto Roy's head, just as he planted my prick against my body and stroked the full length of my shaft with the full length of his tongue.

I dug my fingernails into his scalp, vibrating on the end of his tongue. He licked my pulsating rod up and down, bathing my shaft in wild warmth and wetness – until he had me licked all clean and shiny and boiling, and he pulled my cock back down and planted his lips on the head.

"Yeah, suck me!" I rasped, rubbing his dome like it was a sexual fortune teller's crystal ball.

His black lips flowered over my purple crown and flowed down. I was immersed in wicked emotion, the man consuming just about the entire coursing length of my prick in his wet velvety mouth. His eyes rolled white up at me, my cock locked in the cauldron of his kisser.

He pulled his head back, pushed it forward, sucking on my schlong. I moaned, the man mouthing me in the most intimate manner imaginable. Who says the library is a dry and dusty place where nothing exciting ever happens? This bookish employee was going the extra mile in customer service, this lucky patron getting ready to squirt sweet customer satisfaction.

Roy gripped my hips and really wet-vacced my dong, sucking faster, harder, my cock right down his throat. I clutched his bobbing head and held on for dear life. But, I still wanted more, before I blew out my balls in what I knew was surely going to be an orgasm of pulp fiction proportion. I wanted to taste the man's sweet ass.

Roy gripped my sack and twisted, tugging urgently on my prick with his mouth. It was now or never. I shoved him back, every fiber of my dong and balls telling me to blow taps in his mouth. But, I had my eyes on a bigger prize.

My cock sprung out of his sucking mouth in a gush of saliva and hot, humid air. I pulled the guy to his feet, spun him around, shoved him up against the books face-forward. My dick bobbed angrily, anxious to get off. But, I kneeled at my improvised place of ass worship and tugged Roy's already open jeans down, his white Jockeys along with them.

His dark moons jumped up into my face, thrilling me. I gripped the cheeky pair, reveling in their warmth and smoothness and awesome plushness. And then, I put my mouth where his mounds were, sinking my teeth into one of Roy's buttocks.

He jumped and grunted, as I bit deep into the rich flesh. Tattooed his other cheek with my teeth marks. I chewed on his back meat, filling my mouth and soul. Then I licked, tonguing the extravagant curves of his licorice hills.

I spread the flat of my tongue all over his buttocks, joyfully painting every inch of the baby's bottom skin with my saliva. Roy gripped the shelving and quivered, enjoying the heady ride almost as much as I was.

And when I'd tasted every bloated, ebony inch of his outer buns, I went deeper. I dug my fingernails into the plump, wetted flesh and spread his buttocks wide open. His pucker was an even darker, deeper black, his butt cleavage even smoother than his butt cheeks, as I confirmed with repeated swipes of my tongue.

"Jesus!" Roy groaned, overwhelmed by my bum love.

I lapped up and down his crack, stroking the inner walls of his cheeks again and again, from down on his perineum and up along his starfish all the way up to his tailbone. Going round-the-world on the guy with the world-class posterior.

There was only one last place to explore with my tongue and mouth – his anus. I clawed him as wide apart as I could and his pucker blossomed before me. I dipped my tongue in, squirming the tip against his asshole. His buttocks trembled in my hands. I thrust my tongue in deeper, penetrating into his ultra-pink anus and spinning my poker around and around, rimming and eating the guy.

He tasted delicious, the musk from his balls and sweat from his body adding to the heady stew. I ate him out like a starving ass-man, chewing on his hole, thrusting my entire tongue inside and plowing it back and forth in his chute.

"Please, fuck me!" Roy gasped.

I couldn't deny him, or myself. I took one last loving lick at his crack and then climbed to my feet, slicked up my dick with the traveling tube of lube I always keep in my pocket. Then I stuck a couple of slippery digits in between Roy's butt cheeks, slickening his hole, getting a good feel as I did so. I punched a pair of fingers right inside the man, thrilling at the way his ass gripped my digits. He groaned, begging me to stick him for good.

I grasped my glistening fuck-stick and pushed my shining hood up against his manhole. He and I both groaned. I pushed harder, he pushed back, and my cap burst through his ring and plunged into his anus, followed long and hard and slow and sensual by the entire length of my cock.

I was buried in the man's ass, on fire. I gripped Roy's chest and nuzzled his neck, rutting around in his chute. He grabbed onto his own solid dong and stroked.

I lowered my hands to his hips, my cock being squeezed almost to orgasm by his sucking ass. I pumped my hips, my dong back and forth in his anus. It was sweet, pure, hot pleasure for both of us, cock sawing chute.

"Faster! Fuck me faster! Harder!" Roy cried.

I did as requested, pounding into the guy, rocking him on the end of my pile-driving prick. The books danced on the shelves along with Roy's body, in rhythm to my frantic thrustings. But, there was no old lady to shush this X-rated library learning experience, just two sexually-educated men getting it on at fever-pitch in the stacks.

I stared down at Roy's rippling buttocks, bouncing my thighs off the over-burgeoned pair, pistoning his anus. He jerked, jolted by his own hard-cranked orgasm, bookmarking tomes with hot, shooting sperm.

That was all I could take. I pumped like a madman, banging into his cheeks, my dick sucked and stroked beyond the point of no return. I bleated, and blasted, blowing sizzling semen up against Roy's bowels over and over and over.

We've agreed to continue our exciting research at the library. More in-depth study is definitely required – of each other.

DROPPING
A LOAD
Landon Dixon

I caught fat Ethel's eye behind the counter, pointed at my empty coffee cup. She snorted and ambled on over with the jug, poured me some more of the good 'ol dark stuff. I had a long haul in front of me, and just like my rig needs gas, I needed caffeine to keep going. Trucking was no easy business in the spring of 1938, and I needed to stay on top of the game.

That didn't mean, though, I didn't always keep my eyes open for a little roadside diversion. I swung around on my stool, mug of mud in hand, and surveyed the crowded truck stop. My red-veined orbs quickly focused on one individual in particular – the black coffee kid peering in through the screen door of the joint, licking his lips and staring at the steaming food on the white crockery, flared nostrils working hard to suck in the heady smell. He was hungry, no doubt about it. Just my kind of Joe.

"Lookin' for work?" I asked him, after I'd settled up with fat Ethel and banged on out of the eatery.

He glanced up at me, all nervous and shy, soulful brown eyes blinking. "I'm lookin' for anything, mister. I haven't eaten in three days." He twisted his cap around in his small, dark hands.

He was wearing dusty blue overalls and a white shirt, worn boots, his face and bare arms gleaming ebony, his lips plush and wet.

"Well, today's your lucky day, kid. I'm pickin' up a load of oranges 'bout thirty miles down the road, at the Hoskins spread. Could use some help loadin' it aboard and haulin' it to the San Fran fruit market. You know how to drive a rig, strong enough to lift crates of oranges?"

A bright, white smile broke over his pretty face. "Sure, mister!" he gulped. "My daddy was in the truckin' business back East – before the accident. He taught me all about it."

I nodded. I was old enough to be his father, even though he was over nineteen. But, the lessons I'd be handing out were going to be of the off-road variety. "Okay, hop aboard." I walked over to my beaten-up truck.

"Uh, mister!" the kid yelled. "Can I just go out back to the washroom first?"

"Sure. I don't wanna haul any more weight than I have to." I grinned, watching those tight, appetizing buns in the thin overalls run around the diner.

We made good time. The kid's name was Donell; he'd come out to California just a few weeks earlier, looking to get into the fruit and vegetable hauling business, hearing the land was lush and the opportunities endless.

He was right about the land, dead-wrong about the business. Trucking was a cutthroat racket, competition for loads fierce. I wasn't above sawing some throats myself, which is exactly what my intentions were with Hoskins. I'd gotten a hot, juicy tip that he had over a hundred crates of oranges that were a week away from rotting, so he needed to unload them fast. I'd have the guy over a barrel, and I planned to pluck his fruit cheap.

"I'll do all the talkin'," I told Donell, as I pulled the rig off the highway and onto the dirt road that led up to Hoskins farm. "You just take notes this time, okay?"

He smiled that sweet, shy smile of his, and something blossomed in between my legs.

Hoskins was a tall, stringy guy with a nasty disposition. "Buck-twenty-five a box!? You crazy!? Oranges are going for six bucks a crate, maybe more, down on the *Embarcadero*, and don't you try and tell me different!"

"Maybe, maybe not," I replied laconically, winking at the kid. "But, you got to get 'em there, 'for you can sell 'em."

Hoskins hawked a wad of tobacco down at my shoe. "You can take your …"

"Okay! Let's go, Donell. This guy obviously doesn't wanna do business. I hope he's got the machinery for making orange juice, 'cause that's all that fruit is gonna be good for in a couple of days."

We started walking back up the road to my rig.

"Hold on," Hoskins grumbled.

We kept walking.

"I said, hold on!"

"You're gonna make a big profit, aren't you, Mr. Jameson? Buyin' those oranges for a dollar a box and sellin' them for six?"

We were back in the truck, on the road, hauling oranges now. The kid had moved fast once I'd nailed down the deal, stripping off his shirt in the heat of the sun as he loaded the crates onboard.

I looked at his bare chest, the succulent puffy licorice nipples that capped his smooth pecs, just above the line of his overalls. "Maybe even six-fifty a box. There's a bad strain of the flu going around 'Frisco right now, don't forget."

We hit a bump, the truck and load jostling. I had to keep my eyes on the road.

Donell cocked his head, listening. "I think maybe some crates have come loose, Mr. Jameson."

"Bill," I reminded him. I might be more than twice his age, but I was no old-timer. I turned the rig onto the shoulder of the road. And, now was a good time to prove it.

We climbed down out of the cab, me right on Donell's swishing little tail. He never made it to the back of the truck because I grabbed his arm, spun him around, pinned him up against the side of the rig.

His young, lean body burned hot as the sun against my rugged, needful physique. He looked up at me with clear, questioning eyes. And then, his eyes lost their questions, got a little misty, as I gave him the answers by grinding my cock into his groin, up against his cock. "Mr. Jameson," he breathed.

I slammed my mouth against his, planting my lips on his soft, lush lips. I poured on the loving, boiling inside and out, clasping the young man in my arms and devouring his mouth. His arms tentatively encircled my torso, then hugged tight, when I swarmed my tongue into his mouth and thrashed it around.

We melded together, our cocks connecting and squeezing, his surging up hard as mine. I explored his dripping, pink mouth with my tongue, then rimmed his thick lips, licked up and down the smooth, tender skin of his neck. He moaned, rolling his head against the canvas side of the truck.

I grabbed up his arms and plastered them over his head, exposing his damp, tangy armpits. I thrust my tongue in, licking up and down the flesh and tightly-curled hair of one pit, the other, lapping up his sweat and heat. He was as fresh as they come, and I reveled in the taste, smell and feel of the guy, tonguing his armpits.

I unhooked his overalls. He moved forward a bit, away from the side of the truck, and the straps dropped down along with the overalls, fully exposing his chest. I instantly clutched a pec in each hand and kneaded the warm, ripe, black mounds, giving Donell my outstretched tongue to suck on. He captured it between his lips and really pulled, just as excited as I was now.

I let him tug on my tongue, as I felt up his boyish chest. Then I broke loose and brought my mouth lower, down to his nipples. I swirled my tongue all around one dark bud, the other, teasing them higher and harder, tasting their rubbery textures and pebbly areolas. Donell gasped, shivering in my grasping hands, on the end of my spinning tongue.

Hunger welled up inside me to new heights, and I captured a rigid nipple in my mouth and sucked on it. I tugged, pulled, bit, almost tearing the lovely jutter right off the guy's chest and swallowing it down my throat. I bobbed my head over to his other glistening bud, sucked on that stiffened protuberance until Donell and I just couldn't take anymore.

He squirmed against the side of the truck then squirmed right out of my hands and mouth, dropping down to his knees on the gravel shoulder. "I wanna suck you!" he gasped. "Please, Mr. ... Bill, I wanna suck your cock!"

The kid needed meat, like all growing boys. I batted his scrambling hands aside and cracked open my belt and fly, shoved my jeans and drawers down. My veiny root plant sprung out in front of him, bulbous cap brushing his lips. I shivered when he gripped my swollen shaft with his hot, little hand, shuddered when he tugged on it.

"That's the way!" I groaned, feeling his warm, earnest strokes all through me.

He stretched me further out with every jack of his hand, my dick throbbing under his soft, moist palm, bloated hood straining only an inch or so away from his pretty lips. His hot breath flowed over my groin, my obscenely swelled-up manhood looking huge and hugely erotic in his small hand, in front of his young face. He opened his mouth up wide and slipped his lips over my knob, and I buckled like I'd been socked in the gut.

"Jesus, fuck, yes!" I rasped, the kid swallowing my hood, sucking in shaft.

His mouth was a wet-hot cauldron, consuming my monster erection. I grabbed onto his close-cropped hair and jerked him even farther down my dong, bringing his pouty lips to within a couple of inches of my tightened balls. He gagged, unable to swallow anymore, but what he had inhaled was more than enough to turn me molten by the side of the road.

He looked up me with his watery eyes, his cheeks bulging with my cock locked down in his mouth and part of his throat. I quivered, the pressure intense, skyrocketing. My cock beat wildly inside him, like my heart in my chest.

At last, he pulled his head back, and my dong exploded out of the crucible of his mouth in a burst of hot air and spit. He was right back all over it in an instant, sucking me into his mouth, pulling back, dragging his lips and tongue along my shaft, Hoovering my dick with a raw, honest enthusiasm that left me weak in the knees and the head, breathless.

The pure, sweet cock-sucking went on for a glorious minute or two, the kid gripping my pulsating rod and blowing me from clenched hand on up, over and over. There was no traffic on the highway, just the sun beating down on the two of us, birds singing, leaves rustling.

But for the next part of our road initiation, I required a little more privacy.

So, when Donell pulled me right to the boiling brink with his wet sucking mouth, I scooped him up off the roadside and led him out into a field, behind a covering of trees. My bobbing cock shone in the sunshine, like Donell's nude night-shaded body, when I helped him shove his overalls all the way down.

His dick wasn't quite as large as mine, but it would be a nice, appetizing mouthful nonetheless, once we hit 'Frisco and got a room. Now, I just gave it a couple of affectionate strokes, stirring the semen in Donell's balls. Before I pushed the kid down into the doggy-mounting position, and the bigger dog got in behind.

His ass was as round and ripe as any pair of cantaloupes. I slapped the dark moons, making them ripple, him moan. Then I greased my cannon with spit, shoved a pair of dripping digits in between his ass-melons and scrubbed his smooth crack.

He jumped against my fingers. I probed his pucker, sticking the tip of a finger inside, popping his ring. He wiggled his bum around on the end of my digit in delight, and I went two knuckles deep into his searing sexual core, loosening him up just a bit for the massive, meaty onslaught to come.

I pulled my hand away and gripped my dong, spreading his cheeks with my other mitt. His black pucker winked at me, inner pinkness flashing brilliant. I licked my lips, sweating profusely. Then I steered my mammoth cap up against his tiny starfish, and we both shuddered with the heated impact. I pushed forward, gritting my teeth, the kid's cheeks and body shivering.

"Fuck!" I growled, driving hood through his resisting ring, delving shaft deep into his gripping anus. I didn't stop until my balls kissed up against his bum, my huge spike impaling his swollen bottom.

He undulated his ass. I rutted around, getting all I could of the wicked feeling of his hot, tight chute hugging every inch of my cock. It was as fine a feeling as I've ever felt in my life, just me and the pretty boy under the sun, my cock embedded in his ass.

I gripped both of his hips, pumped mine, fucking his bum. He groaned and banged his fists into the field. I went slow and sensuous, stroking long, pulling out to the cap and then plowing all the way back in again, over and over. His ass sucked on my cock just as much as I plugged it.

"Fuck me harder, Bill! Faster! Really fuck my ass!"

He couldn't wait. And neither could I.

I dug my fingernails into his flesh and flung my hips back and forth, ramming his butt, reaming his chute. His cheeks rippled with the heavy impact of my thighs banging against them, his body rocking to my frenetic rhythm, my axe splitting him in two.

I hammered his dusky, peachy bottom, pistoning his chute. The blazing friction was incredible, my thrusting cock going numb-hard in his swallowing anus. He took it and loved it as much as I did, grabbing onto his own flapping cock and fisting.

It was too much. My balls boiled, my cock surging with imminent explosion. I wanted the kid to taste the fruits of his labors. So I ripped my dick out of his gaped ass and spun him around, speared into his open mouth.

"Fuck, yes!" I howled, going off in the kid's mouth, blasting fiery cum right down his throat.

He gripped my balls and sucked on my cock, squeezing, draining every last spurt of semen out of my body and gulping it down. As he jacked white-hot jizz out of his own dark meat, spraying up into the air again and again.

He brought me to my knees, into his arms.

Which is when I heard my truck start up, glimpsed it rumbling off down the road. I scrambled to my feet and raced after it, cursing myself for leaving the keys in the ignition, for getting so completely diverted in the first place. They didn't call it 'thieves' highway' for nothing.

Then I got another kick in the crotch, when I looked back and saw a dusty car pull up and Donell jumped inside. They roared past me, the kid sticking a hand out the side of the fast-moving vehicle and waving and yelling, "Thanks for the load, Mr. Jameson!"

CAMPUS RUMPUS
Landon Dixon

Jeremy and Ian were in Jeremy's dorm room, sitting at his desk pushed up against the wall, Jeremy frustratingly trying to drill the fundamentals of chemistry into Ian's head. It was no easy task.

"See," Jeremy said, "when a base and an acid ..."

"Hey, why don't we take a break?" Ian interrupted. "My head is spinning." He slapped Jeremy good-naturedly on the shoulder, almost knocking the studious young man's glasses right off his face.

Jeremy was small and slender, with dark, velvety skin and a delicate, fine-featured face, intelligent brown eyes. The exact opposite of Ian, in other words, who was a blond-haired behemoth with a boulder of a head and a jutting granite jaw, grey eyes, freckled skin, a muscular body built for the defensive line of the college football team, where he really excelled. The mismatched pair had come together thanks to the university-mandated tutoring requirements it bestowed (or belabored) on its more brainy students, to help out those less academically but more athletically gifted.

Jeremy sighed and set down his textbook and scientific calculator. "You've got an exam coming up in a week, you know," he reminded the buzz cut giant.

"I also got a football game coming up on the weekend," Ian countered, scooping a pigskin up off the floor of the dorm room. "What say we chuck the old ball around, huh? Loosen up the muscles – brain and body."

"The human brain doesn't have any muscles. It's ..."

"Come on!" Ian's whack on the back sent Jeremy sprawling across the table.

Out on the grassy field behind the old dorm building, Ian heaved the football to Jeremy, a tight, perfect spiral despite the big guy's ham-fisted approach to the game. The ball passed through Jeremy's tentatively extended arms and punched him square in the chest, knocking him backwards onto his butt. Had his eyes been open, he might've had a better chance of catching the ball, perhaps.

As it was, the football rebounded off the tumbling young man at a right angle and bounded all the way down the bank of the river that ran alongside the university.

Ian lumbered over and grabbed one of Jeremy's small hands in one of his huge mitts, heaved him to his feet, just about wrenching the science major's shoulder out of its socket. "You almost caught that one," Ian said. "Next time, use your hands." He grinned solid white rows of teeth and jogged over to the riverbank.

Jeremy stood in the early evening sun rubbing his chest, the grass stains out of the back of his pants. He looked at the watch on his thin wrist, wondering what was taking Ian so long. The guy seemed to be moving even slower than his comprehension of elemental chemistry.

It was a warm night, perfect studying weather. Jeremy had an exam of his own to ace in physics in two days. So, finally, after at least one minute had passed, he threw up his hands and trotted over to the riverbank, looking down.

Ian was stretched out on the grassy flat at the water's edge, flat on his back.

Jeremy snorted and scrambled down the bank, stood over the sunbathing giant. "Playtime is over, Ian. We have to get back to work."

One of Ian's eyes popped open. He squinted up at Jeremy. Then one of his thick arms reached up, hand gripping Jeremy's wrist, pulling the man down onto the grass next to him. "Hey, lie down a sec and enjoy nature," he rumbled. "That's biology, right?"

Jeremy was thrown onto his back on the soft, warm bed of grass. "We aren't studying biology, Ian," he grumbled, scrambling to get back to his feet and into his textbooks.

Ian rolled over on top of him, pinning him to the ground. He grinned in Jeremy's face, eyes twinkling, huge, heavy body enveloping

116

Jeremy's small, thin frame. "Anytime you want to get up, just go ahead and try," he teased.

Jeremy squirmed, twisted, wriggled, but it was no-go. The solid mass on top of him was unmovable, the muscled arms locking his arms up over his head unbendable. Sweat bathed his face, and he blinked it out of his eyes, looking up at Ian looming large above him.

And then both young men felt what all of Jeremy's struggling against Ian's hot, hard body had really wrought – a raging erection in Jeremy's pants, pressing up against Ian's groin.

Jeremy went limp everywhere else, staring worriedly up into the footballer's eyes. Try as he might, he couldn't control the reckless flow of blood into his cock; it went harder, bigger, thicker, pumping up against Ian. Both men felt it, no way around it.

Ian scowled down at Jeremy.

Jeremy bit his lip.

Ian's lush mouth broke into a wide grin.

Jeremy's pretty face registered fearful surprise.

"Looks like you are interested in football, after all, huh?" Ian breathed into Jeremy's face. He pumped his hips, driving his cock into Jeremy's erection.

Jeremy could feel the other man's swelling excitement, rubbing against his full-blown enthusiasm. He closed his eyes and moaned softly, the wonderfully warm sensation of one man's cock stroking against another man's cock filling his body. He shimmered with swelling pleasure from head to toe. Then he started, when he felt Ian's soft, wet lips press down into his.

Ian kissed Jeremy's plush lips, lightly. Then harder, more heatedly, mashing his big mouth against Jeremy's pert mouth, consuming the undulating young man. He thrust his tongue into Jeremy's mouth and thrashed it around.

Jeremy was overwhelmed by the power of Ian's passion, the relentless thumping of the man's hard cock into his hard cock. He feebly tried to fight Ian's tongue with his own, but his sticker was pushed aside, so he just lay there and reveled in the onslaught of Ian's tongue swirling around and around in his mouth.

Ian pulled back, up, lifting his suffocating body off of Jeremy. He crawled down to Jeremy's crotch. "Let's see what you got going on down here," he growled.

Jeremy whimpered, as the big man tore his belt open and ripped his fly down, skinned his pants and underwear down his legs, Ian lifting Jeremy right off the ground with the strength of his movements. Jeremy's cock flopped out into the open, onto his stomach, stretching out long and black as licorice.

"Wow, for a little guy you're really packin'," Ian marveled, staring at the night-shaded tool.

Jeremy gulped, his cock quivering like the rest of his body, anxiously anticipating the impact of Ian's hand or mouth on his most sensitive organ. There was no escaping it now. He was going to be ravished by the big man, any which way the big man wanted, which was just what Jeremy wanted. He jumped a couple of inches off the grass when Ian gripped his throbbing shaft with his huge, hot hand.

Ian stroked, shifting his paw up and down the pulsating dong, squeezing it tight, pumping it hard, admiring the size and texture and coal-black color. Then he dropped it, shoved Jeremy's legs apart, bent down in between and licked the young man's pube-pebbled balls.

"Ooooh!" Jeremy moaned, the slap of Ian's wet tongue on his scrotum jolting him with feeling. He rolled his head around in the grass, the man vigorously licking his nuts, tightening his sack with sensation to the point he thought it and he would burst.

Ian devoured Jeremy's pouch, tugged on it.

Jeremy's eyes popped open. He stared down the length of his heaving torso and twitching prick, watching Ian suck on his nut sack. The heated tug, the big man's agile tongue probing and juggling his balls, made Jeremy surge with pleasure. His cock arched up into the air, precum oozing from the gaping slit.

Ian pulled his lips slowly off Jeremy's balls, leaving the man's sack glistening under the sun. He went lower, gripping Jeremy's thighs and diving his tongue deep in between the man's legs, licking at his perineum, stroking the thin, sensitive bridge between penis and anus, curving his long tongue up to lap at Jeremy's crack.

Jeremy's entire body arched along with his cock, willfully urging Ian to tongue his erogenous zones, quivering all over with excitement. Ian's rough searching mouth-organ found Jeremy's pucker, squirmed against it, the man blowing hot air out of his nostrils and against Jeremy's balls.

"Oh, God!" Jeremy gasped, shaking.

Ian dragged his tongue back along Jeremy's crack and perineum, up over his balls and along his shaft. He spread his thick, red lips over Jeremy's blue-black hood and pulled it inside, upwards.

Jeremy gripped the turf on either side of his body, tearing at the grass, as Ian brought his cock up and swallowed it down, the man's head dropping, mouth consuming. The pulsing length of Jeremy's ebony tool was disappearing from view, devoured by Ian, until there was nothing left to the naked eye but Jeremy's squished balls, his dong locked inside the wet-hot cauldron of Ian's mouth and throat.

Jeremy moaned, pounding the ground with his little fists. His body beat to the frenzied beat of his cock in the other man's mouth, out of control. The damp, searing pressure was incredible, unbearable.

Ian lifted his head, dragging his lips along Jeremy's thundering shaft, right up to the bloated knob. He held the man's cock up there for a moment, the shaft gleaming, then he dropped his mouth downward again, sucking up Jeremy's cock again. He did it over and over, blowing Jeremy deep and devastating, blowing apart what little sexual self-control the young man possessed.

"Ooooh, Ian, I'm coming!" Jeremy managed to bleat in the nick of time.

Not that it mattered because Ian only grinned from around the length of dark meat, inhaling it whole again, asking to be blasted. Jeremy bucked, exploding in the other man's molten mouth. He jetted with absolute joy, jumping up off the grass on the geyser of his ecstasy, spraying Ian's throat and mouth full.

Ian swallowed almost it all, taking the heated spurts deep. He gripped Jeremy's balls and squeezed and sucked everything out of the radically trembling man that he could, leaving himself with a mouthful of sperm. Then he flipped Jeremy over, spat some of the slippery semen onto the man's butt, then onto his own hard cock, which he pulled out of his jeans.

Jeremy hugged the ground, quivering with the aftershocks of all-out orgasm. He barely heard Ian growl, "I'm going to fuck you now!" But, he felt it, knifing into his cloud of bliss, as Ian pushed his cum-smeared cockhead in between Jeremy's taut cheeks and up against the man's asshole.

Ian gritted his teeth, gripping his huge, swollen-angry pink pole at the base, shoving the mushroomed purple tip against Jeremy's pucker. Jeremy's dark cheeks cushioned Ian's cock, his ring holding tight. Ian pushed harder, applying enormous, unstoppable pressure. Until Jeremy's rim widened, Ian's hood plunging through, inside Jeremy's anus. Hard-driven shaft followed immediately, sinking inside scorching hot chute.

Jeremy chewed grass, wallowing in the wicked sensations of another man's cock filling, stretching his ass. The feeling was intense. His bung swelled to the bursting point. Until, finally, Ian's blond-dusted balls kissed up against Jeremy's trembling butt cheeks, the immense dong buried full-length.

Ian didn't waste any time. He planted his hands on either side of his gasping fellow student and pumped his hips, thrusting his cock back and forth in Jeremy's anus, fucking the man like a dog fucks its bitch. Right out there in the open under the sun by the edge of the river.

Sweat poured off Ian's face and down onto Jeremy's neck, the sharp, wet crack of Ian's thighs against Jeremy's cheeks rending the sultry night air. The big man pounded his cock into the prone man's ass, reaming Jeremy's chute, relentlessly, powerfully. Jeremy's ass cheeks were shocked over and over by the crash of Ian's body against them, his own body shivering wickedly with the savage, burning sluice of cock in bung.

"Fuck, yeah!" Ian roared, pumping harder, faster. He pile-drove Jeremy's ass, plundering the young man's anus for all he was worth.

It went on and on – to the point where Jeremy just about passed out from the punishment. He gasped for air, suffocating, his head spinning, body ablaze. He'd never been fucked like this before. His whole butt had gone numb; he was just a sucking hole, for a man to piston until he blew out his balls, poured liquid fire inside.

"Fuck, I'm coming!" Ian cried, pumping in a frenzy.

He frantically sawed Jeremy's chute. Then jerked, jolted by the white-hot orgasm that welled up from his flapping balls and blasted out the tip of his churning cock. He shot burst after burst of sizzling jizz into Jeremy's bung, shaking uncontrollably up above the man's laid-out body.

Jeremy felt the heated splashes against his bowels, his body flooding with a new kind of bliss. His own cock spasmed, leaking semen into the grass.

Ian pulled up, his cock sliding out of Jeremy's devastated ass. Sperm oozed up along with the drained dong, and Ian went back down on his hands and knees and licked his own cum out of Jeremy's crack, sucking it out of the man's rendered asshole. Then he flipped Jeremy over on his back again and went full-length over top of the guy, like it had all begun.

Ian kissed Jeremy's gaping mouth, opening up his own mouth so that the cum flooded inside. They swirled the semen and their tongues together, cocks pressing tight.

"Back to the books now I guess, huh?" Ian said, grinning, licking a string of jizz off Jeremy's lips and swallowing it down.

"Yeah," Jeremy groaned, staring up into Ian's eyes, basking in the salty taste and musky smell and rugged feel of the big guy. "But we'll need to take plenty of breaks. You've taught me that."

DIRTY COP
Shane Allison

The stench of piss comes from urinals unflushed. I pull the neck of my shirt over my nose to avoid the smell while I fondle my dick between fat fingers. It ails for the vacancy of a warm mouth. I've been told that this bathroom is the best cruise spot on campus where some serious money can be made. I'm here to find out if the rumors are true about all the trust fund college cock that frequents this place, or if smoke is just being blown up my ass. I peek through the slit of the occupied stall in an attempt to get a look at the guy next to me. The glory hole between us has "Make this hole bigger" sprawled in black ink above it. I pull out my purple Sharpie and scribble my cell number for blow job "$ervice" in bubble penmanship. It isn't much but is large enough to catch a glimpse of the horny piece of trade giving himself an afternoon hand job. I can see him piercing back at me. I turn on my toilet in his direction to give him a better look at my dick. A drop of precum forms at the piss slit as I tip it up to my belly. I slide my left hand beneath my tender sac, massaging my balls.

I stand up off the commode, and spread my ass, so he can see my hot goods. It turns me on to hear his dick slap against his palm. I run my finger along my booty to show him my ass(ets). I like being watched; I'll put on a show for anyone for the right price. I sit on my toilet and tap my foot to let him know that I'm up for anything. He slides his index finger along the bottom of the partition. I lift my sleeveless shirt up above my gut. My dick is thick and throbbing, hungry for a stranger's mouth, starving for a man's butt. Who knows where that finger has been: caressing the supple helmet of a dick uncut, perhaps? Maybe up an ass big enough to shove a watermelon through? I hope his dick is enough to make my prostate purr. I stand off my toilet again with my underwear and jeans down below thighs and knees, roped around ankles, and glide my dick beneath the divider. *I'll give 'm a taste*, I think to myself. His hand is hot and tight around the shaft as he jacks me off.

"Suck it," I whisper below my breath.

His clothes rustle along the tiles; his belt buckle of heavy metal clangs against the floor of dried cum. I look down at his face. He's a gorgeous, b-boy thug with a shaved head. His hairline is neatly trimmed as if he's just come from the barber. His skin is the color of sunshine that mixes nicely with my tender sheath as it skims along voluptuous lips, darting in and out of his mouth. *Damn, you can suck a dick*, I think. My legs ache as I shove them further beneath his stall. I pop my pierced dick out of his yapper, stand off my skinned knees, and pull back the latch to my door.

"Come into my stall," I murmur.

He ducks in holding baggy shorts up over his ass, his dick that peeks from the slit of his zipper, curves up slightly instead of sticking straight out like most of the cocks I've had. My mouth is already watering for him.

"You can suck me," I tell him. "But this dick ain't free."

"How much?" he asks.

"Fifty," I reply.

He pulls two twenties and a ten out of his jean pocket and hands it to me.

The cruiser sits on my toilet and runs his hand under my shirt, caressing my belly before taking my dick, tilting it up to his lips. I lift my tee-shirt out of his face as he blows me.

"Suck it," I order, as I ram his head deep within my stinking musky forest of pubes. To hear him gag is sweet music. I push his hand away in his attempt to control the crazy inches that's being rammed down his throat.

"C'mon, dude, show me you can take it."

When we hear the door open, it startles our lusting hearts causing us to pause, our blood to slow. We hear boot steps tramp across the gritty floor strewn with tufts of tissue and paper towels.

"You two in the first stall, I need you to open up; let me talk to you."

"It's a cop," I whisper with wide-eyed shock to the cock sucking cruiser. The last thing I need is to get arrested again being that I'm on six months probation for whorin'. We both freeze. The slurps from the cruiser's blowjob have fallen silent.

"We jus' talkin'," the cruiser says looking at me.

"Open up... now," he orders.

We fasten, button and buckle our clothes as quick as we can. I slip the latch out of the metal hole of the door of my stall.

The cop, dressed in a brown polyester uniform, is built and buff with black, greased braids protruding from beneath the rim of his hat. He's bigger, and towers over us. Officer Will Gray is etched in white letters on the nametag that's pinned on the right side of his breast.

"Let's see some identification."

We both reach for our wallets in the back pockets of our pants. I pull out my driver's license that's snug between my voter's registration and a business card that was given to me by my public defender.

"Derrick and Carlton," he says. I think to myself, so that's your name?

"So what were you two doin' in here?"

"We're jus' talkin'," says Derrick.

"It didn't look like you were talkin' to me. We've been gettin' complaints from the staff about suspicious behavior in this bathroom. Are you both students here?"

"I'm a junior," says Derrick.

I lied and told him I was a senior.

"All right, both of you turn around."

"C'mon, man, we weren't doin' nothin' said Derrick.

"Shut up and do what I tell ya, and there won't be any problems. Now put your hands on the wall."

Thick pearls of sweat trickles down our cold panicking faces.

Officer Gray pads us down for weapons. He looks at me with dark, suspicious eyes.

"You look familiar; where do I know you from?" he asks.

"No place," I reply.

"You don't have anything in your pockets that will stick me, do you?"

"No," I say.

My dick gets slightly hard as his hands slither between my inner thighs. His fingers are only inches away from my crotch.

I look over at Derrick when I feel something being poked in my spine.

"You ... lock your fingers," the officer says in a snide tone.

"Are you arrestin' us?" Derrick queries, looking over his shoulder.

"Turn around." He forces Derrick's head back toward the wall.

"Bro, what is this?" I ask.

"Keep your hands up, and I ain'tcha bro." Officer Gray runs his night stick under my shirt.

"Man, what are you doin'?" asks Derrick.

"Shut up and keep your hands on the wall."

I knew I should have gone home, I think to myself.

"Spread your legs." He pushes my feet apart.

He runs his nightstick between my legs, sliding it beneath my balls.

"Both of you ... strip."

"What?" I say.

"Take your clothes off."

We disrobe, leaving nothing on but a pair of socks. I'm terrified thinking that this guy is some homophobic fag basher out to beat us both to a bloody pulp.

"Nice," Officer Gray says, poking at our booties with his nightstick. I wasn't sure about Derrick, but my dick was good and hard pressed between the wall and my belly.

"Turn around," he says.

With our hands in the air, we turn around Officer Gray. My boner that sticks out in his direction like a compass doesn't embarrass me. I notice that Derrick's spit has dried from my dick. The policeman examines our hard-ons with hands covered in pitch gloves.

He looks at me and says, "I looked under and saw y'all two engaged in a lewd act."

"I swear we weren't …"

"Hey, hey, hey," he says. "Don't lie to me. I saw him givin' you head."

I was shocked by the way he spoke. Officer Gray looks to Derrick.

"If you lie to me, I'll take your ass in. Were you or were you not performing oral sex on him?"

Derrick drops his head, looks to the floor and says, "Yeah."

"He's lyin' I …"

"Shut your mouth!" He yells. "Now listen up. There's a way you two fags can get outta this shit storm you're in."

"Yeah, what? Anything," Derrick says.

"I wantcha to show me how you suck dick."

"What? No fuckin' way!" I tell him. "How do we know you still won't arrest us?

Officer Gray shoves me down on the toilet against its metal pipes.

"You don't," he replies forcing my thighs apart.

Derrick places his hand calmly on his arm.

"If we do this, will you let us go, man?" he asks.

Officer Gray doesn't take his eyes off me.

"Maybe," he replies. "If you suck it real good."

Derrick looks to me and says, "Let's just do what he wants."

"Listen to your boyfriend," he says to me.

"He's not my boyfriend," I tell him.

Officer Gray presses the nightstick harder against my Adam's apple.

"You know you've got some mouth on …"

"Okay, man, I'm doin' it, look," says Derrick, as he tilts my dick to his voluptuous lips. He opens up and takes me in his mouth.

"How does his mouth feel?" Officer Gray asks, tweaking my nipples. "You like gettin' your dick sucked?"

My contempt for him fades as I enjoy the blowjob that Derrick is giving. I take a chance and grope the cop's bulge.

"You wanna suck me, boy?" he asks.

I bend over and lick his polyester crotch.

"Take it out," he tells me. "Take my dick out."

I unzip the zipper and ease my hand down into its copper gape. His dick is firm; my adrenaline is running through me like volcanic lava knowing that I would soon have a policemen's cock in my mouth.

Derrick reaches around and pinches my cheeks that flows over the black rim of the commode, steady slurping upon me.

I hook three fingers into the elastic of his Fruit of the Looms, tugging them down past a bushel of pubes. His dick pops from the waistband with a meaty, mushroom crown.

"Think you can handle this?" Officer Gray looks down and gives me a shit-grinning smile. His dick is musky with sweat. I'm scared that he'll crack my skull, but ready, willing and hopefully able to work the slab that hangs between his thighs. I slowly work the head into my mouth. The ridges rub against my lips. I work up more spit to lube it up as I slide down, devouring two, three, four more inches. The muscles in my mouth begin to ache a bit as he overpowers me. I go in deeper; more inches of dick disappear.

"Whatta mouth," Officer Gray says. "Whatta … mouth."

I swirl down and up, down and up, noticing in the mirror, the slobber that runs along the underside of his dick. Derrick is still at me trying to get me to blow my load. I damn near forgot that he was between my legs being that Officer Gray was hard at work knocking his dick against my poor old tonsils. I gag a few times, but keep at it.

"Don'tcha puke, punk," he says, gyrating his hips into my face.

"Squeeze my ass," he tells me. I take my right hand and pinch the cop's chocolate ass cheeks.

"Hard," he demands. In order to keep with the pace of my blowjobs, I squeeze his booty when I go balls deep. My own hole is wet with sweat, anxious for plowing.

When I back off Officer Gray's dick, a web of spit runs from my lips to his chunked cock. I'm dying to feel this cop's dick fucking me. He plays with my chocolate chip nipples. The scent of sex hovers above our naked bodies.

"You get fucked?" the cop asks.

I slide off his dick and say, "Sometimes."

I usually charge two-hundred for anal, but what could I do? He was a cop.

"Well, you gettin' fucked today. Get up," he says, tapping Derrick on the shoulder. A trail of spit trickles down Derrick's chin and neck of stubble.

My asshole is ready to swallow that porno star dick. I stand up and move to the sink. I bend over and spread my legs. Officer Gray hangs the nightstick on the metal rail screwed to the handicap accessible wall of the stall. He unbuckles his belt that holds his pistol. I don't doubt that it's loaded. He unfastens the copper rivet of his pants. They drop to his feet. The buckle clangs on the tile floor.

"Don't move or I'll have to stick my gun up your ass," he tells me. "Hell, you'd probably like that shit." He scoots up behind me. His dick is warm as he smears the head of it from one butt cheek to the next. "I hope ya'll got rubbers," Officer Gray says.

Derrick pulls a red packet out of his tattered jeans pocket and hands it to him. The big dick cop tears across the edge with his teeth. His dick rests upon my ass as he pulls out the lubed latex.

"This betta not be that cheap sheep skin shit," he says to Derrick.

Get that thing in me, I think to myself.

I can feel Officer Gray's angry fingers creep in, prying my cheeks ajar. Derrick sits on the toilet and whacks what looks to be nine inches of light-skinned dick. I brace the edge of the sink for the cop's cock.

My rectum pulls and stretches as he works it in me slowly. It hurts like hell, and I try to relax all my muscles. My eyes are red and watery as Officer Gray's dick devours my ass. I'd give anything to see him explore my middle.

"Let him blow you," he says to Derrick. He walks over and stands at my open mouth while Officer Gray pounds me hard from behind. Derrick parks his dick in my mouth, fucking my face while the cop impales my booty. His precum is salty on my pallet. Gray laughs knowing that both ends of my body are getting poked.

"You got a fat ass, man." Officer Gray says.

He says he hasn't jacked off all day, that he usually finds a secluded place to park to blow off a wad, but hasn't had the time since he's been busy patrolling the campus.

"Damn, I been bonin' for an ass like yours." He thrusts his dick through me.

Derrick continues to snake it down my gullet, holding it there until I gag.

"I'm about to come," he says, as he rapes my mouth. He pulls out; a thick string of cum shoots across the side of my face, into my hair. I take his dick and pump the rest of his cream off into the sink.

"I'm gettin' close to shootin' off," the cop warns, as he pushes and bucks through the remnants of my insides.

"Oh shit, I'm comin'! I'm gonna shoot, dude!" he yells.

"Shootcha juice," Derrick says.

"Ah, shit!" the cop hollers.

His face grimaces, eyes squint shut.

He pumps cum into the rubber that slides along the sore walls of my ass.

When he's done using me, Officer Gray slips out. I collapse into the sink.

"Jesus, you can fuck," I say.

He unrolls the cum-filled rubber off his dick and slings it in a trashcan of wet, brown paper towels.

"That was hot," the cop says, pulling his pants up over his booty. I try to get dressed, but every muscle in my body screams.

"So, are you going to take us to jail?" Derrick asks.

"Well …you're free to go." He looks over at me as I pull my jeans over my spent ass. "But you … you stay."

Derrick takes one last look at me and walks out of the bathroom.

"I knew you looked familiar. I busted you last month over on Park Avenue. I'm takin' you in. The guys at the station are gonna love you."

DOUBLE-DICKED BY A FEW GOOD MEN
Donald Webb

I'm lying on my bed, with my legs widely splayed, beating my meat. Two of my fingers, lubricated with spit, poke about in my chute. Bearing down, I dig deep enough to feel the edge of my prostate. If only my fingers were longer! The smell of my ass, when I bring my fingers to my mouth for more lube, is a real turn-on. I'm not ready to come; I'm enjoying my jack-off session too much. If I want, I can go on for hours. When I know one stroke more will take me over the edge, I pause for a few moments.

After raising my legs, and placing my knees on the bed next to my head, I lick precum off the crown of my long dick. A silvery thread connects my mouth to my cock when I back off. An ache in my neck forces me to lower my legs.

In sexual nirvana, I tug at my nuts and finger my hole. A loud banging on the front door brings me back to reality. I'm trying to ignore the intrusion, but the clamor persists, so I pull on a pair of running shorts and slip on my sandals.

Stomping downstairs, I yell, "Keep your hair on ... I'm coming!"

When I fling open the door and see a Marine on the threshold I'm at a loss for words. Dog tags glisten on his naked mocha-colored chest. Camouflage trousers sag below his prominent hipbones. His hat, pulled low on his brow, shadows his face. A blouse hangs from one hand. Muscles undulate when he uses the blouse to wipe sweat from his chest.

His manly aroma drifts toward me when my breath catches in my throat. Trying to clear my mind, I shake my head. Am I dreaming, or is this hunk really posing in my doorway?

Just when I'm about to reach out and touch him, to see if he's real, or if he's a figment of my imagination, he says, "What's a matter, Mikey ... you don't know me?"

It's my best friend's older brother. It's been a while since I last saw him, and he's filled out, a lot.

"Riley," I say. "Is that really you?"

He laughs as he lifts his arms and flexes his biceps. His ribcage expands, accentuating his narrow waist. "You like the new bod?"

"Yeah ... you look so ... um ... different."

Smiling, he clasps his hands, leans forward, and puts his bulging deltoids on display, like he's on stage at a muscle show.

"What're you doin' here?" I ask.

He relaxes, removes his hat, and scratches his scalp. "We're shipping out to Afghanistan on Monday morning, so I'm home for some R&R."

My face flushes when he glances down at the tent in my shorts and asks, "What's goin' on?"

"Just reading."

"Looks like you be doin' more than just reading."

If you only knew!

"You alone?" he asks.

"Yeah, folks are away."

"I'm locked out," he says. "Ain't no one home."

"They're in Florida."

"What the fuck I'm supposed to do now, Mikey?"

"I'm taking care of the place. I'll let you in."

After retrieving the key to his house, I follow him off the verandah. He stumbles on the stairs, so I put a hand on his upper arm to steady him. The skin covering his huge biceps is smooth as black velvet.

"Boy," he says with a giggle, "am I drunk."

He places a brawny arm around my shoulders, I put my arm around his waist, and we meander across the lawn to his house. Even though I'm five-eleven, I feel like a midget next to him. His hot torso presses against my bare skin. His armpit, a few inches from my nose, is giving off a heady scent. My cock stiffens when I think about licking his pits.

We stagger up the stairs to his front door. He leans on me as I open the door, switch on the hallway light, and help him inside. I'm too excited to break contact with him, so I haul him down the hallway into his bedroom.

When I release him he falls back on the bed. "I feel like I'm still movin'," he says when I lift his legs onto the bed and straighten him out.

After turning on the bedside lamp, I stare at him for a few minutes. He seems to be drifting off, so I turn to leave. I could stand there all night looking at his spectacular body, but that could prove to be dangerous.

"Whoa, Mikey, what's your hurry?" he says patting the bed next to him. "Sit and fill me in on all the gossip."

I'm terrified I'll do something stupid and get clobbered, but he keeps patting the bed, so, like a trained dog, I sit.

The touch of his thigh against my leg sets me on fire.

"You got a girlfriend yet?" he asks with a grin on his face.

I shake my head. "No. Too busy with college."

He exposes his hairy armpits when he places his hands behind his head. Once again, I am tempted to lick them. His obsidian-colored eyes stare at me, giving me a knowing look; reminding me of the time he walked into his brother's room and found his brother and me having sex. We were shocked, but he was cool. "Next time lock the door, brutha," was all he'd said.

Now, here he was, lying on the bed next to me. "You're full of crap, Mikey. I know you're into guys."

He brought up the topic, so I take advantage of the opening. "You ever had your dick sucked, Riley?"

"You mean by a guy?"

I nod.

"I look like a fag to you?"

"Nah ... just wondered ..."

"You like sucking cock, Mikey?"

"Fuck yes. There's nothing I like more than having a big dick down my throat ... specially a black Marine's," I add with a nervous giggle. "You wanna try it."

He stares at me for a moment or two, like he's giving it some thought, and then he closes his eyes and gives a big sigh.

I'm petrified to put the make on him – he could crush me with his big arms – but I can't stop myself. As usual, I let my dick do the thinking. My hand gropes his muscular thigh. He doesn't object, so I slowly move my hand onto the mound between his legs. He's getting hard. With trembling hands, I loosen his trousers and tug at them. He lifts his hips, so I can pull his trousers and shorts down to his knees. His big, uncut dick, flops onto his beefy thigh. A set of big nuts droop to the bed.

The aroma emanating from him sends me into orbit. I can't believe I'm going to do him. I've dreamed about it for so long. Precum oozes from the hole in his dickhead, so I slurp the juice into my mouth. I chew on his pliant foreskin until it retracts, and his rod expands to a good eight inches. Bloated veins encircle the chunky shaft.

My tongue twirls around his tasty knob, and then I open wide and engulf the head of his dick. It's impossible to deep-throat him, he's too big and hard, and the angle's all wrong, but I persevere until my jaw aches. His sac is surprisingly smooth when I suck his nuts into my mouth. I push his legs up to his chest, so I can taste his butt.

His eyes pop open. "Whoa, Mikey. What you doin'?"

He tries to lower his legs, but I'm too quick for him. I bury my face in the warm moist place between his muscular mounds and nibble on his hole. He tastes like I knew he would, so I give his perineum a tongue bath, licking him from end to end. My tongue probes his slit. He's real tight.

When he emits a long drawn-out groan I look up at his face. His eyes are closed, and he's probably dreaming of pussy, but I don't care, I'll have him any way I can.

After rimming him for a good five minutes, I sit back and admire the view. His boots are in the air, and his camouflage trousers are bunched around his ankles. There's no doubt that it's a Marine I'm rimming, and I can't believe it.

He opens his eyes and looks at me. "Don't get any ideas, Mikey. That's virgin territory down there."

When I lower his legs, and resume blowing him, he once again closes his eyes. His huge knob, suddenly breaking through the stricture in my throat, slithers all the way into me, not stopping until my lips contact his pubes.

His mouth is wide open, and his head is arched back.

"Does it feel good?" I ask as I come up for air.

"Oh fuck, Mikey," he says. "I gotta admit, it feels great."

He lets out a long groan when I resume blowing him. He's gasping for air like he's getting ready to blast a load down my throat, when a voice says, "I see you talked him into giving you a blow job. I hope he can handle the both of us?"

We look towards the voice. It's another Marine. This one, tall and slender, is dressed in full utility uniform. He's leaning against the wall, pelvis pushed out, thumbs hooked in the waistband of his trousers.

"Hey, Lenny," Riley says "Where ya been?"

I'm shocked at the sudden appearance of another Marine, but not shocked enough to object. It's obvious they've discussed me, and this is all planned.

Riley and I watch as Lenny rubs his hand over the prominent bulge in his pants. He opens his fly and pulls out his long milk-chocolate-colored dick. He grips it at the base with one hand, and then slaps it onto the palm of his other hand. The noise carries across the room. I lick my lips.

"What you be looking at, whitey?" he says. "One brutha's cock not enough for you? You be wanting this one, too?"

I nod.

He walks over to the bed, and the two of them high-five, like they just won the lottery.

He climbs onto the bed and plants his boots alongside Riley's head. He leans against the wall, pushes his trousers down his legs, and strokes his dick. His rod isn't as thick as Riley's, but it's longer, inches longer. He places a hand behind my head and pulls my face towards his crotch.

"Suck that dick, boy," he says.

My mouth opens wide, and I suck the purple-colored knob. He exerts more pressure on the back of my head. "All the way down, boy," he commands. "You can do it."

Unimpeded, his dick slides down my throat.

"There you go," he says. "I knew you were gonna do it."

Riley starts fingering my hole. To facilitate his probing, I spread my cheeks.

I'm gagging on Lenny's cock, but I'm loving it. I've never had a dick that far down my throat. Lenny plays with his own hole while he pounds my throat. He pulls his saliva drenched dick out of my mouth and rubs the fingers that have been in his asshole over my lips. I take a deep breath and lick his fingers.

"You like the taste of my ass, boy?" he asks as he slaps my face with his dick.

"Yes, sir," I mumble.

"What's that!" he bellows.

"Yes, sir!"

"You wanna eat my ass?" he asks.

"Please, sir," I say. "Let me eat your ass."

He turns around and spreads his cheeks. His butt is smooth, but there is a swath of hair running from his coccyx to his nuts. He uses his fingers to pry open his moist hole and expose the pink lining of his chute. I lean forward and lick him. I adore his funky taste. I chew on his crater and fuck him with my tongue. He's wide open and receptive to my probing.

"That's it, boy," he says when I slip a finger into his hot cavity.

Riley's watching me fingering his Marine buddy.

I'm encouraged by Lenny's passiveness, so I slip two more fingers into him. His asshole gyrates around my fingers. It's obvious he's had more than fingers up his butt, and I'm wondering if I'm going to get to fuck his Marine ass.

"There's safes and lube in the drawer," Riley says to me. "Put one on my dick."

Lenny turns around and watches as I use my mouth to roll a safe down Riley's shaft. I then lube my ass. I straddle Riley's hips, place his dick-head at the entrance to my channel, and sink down to his hips. He's where I want him.

Leaning back on my hands, I fuck myself. Riley's big knob gives my prostate the attention it's needed all evening. My hard-on bounces up and down as I ride Riley's dick. Precum oozes from my meatus and drips to Riley's abdomen. He bends his knees up and I fall forward onto his body. He pounds my hole, in and out, in and out, like a piston on a steam engine.

Lenny squats down, over Riley's face, and holds his dick at my lips. I wonder how Riley's going to react with Marine butt in his face, but he's cool with it. Lenny's dick slides back down my throat.

"You want I should fuck your white ass?" Lenny asks after a few minutes.

"Please, sir," I say. "Fuck my ass."

He climbs off the bed, rolls a safe down his shaft, and lubes up. I'm anxious to feel him deep inside me. Oh, shit, I think when he spreads Riley's legs and crouches behind me. I didn't mean at the same time, but I'm so turned-on I can't resist. I want to see what it feels like to be double-dicked by a few good men.

Riley's abdomen feels like a washboard when I lie on him and force myself to relax. He doesn't move as my hole stretches to accommodate Lenny's girth. The pleasure/pain is so intense I sink into a stupor. When I come back to reality, they're pounding my butthole, and I've never had it so good. The thought of their Marine dicks rubbing together as they fuck me, blows my mind.

My cock is sliding back and forth over Riley's six-pack and I'm rapidly approaching orgasm. I raise my body to relieve the pressure, but it's too late, I've been holding back too long. Jism spurts uncontrollably from my dick. Riley's eyes pop open in surprise when the first two volleys hit him in the mouth. I fall forward and lock my mouth on his mouth. He tries to resist – I guess Marines don't kiss men – but I hold his head in place. My tongue explores his mouth when he gasps for air, giving me a taste of my own cum. He's squirming under me, and I can feel him planting his seed in my core.

Riley's dick slips from my hole when Lenny grabs my hips and pulls me up into a doggy position. His long shaft bores further into my chute as he rams me. I'm more open than I've ever been before. Lenny nibbles on my ear. His hot breath sends tingles through my body. He's hyperventilating by the time he creams. I wish that I could've taken them bare, so their DNA could combine inside me. What a child that would make!

Lenny collapses on the bed next to Riley, so I crawl between them, and fall into a deep sleep.

Sometime later, I awake with a full bladder. When I return from the bathroom, Lenny is lying on his left side. His face is buried in the pillow, with his right leg drawn up to his chest, so I bend over and lick his moist hole. My tongue slips in, and I can taste his juices. He is wide open, so I slip a couple of fingers into him. He reaches down and lifts his ass-cheek. I continue probing for a short time, and then I slip on a condom, lube my dick, and climb between his legs. He groans when I slam my dick into his silky chute.

I'm long-poling him, when he says, "Oh, yeah, you jarhead, fuck that hole."

Fuck, I hope he doesn't look and see it's me plowing his furrow.

Riley scrambles off the bed and comes around to our side. I'm wondering what's going down when he rolls a safe down his rod. I'm hoping he's going to shaft me, but that's not what happens. He shoves both Lenny and me over, until I'm flat of my back and Lenny is lying on my abdomen. I'm still balls deep in his channel.

"What the fuck?" Lenny says when he realizes it's I fucking him.

"I know what you need, brutha," Riley says as he pushes Lenny's legs up to his chest and straddles my thighs.

Riley's dick slithers alongside mine when he pushes it into Lenny's receptive chute.

Lenny, groaning and thrashing around on top of me, like he's had too much Spanish fly, bellows, "Fuck me, fuck me!"

Riley kisses Lenny and then he drops his head down and plants his lips on mine. We've gone too far for him to pretend he doesn't like kissing men. He's gasping for breath, and I can feel the tube in his thick dick pulsing as he shoots his load.

He withdraws his dick and deep-throats Lenny.

When Lenny's channel suddenly clamps down on my rod, Riley pulls his mouth off Lenny's rod, and we both watch as Lenny's juice squirts over us.

It's all too much for me. I can't hold back any longer. I give a couple more shoves into Lenny, and then I'm over the top, planting seed deep in his Marine butt.

We collapse in a heap.

They still have one more day before they ship out, so I'm hoping they're going to spend it with me.

If this is what the Marines are about, maybe I'll head down to the recruiting office on Monday.

GOODNESS OF HIS HEART
HL Champa

The GPS in my car called out the next set of directions, but I didn't really need them. I had been traveling to Stephen's office for months now. The butterflies I felt on the first visit were still there, but for a very different reason. Stephen was our college's wealthiest donor, and my boss wanted me seeing him as much as possible. They were looking for a seven-figure donation, his name on the side of a building and a healthy increase to their bottom line. I always came back from Stephen's with a check, but not for the reasons that my boss thought. I was the first to admit I was a lousy fundraiser. But, I gave Stephen what he wanted, and he gave me what I needed to keep my job. I pulled into the concrete of the parking structure, my wheels squeaking on every turn. Stopping the car, I straightened my tie, even though I knew it would soon be crumpled on Stephen's floor. I could only imagine what he would want today, what I would have to do to get the college an extra few grand for the quarter.

# # # # #

My boss, the illustrious Dean of Fundraising, heard about Stephen the same way everyone else did. He had gotten rich selling some computer program to the world and had spent the years since graduation throwing his money around. One week he'd be in Europe buying horses, the next he was back in town cutting the ribbon on a new wing of the hospital; which of course, had his name on it. Everyone loved him, but especially my boss. He came into a weekly staff meeting and threw a copy of *Black Enterprise Magazine* on the table, which featured Stephen's smiling face. It was official; he was the biggest celebrity our tiny, traditionally black college had ever seen.

Once my boss found out we had graduated together, he saw the perfect opportunity to get some of that considerable money for the college. He set up an appointment immediately for me to go see Stephen. I wasn't confident in my ability to convince him to donate his money to our small time college. He probably didn't even want people to know he had attended such a non-prestigious school. Besides the fact that it wouldn't get him any media attention, Stephen and I didn't exactly have the best history in the world.

Stephen and I had spent four years competing for everything. Grades, friends, lovers; they were all fought for. Unfortunately, for me, Stephen usually won. I had spent all my time chasing after his success, trying to duplicate it, or at the very least, keep him in my sights. I knew it was immature, but competition between the two of us became our normal routine.

There was only one place where Stephen and I were almost equals. He and I managed to bed many of the same guys, exchanging them back and forth with staggering regularity. It wasn't a matter of who had gotten there first, but who left the best impression. My reputation was solid, but Stephen never could settle for being second best. Right before graduation, he proved his point by stealing and bedding the only real boyfriend I'd ever had. At the time, I was devastated. I thought it was only because of my boyfriend cheating on me. But, I soon realized it was more than that. Underneath all the antipathy between us, I suspected there was also a mutual attraction. It went unfulfilled all those years, constantly denied by us both.

Stephen was the one guy I could never have. And, the one guy I always truly wanted. I never told him, but my true feelings for him were hard to ignore. So, I masked my lust with anger and sarcasm. Stephen did the same thing, but of course he did it better. After graduation, we lost touch until my boss threw him back into my life. He knew I worked at the college, and he knew that every time he sent in his alumni updates, I was the one who had to publish his latest milestone. Every write-up was a slap in the face. My life paled in comparison to his, and my anger grew every time I was reminded of that fact. But, soon it wasn't just the alumni magazine he was appearing in. When he hit the front page of *The Wall Street Journal*, everyone knew what a big deal he was.

This time, I had nothing that could compete with what Stephen had. To make matters worse, I was going to have to beg him for money. I couldn't think of anything worse.

# # # # #

The first time I went to see Stephen, I was nervous. When I walked into his office, after waiting for nearly thirty minutes, I was impressed immediately. The space was nothing short of amazing, with awards and accolades lining the walls. His demeanor was polite, but the glint in his deep brown eyes told me what I already knew – that he was better than I. I sat down in the cushy chair opposite his desk. He let me go through my speech, about giving back, tax write-offs and the like.

He sat behind his huge desk and smirked the entire time. I tried not to be distracted by his lips, which he wet with his tongue every few minutes. The action nearly took my breath away each time, but I managed to keep my composure. He looked even better than he had back then, his dreadlocks traded for a business-like close crop. His thick black lashes fluttered as he tried to follow my meandering speech, clearly bored by my pitch.

I could tell he was humoring me, and any second he would give me the brush off, and I would have to go back to work and explain why I didn't close the deal. I stopped talking and waited. And waited. Stephen let nearly a minute tick by in uncomfortable silence before he spoke. I was hoping to see him pull out his checkbook, but instead he leaned back in his chair and looked at me with appraising eyes.

"Wow, it is great to see you, Darren."

I smiled a bit, but quickly crisped up when I realized he was patronizing me.

"Yeah, you, too, Stephen. You've clearly done very well for yourself."

He looked around the room as if the thought had never occurred to him. His smile was the same one from all those years ago, the superiority of knowing you are always the winner. But, damn it, he was still so cute.

"Darren, you've done well, too. Nothing to be ashamed of. How is the rest of your life going? You seeing anyone?"

The question hung in the air between us, but I knew what he was really saying. He wanted to know if I could still get guys, or if I had lost my touch. I couldn't bear the thought of confessing how long it had been since I'd had anyone in my life. So I resorted to the only thing that would shut him up. Lies.

"Yeah, well, no one special. But, I still see my fair share."

He nodded, and I wondered if he could tell I was full of shit. He gestured to the photo on his desk of a young man, all dark hair, perfect cocoa skin and bright white teeth. He looked no older than twenty.

"This is Garrison. Isn't he adorable? I met him in Jamaica last year."

I couldn't speak. I nodded and smiled. The bile rose in my throat as I thought of Stephen and his boy-toy. I was jealous of Stephen's success; there was no question about that. Now, I found myself jealous of a guy I had never met. I busied myself in my briefcase as he told me about their recent trip to Aruba to celebrate their anniversary. I waited for him to finish and attempted to salvage a little bit of my dignity.

"Well, Stephen, I can see you're a really busy man. So, I'll let you think over our proposal, and I'll give you call next week."

"Darren, you're not really going to walk out of here without a check, are you?"

"What?"

"I'm just saying your boss won't be too happy if you come back to the school empty handed. I mean, I give money away like candy. If you don't close this deal, your boss is going to be angry. He told me as much on the phone."

"He called you?"

"Yeah, yesterday. He was going to come to this meeting himself, but I specifically requested you, Darren. I guess he wasn't all that confident in your abilities."

I looked away, not wanting to see the damn smirk on his face. He loved the fact that my own boss didn't think I could get any money from him.

"Don't feel bad, Darren. He just wants to make sure you bring back the money. I don't blame him."

"But, you're not going to give me any money are you? That's why you did this. You wanted me to walk out of here with nothing. God, you always were such a bastard."

He got up and walked around his desk, stopping right in front of me. I looked up into his dark eyes, feeling smaller than I had in years.

"Is that really what you think of me, Darren? I didn't bring you here, so I could make you look foolish."

"Sure."

"I'm planning on giving the college plenty of money. But, there is something I want in return."

"I knew it. What? What the hell do you want me to do, Stephen? Beg?"

He paused and took a long sip from his drink, before turning back to me. The smirk was back, and I swallowed hard as I tried to decipher the cryptic expression on his face.

"That's exactly what I want you to do."

"You really think I'm going to beg you for money, Stephen?"

"No, I want you to beg me to fuck you."

His hand dropped to his belt buckle, and I watched the leather come undone. I was speechless as his zipper dropped.

"Come on, Darren. I know you've wanted me since way back. I'll give you what you want, if you give me what I want."

I knew I shouldn't. My job might have been hanging in the balance, but I knew I should get up out of the chair and walk out of his office forever. My mouth was dry, and my mind was whirling. My sweaty palms rested on the padded arms of the chair, and I watched Stephen draw his full lips into a smile.

"Well, come on, Darren. What are you waiting for?"

I didn't know what I was waiting for. My cock stirred in my pants, thinking about finally having what I'd always wanted. With a heavy sigh, I dropped to my knees in front of the chair, my hands grabbing the expensive Italian wool pants at his hips. I looked up at him, knowing there was no turning back. Sliding them slowly down, his cock came into view, the thick purple-black head glistening with a drop of pre-cum. His fist was around it in an instant. A few jerks of his hand, and it was bigger and better than I had ever imagined. My mouth opened instinctively, and I inched closer to him. But, he just pulled away. His hand slid around my neck, forcing my eyes up to his.

"Come on, Darren. I know you want to suck my cock. All you have to do is ask. Come on. Ask me like a good boy."

"Stephen, please."

"Please, what?"

"Please, let me suck your cock, Stephen. Please."

I was still staring at his eyes when I felt the head of his cock rubbing against my wet lips. My eyes dropped when his cockhead eased past my lips and into my mouth. Stephen's hand was firm on the back of my head, pushing me forward onto his hard cock. I could taste him, the salty sweet flavor filling my senses. My hands slid up and down his thighs, feeling his muscles flex and relax as I moved my mouth.

"Put your hands behind your back."

I hesitated, but despite my brain screaming out objections, I moved my hands behind my back. I was no longer sucking him off. He was fucking my face, my control of the situation completely gone. My cock strained against the confining zipper of my dress pants, my knees starting to ache from the position I was in. Stephen's cock nudged the back of my throat, making tears drip from the corner of my eyes.

"Look at me, Darren."

I forced myself to look up at him, his eyes devouring me as he kept thrusting his cock inside my mouth.

"God, you look so fucking hot. I wonder how much your pretty little mouth is worth for the school."

I couldn't stop myself from groaning around his cock. No one had ever talked to me like that before. That smirk was still on his face, but for the first time in my life, I didn't mind. Abruptly, he pulled his cock from my mouth, slapping it gently across my cheek.

"Get up."

I got to my feet, just in time to see Stephen sit down in my chair.

"Take off your clothes, Darren. Let me see what I missed out on back in college."

Tugging on the silk of my tie, I could feel my hands trembling. My fingers trembled as I opened the buttons of my shirt. His eyes bore into me, as I threw my T-shirt aside. I had never been insecure about my body, until Stephen's eyes were roaming all over me. My fingers were almost numb as I started to open my belt. But, he didn't let me finish the job.

"Don't be scared, Darren. I won't hurt you. Too much, anyway. Turn around and put your hands on the desk."

I did what he told me, this time with no hesitation. I heard his footsteps, and then I felt his breath hot against my ear. His hand rested on top of mine, and just the tip of his tongue swept over my earlobe.

"So, Darren. Wanna earn a little more money?"

"Yes. God, yes. I'll do whatever you want, Stephen."

"That's good. Didn't take much to turn you into my bitch, did it?"

The words should have felt humiliating, but instead, they just added more fuel to my fire. I couldn't answer him; there were no words for what was going through my head. I pushed my ass back against him, but he remained just out of my reach.

"Let's see how far you're willing to go."

His hand pressed firmly into the center of my back, pushing me down onto his mahogany desk. My face rested on the large calendar, filled with appointments and red pen marks. Stephen reached past me, and I heard him open a drawer. The familiar click of the top of a lube bottle rang in my ears, but I didn't dare look at him. A small tug and my pants fell down to my ankles.

"God, Darren. You have a sweet ass. I hope our alma mater appreciates it. After all, it is the reason you're here. But, I need to hear something first. Come on, give it to me, baby."

"Stephen, please. I want you to fuck me."

He shocked me when he pulled me back by my shoulder. My face was right next to his, the pain shooting right down my spine to my cock.

"One God-damned please? You call that begging? I need to believe it, Darren. How bad do you want to keep your job? Do you want that as bad as you want to get fucked right now?"

"Stephen ..."

The whimper that came from my mouth surprised even me. I had never heard myself so weak, so timid before. He had reduced me to something I never thought I'd be. The weirdest part was how much I liked it. His hand slid to my neck and tightened, and I yelped as the pain increased.

"I need you to fuck me Stephen. I don't care if you don't give me a dime. I just want you to fuck me. Please, Stephen. God, please fuck me. Please?"

He released me, and I fell back onto the desk. I kept babbling, pleading repeatedly to feel him inside me. When he worked one cool, lubed finger into my ass, I moaned loudly against his desk. He moved his big finger slowly, pushing and pulling at a snail's pace, letting me get used to it. One finger quickly turned to two, and by the time it was three, I was pounding my fist against the wood. My cock ached to be touched, but he didn't oblige me. My hips moved back against his hand, trying desperately to speed him up.

"That's it, Darren. Fuck my fingers. That check is getting bigger every minute."

The school, my job was the furthest thing from my mind. I just wanted to feel his cock in my ass, and finally come.

"Stephen, please. I can't take much more of this."

He laughed, removing his fingers from my ass, leaving me feeling empty. I groaned in protest, which only made him laugh more. I should have been mad, but I couldn't feel anything except lust.

"I guess I'll take pity on you, this time Darren. Next time, I don't think I'm going to be so nice. But, I've been dying to do this, too."

I heard Stephen tear open a condom wrapper, and a strong feeling of relief swept over me. His strong hands gripped my hips, the head of his cock prodding at the pucker of my ass. As I took a deep breath, his dick inched forward, stretching me to the point of discomfort. His cock was big, but I was desperate to take it. My forehead dug into the desk, my hands balling into tight fists. Suddenly, something inside me gave way, and I felt my whole body relax. Stephen was in me to the hilt, and finally his hand wrapped around my stiff and swollen cock.

"You are so fucking tight, Darren."

I waited for more wicked words, but none came. The only sounds that passed between us were the moans and grunts of pent up passion. His hand was moving quickly, his cock, even quicker than that. Sweat washed over my back and neck, my eyes pinched shut tight. I knew I wouldn't last; it had been far too long since I'd been fucked properly, and my desire for Stephen was just too much to take.

"Come on, Darren. Come for me."

I pushed back against him as hard as I could, his cock buried inside me as deep as it would go. His fist made one last jerk, one last twist over the swollen, sensitive head. I muffled my cries with my own hand, fearing a scream would make people wonder what was going on in Stephen's office. My cock spurted into his hand, my ass contracting around his thick, thrusting cock. Stephen collapsed onto my back, his own orgasm following right after mine. He lay heavy on top of me, but I couldn't have moved even if I wanted to.

He finally pulled away, cleaning up and dressing quickly in silence as I found the strength to pick up my strewn clothes. Before I was finished buckling my belt, he had his checkbook out.

"Is twenty grand enough for now?"

I nodded, my body still shaking. He wrote his signature with a flourish and tore the check out. He handed it across the desk to me, and then stood up to button his shirt. I folded the check and put it in my pocket.

"I hope to see you again soon, Darren. I think the college could really benefit from this relationship."

His face was back to a smirk. I knew exactly what he meant.

"Yeah, I think so, too, Stephen."

I returned to work that day with more money than I had managed to raise in months. And, a monthly appointment set up with Stephen.

# # # # #

As I pulled into the parking garage of Stephen's building, the GPS alerted me to my arrival. I felt those nervous pangs in my stomach grow more intense. The school wanted to get Stephen to donate enough to start a scholarship. I knew this one was going to cost me.

Big.

COVERED
WITH BLOOD
AND FAT
Derrick
Della Giorgia

The Jeep emitted a loud hiccup from the depth of its metallic stomach and came to a halt. One, two, three, four. Each second brought on us one more degree. I felt the thin skin under my eyes burn first and then sweat. Still. We all waited immobile and speechless. Only Kito's slender fingers kept maneuvering the ignition key, hoping the old vehicle we had been assigned would start again. When we all realized that was not what was going to happen, comments started raining in every language. *"E adesso che facciamo?"*, *"Et maintenant?"*, *"Como vamos a hacer?"*

Kito turned towards us and said: "No problem."

A 100 miles away from the village. Equally distant from water, food and shelter. Kenya Safari Vacation Packages: the vacation of your life. The web page revived in my overheated brain. The sun coming down without affecting the temperature, the earth tones of the vegetation, the vastness in every direction, the sky that looked like a lid on top of us. All the promises were kept. Of course, now we also had the olfactory stimulation, the hot caress of the air and the sensation we had turned deaf. The silence was so sharp and impenetrable that I started praying for the motor to awaken and bombard me again with its mechanical cursing. "What are we going to do?"

For the first time perhaps obliged by the situation, I noticed Kito's skin was of the most beautiful black I'd ever seen. Immaculate, soft and delicate, it smoothly wrapped his elegant physique. His arms were long and defined, magically decorated by many multicolor beaded bracelets. His movements were almost liquid in the long red dress that exposed his chest on the sides and below his neck where more beads concentrated in a chromatic order.

"They are coming to get us with another jeep. We only have to wait a bit. In the meantime, you can take pictures." Not too far from us, a dozen elephants were enjoying the same patch of Kenya as we. He smiled and closed his eyes, transmitting peace to all the insatiable monsters he was in charge of.

He was taller than I. My sun glasses barely reached his shoulders as he helped me out of my seat. Michele would have never done that for me. With him it was a continuous fight, a race. He only cared about being better than I. More beautiful, smarter, more successful. Michele had to know more things about Rome than I did, even though I grew up by the Pantheon and he came from Firenze. Michele didn't want to go to Africa because only rich brainless people would go to Africa and waste their money in a village. "I want to live there for at least six months." His rules were strict. My life with him was horrible. Needless to say, the first thing I did after we broke up was literally run to my travel agency in Trastevere and get myself a nice Safari in Kenya, together with all the brainless rich people who couldn't afford to leave their jobs and move to Africa for six months.

"When are they gonna get here, you think?" I asked while I was still close enough to his neck. A second longer and I would have kissed him. The curiosity of knowing what his skin would taste like percolated through my thoughts, annulling anything smarter I could have told him.

"Maximum two hours." He accompanied the word two with his two long fingers.

"Kito, could you please help me get out?" The Ramirez's daughter requested the tour guide's attention. So far she had taken more pictures of him than of the animals we'd encountered. She had pushed onto his face her blonde head of hair at every possible occasion, and she now wanted to have his hands on her plump twenty-something body. Her laughter reached higher and higher notes as their interaction strengthened.

"Margarita." Kito simply called her name out loud, offering his support.

Eight people wandered away from the vehicle ready to press all kinds of buttons on their cameras as they approached the family of pachyderms. Kito jumped back behind the wheel and rested, his arms under his head and his elbows up in the air.

"My name means precious in Swahili. I will be very precious to you during this trip. You are computer and supermarket people and have probably forgotten the laws of nature. I was born and raised among these creatures. I speak their language; I read their intentions; I know their danger. Please, keep that in mind." Kito had introduced himself before leaving the village to our just awakened and still tired faces. He was a Maasai, but spoke also the two official languages in Kenya: English and Swahili. He'd been working in the village since he was a child, and he dreamed of visiting Europe, a long trip to learn about "computer and supermarket people," as he referred to us. His eyes were sincere and sweet, but he was no fool.

Two hours later, we were on the new Jeep on our way back to the village. That night, I ate alone, avoiding my Safari companions and analyzing my relationship with Michele. After all, Africa was the right place for a good introspective session, especially if you were past the group dancing that followed dinner every night.

I switched my iPod on and completely isolated myself. I took a long walk, determined to count all the stars on my path. *Negrita's Rotolando Verso Sud* on repeat. Every name, a man. And every man is only what he will discover following the distances within himself. The Tuscanian band's words were so appropriate. I had to discover my inner distances. It wasn't Michele's fault either. I still wasn't attuned to my surroundings. A full smile formed on my face. A fat yes spilled out of my lips dried up by so much thinking.

"How are you, Rocco?" Kito's sclera floated midair around me as he approached me. Only a few seconds later, my sight adjusted, and I recognized his long-limbed silhouette.

"Hi, Kito. What's up?"

"I was outside, and I heard your music."

"I'm sorry if I disturbed you. But, I was using my headphones. How did you ... where were you?" I couldn't believe I'd been so loud. Michele often complained my volume was annoying, but we were out in the open now. Was he serious?

"You forget how important sounds are to me. I can tell you what time of the day it is, where I am and what is going on by just listening ..." His fingers reached his temples, and he started listing all the animals that were sharing the night with us. Then, he gently landed his hand on my left ear and continued: "Unlock your senses. Don't be afraid of the silence. Relax your hearing and everything will come to you. Amplified. It is only a matter of exercise. Come with me." He freed my hands of my iPod, put it in my pockets once he realized I wasn't going to move and held my hand to show me the way.

He took me to the tent where he used to spend most of his free time. We sat inside in the dark.

"Don't worry. Soon your eyes will become stronger, and you will be able to catch the white light of the stars."

"You're right!" As soon as he was finished, I was able to see his face and the cushions we were sitting on. Again, I felt that impulse to try his skin.

"Do you hear the lion?" In the distance, the big cat was imposing its law.

"What if it finds us?" I made a joke, but secretly I wondered how he would defend us from the hungry beast.

"You will be dead, and I will have to cover you with fat and blood." He laughed.

"What?" He wasn't so elegant anymore. He wasn't that different than any other sarcastic "computer and supermarket" guy I knew back in Rome.

"You see, us Maasai do not give much importance to the body once life flies out of it. We give it back to nature. We feed other creatures with our dead ones. And to make sure they don't remain uneaten, we cover them with blood and fat to be more appetizing. To have a dead family member that stays uneaten is considered a dishonor."

"Well, thank you for the lecture." I didn't know every word was true and thought he was only making fun of me. So, I got on my knees and proceeded towards the side of the tent that would let me out.

"No, stay." Kito's arms wrapped me from behind and swallowed me into his embrace. I found myself nested in his small but athletic lap, his wise lips already going up and down my neck. "*Busu* in Kiswahili means kiss. How do you say that in Italian?"

"*Bacio.*" I managed to answer before showing him. His skin was smoother then it looked. I licked it. It tasted like sun and life.

An hour of kissing later, I perceived the uncontainable pressure in many a spot in my body. The excitement – taken to such extent – turned into pain, my flesh into a device that created electric waves every time Kito's sweet breath returned to me. He told me to wait when I insinuated my hands under his dress. He told me to wait when my tongue went anywhere below his neck. He told me to wait as I moved to acquire a position that would facilitate more intimacy and action. "Make your body stronger. Take full advantage of your senses. You will enjoy a longer lasting pleasure. You will receive the meaning of it."

"Take your clothes off now." He ordered me and stared at me, waiting for me to obey when he saw I couldn't keep inside me what he'd caused.

Once I was sitting naked inches in front of him, he did the same thing. My erection pointed at him and his at me. We looked like warriors on the verge of attacking their enemy, imbued with tension but still immobile. As I'd imagined, his body was perfect. Every muscle, every fold, every curve spoke of sex. He handed me a beaded bracelet and kept one for himself.

"Put it on." He slowly adjusted that circumference to the dark spear I couldn't avoid to desire. "It feels good." Then, he reached over me and took my beaded cock into his hands stimulating it in a way I'd never experienced before. As if playing a musical instrument, he applied pressure on sensitive spots I didn't know I had. "Will – you – do – the same?" He interspersed his words with long kisses. "Please?"

My clumsy hands didn't seem to have a rhythm, at least not the perfect rhythm his produced. My palms slid up and down the beads and his turgid stick. Again and again, but that didn't quench the desire that kept devastating my mouth. Now I wanted to suck him. But he refused to let me go down on him. In vain, his caresses brought my chin back up, my lips back to his. The more that game lasted, the faster my heartbeat, and eventually I left him no choice. With that violence well known to lovers, I bent on him kissing his knees with the adamant intention of giving him something back.

"Tell me if you like it." I spread my saliva on his inner thighs and obliged him to fuck my mouth. "Put your hands on my head and let me know what you feel." Kito reluctantly positioned his wrists on the back of my neck and emitted some deep respiration noises that assured me I was doing the right thing. "Hold my head tight!" Now it was me ordering. Soon, my head was locked in his grip, forced to swallow him until I felt the hard beads hitting my teeth. His juice commenced to descend down my palate, giving more flavor to our act.

"I've never done this before with another man." He confessed to me, instants before entering my body. My entire torso plummeted on his painful weapon until I felt the bracelet wrapped around it slowly entering me, too. Kito pressed his hands on my ass and pushed more.

My white skin was glued to his dark body and sweat starting flowing down between us, making our friction faster and more intense. My cock was trapped in our abs and sprayed white milk on his chest long before he was ready. But I kept going, the pleasure continuing endlessly.

"I'm ready." Kito warned me. "This is for you." He slid out of me and started bursting, our four hands helping the flow as much as it was possible.

"I'm dead!" I whispered before falling asleep in his arms.

"Shall I cover you with blood and fat?" He answered, kissing me one more time.

SORRY MAN, MY BAD
Michael Mandrake

D'Andre got on the crowded train with his briefcase in one hand and iPod in the other. He winced when an old woman bumped him with her huge bags.

"Sorry, young man," she smiled as she walked away, doing the same to others.

How he wished that the "El" were not always so packed this time of the morning. He swore that one day he was just going to have to buckle down and drive to work. Even though parking was so expensive downtown, it might be worth it, so he could avoid this.

As the doors closed, he moved toward the middle of the car. He sat the case down while twiddling his fingers to the sound of Jill Scott coming out his earphones.

"This is sixty-ninth. Please, exit the doors on the left." Pause. "Doors closing."

Damn, that is annoying, he thought.

As the train proceeded to move again, he felt someone bump him with their book bag. Again, he tensed turning around to see whom the culprit was.

"Sorry, man, my bad," the other man said. Their eyes met for a split second when the other man stopped to stand on D'Andre's left side.

D'Andre turned up the volume on his player while glancing back at the young brother again. *Damn*, he thought. He shook his head then looked out the window at the buildings outside. The man didn't notice him staring; he was reading *The Times*, while trying to hold on to keep from falling.

Again, D'Andre peered over at him, looking at how attractive he was. The brother was smoking; caramel colored skin, hazel eyes, and from what he could tell through the clothes a lean body. "Mmph..." he said, as he gazed back out the window.

LOUDSPEAKER "This is thirty-fifth. Please, exit the doors on the left." Pause. "Doors closing."

The man looked up from his paper returning D'Andre's gaze. "Hey man, what's up," he said, as he shrugged his shoulders flashing a somewhat irritated look.

D'Andre closed his eyes trying to think quickly for an explanation as to why he was staring this brother down. "Hey dude, I was just noticin' your Sean John fit. It's live man. Where did you get it from, and how much was it," he asked with a wide, closed mouth smile.

Seemingly, the man softened his stance, putting the paper under his arm. "Aw, I don't really remember how much I paid for it, but I know I got it from Ricco's in The Plaza," he said, smiling back.

D'Andre breathed a sigh of relief when the man believed his little white lie. "Cool man, I'm gonna have to check that place out. Thanks, bro."

"No prob, man. Hey, is that the latest Jill Scott you listenin' to?"

D'Andre was happy that the man wanted to continue talking with him. *Any excuse so I can look at the brother*, he thought. "Yeah, it's just as good as her first one. She can really blow, can't she?"

"Yeah, I saw her in concert a couple of years back. The sistah puts on a great show." His pearly white teeth made an appearance, and D'Andre felt compelled to show his as well.

The two continued to chat, seemingly forgetting they were on a crowded train. During their conversation, they found out they had a lot in common: live music, mostly jazz and R&B along with spoken word clubs, writing poetry, and Cajun food restaurants. When Clark Street came up, they noticed they were getting off at the same stop.

"Where you work at, Taj," D'Andre said as they trotted down the stairs. While they talked, the young man told him his name.

"I don't work, D'. I go to school at the Art Academy on State Street." D'Andre was flattered that Taj felt comfortable calling him D'. Really, only his close friends called him that.

"Aw, really? What's your major?"

"Game design and development; that's where the monies at now D'. Man, I'm sorry I keep calling you D', and I don't even know ya that well."

D'Andre smiled and shook his head. "Naw man, it's cool. You're right about game design, though. There will always be a market for video games."

"True dat."

As the men continued to walk up Clark Street, D'Andre saw he had passed his building. When they came up on Starbucks, both men stopped, and D'Andre looked at his watch. It read nine-fifteen; his start time was nine-thirty. *I got time to grab coffee with Taj*, he thought.

"Hey D', are you late for work?" Taj pulled out his wallet, getting out some money.

"Naw, I don't have to be there till nine-thirty, plus I got a seven minute window."

"Oh cool. You wanna grab a cup of coffee before work?"

"Sure, I'll buy though, man."

D'Andre opened the door moving aside, so a woman with her baby could walk out, then he waved Taj in. As Taj walked past, he checked out his "fit" examining how nice and snug it was in all the right places.

When they walked up to the counter, Taj ordered a tall Italian Roast while D'Andre asked for a *vente* regular with cream. After putting a bit of sugar in his coffee, the two walked out and stood on the side of the entrance. D'Andre hated that he had to go to work leaving Taj.

D'Andre Ward didn't have many close friends left, when he divorced his wife and came out to everyone. His dad disowned him, saying he could never love a gay son because being gay was against God's word. Unfortunately, his mom passed away from cancer when he was twenty.

The only true confidants he had were his best friend, Todd, a white guy whom he roomed with at college, and Marcus, who worked with him at the firm.

"Thanks for the coffee, D'. Hey, um I'm sorry for comin' off kinda' hard bro. I've only been up here three months, and I'm pickin' up the habits already. I'm from the South; down there everyone speaks and/or smiles at one another. Up here, people ain't so nice. My first day I spoke to a brotha, and dude straight up gave me the nastiest look. After a few more of those, I got the hint," he laughed sipping his coffee.

"It's cool, Taj. I know what you mean, believe me. In Chi, brotha's are always on the defensive." D'Andre drank while looking at his watch; he was three minutes from being considered late. While he turned up the cup again, he tried to think of a way to see Taj without asking him out. "Hey Taj, I gotta run, but maybe we could chat again since you're new to the city." D'Andre took out his card case to hand him one. "See ya' around OK?"

"Yeah man, thanks for the coffee."

D'Andre ran across the street and out of the sight of Taj. While finishing his, Taj noticed that D'Andre was running back toward the train station.

"D' the lawyer was checkin' me out," he said, looking at the card with a sly smile.

Taj Redmond was attending art school on a scholarship from a Native American empowerment organization from his home state of Louisiana. At age twenty-two, he had finally left the home of his grandmother who raised him since he was five. His mom was a descendant Natchez Indian tribe, and his father was black. Both of them were killed in a car crash that left Taj an orphan.

Neither his mom's nor dad's siblings wanted to take the responsibility, which left his grandma to care for him. Grandma spoiled Taj, giving the boy everything while letting him do whatever he wanted. He took advantage, going out clubbing and down low parties where he wasn't old enough to be.

Taj considered himself straight, but bi-curious. Girls were crazy about him, but he did not feel the same for them. He had some of the fines ladies in his bed because they loved his hazel eyes, lean body, and long light brown locks. When he left New Orleans to go to school in Chicago, they were quite upset.

The only person that knew about his curiosity was his best friend, Jeff, who grew up with him. Jeff was a straight white boy that loved black women. Jeff was cool with the "scene," though. He would go out with Taj, but would make it clear to all that he liked girls.

Taj threw the empty cup in a trashcan before putting the card in his back pocket. *Maybe I'll give D'Andre a call this afternoon,* he thought. Taj ran over to the school, up the stairs to class.

# # # # #

D'Andre twirled his pen around his fingers, while reading over his latest case. He threw the pen across the room, closing the folder on his desk.

"Shit."

Disgusted he got up and walked to his window. D'Andre looked in the direction of the school, where Taj was. *What the hell? I don't even know this kid, and I am already thinking of him. Taj is definitely straight; I need to stop.*

As D'Andre was about to sit back down, his Blackberry rang; it was a number he didn't know. He pushed the connect button and spoke.

"Hello, this is D'Andre Ward."

"D', it's Taj. How's work today man?"

D'Andre's serious look changed when Taj's voice came through the other end.

"What's up man? Sorry. I was in a rush. Work is work by the way. How's school?"

"It's good bro." Taj thought about what he should say next. He really wanted to let D'Andre know that he was interested in getting to know him better, but he decided to invite him out for lunch instead. "D', do you wanna have lunch with me?"

Surprised, D'Andre stood in silence as he heard the invite from Taj.

"Hey bro, I'm sorry for comin' off like that. It's just that you were so friendly, and I hadn't met many nice people yet." Taj thought he might throw that in there, so he wouldn't let on that he was interested, nor that he knew D'Andre was checking him out on the train.

Not to mention Taj had met plenty of nice people, but when he stepped off the bus from New Orleans, he decided he wanted something real; he wanted to fall in love, and would sacrifice casual sex to get it.

"Uh no, man, its' okay, I feel ya'. Sure, we can have lunch. What time?"

"Can you meet me in front of the school at about two?"

"Sure, any place you'd like to go?"

"I'm a poor college student, so if you don't mind McDonald's. That would be fine."

"Eww, McDonald's is gross. If you like Chinese, let's go to Woo's Wok; I'll buy."

Taj smiled at D'Andre's willingness to pay again. "D' you paid for coffee this morning. I can't allow …"

"Like you said, you're a poor college kid in a new town. I insist."

"Okay D', since you insist. I'll take Chinese ova Mickey D's anytime. I gotta go to class. I'll see you at two."

As soon as he hung up, D'Andre exhaled. He actually did have lunch plans with Marcus, but he could do that any day. It wasn't all the time you would meet a beautiful young brother that would allow you to take them out without getting homophobic.

# # # # #

Once they ate together that day, they seemed to get more comfortable around each other. From then on, they would meet at the train station at seventy-ninth to take the El. Taj lived in the area, but D'Andre just parked his car around there to save on gas. Really, D'Andre wanted to ask Taj if he would like to carpool, but he thought that Taj might take it the wrong way.

They would meet for meals, whenever they were both available and talk on the phone about music, sports, food, and life in general. Both men were playing their cards carefully. They had not talked about sex or anything about relationships. They did know of each other's family situations; however, D'Andre didn't tell Taj the real reason he divorced his wife.

D'Andre was racking his brain as to why this kid was opening up so quickly. It bothered him so much he talked to Marcus and Todd about it. Even though Todd was straight, he would listen to D'Andre's man problems all the time and offer his best advice.

"D', why don't you just ask him, instead of driving yourself up a wall? I mean, obviously the kid likes you," he said, during their last conversation.

When he tried to talk with Marcus, he was no help. "Listen D', I love ya, but I just can't talk to you about tryin' to get anotha brotha in bed."

Seemingly, the attraction between them was apparent; nevertheless, both were afraid to make the first move. Finally, after three weeks of aching hands from jacking off while having wet dreams of the young man, D'Andre decided to go for broke. Taj will like me as a friend, or he might want something more, I'll never know unless I ask, D'Andre pondered after sitting home alone one night.

Finally, D'Andre dialed Taj on a Friday, to ask him out for a meal.

After three rings, Taj answered in his usual friendly tone. "Hey D', what's up my man?"

D'Andre always smiled when he heard Taj's slightly southern accent. "Hey Taj, listen, I was wonderin' if you wanted to go out to dinner tonight."

Taj was silent as he processed what D'Andre had just asked him. Inside he was yelling like a little schoolgirl. He had been waiting for him to ask ever since they met three weeks ago. Trying to contain his excitement, he cleared his throat. "Yeah sure, um where?"

"I thought since we both like Italian, we can go to Ciao Bello downtown. Is that cool?"

Taj smiled running his fingers through his hair. "Yeah, that would be great."

"Cool, I'll pick you up at seven-thirty."

"Cool man, see ya then." Taj pushed his disconnect button while stroking his goatee. He closed his eyes thinking of how gorgeous D'Andre was. The brother had so much going for him. Not only was he hot, but he also had a career with probably a nice house to boot. D'Andre's age didn't bother Taj either; the man was in great shape for age thirty-six.

Taj had never been by his house, and even though D'Andre dropped Taj off at home, he'd never been inside. They had really played it cool, yet maybe tonight after a nice romantic dinner, things would heat up.

Taj chuckled to himself as he walked into his bedroom. He looked in the closet grabbing a pair of black slacks and a long sleeve shirt to wear. He dropped them on the bed before looking in the mirror.

"I'm here for ya', D'." He flexed a bit marching towards the bathroom for a shower.

D'Andre picked a pair of black trousers and a well fitting tee out of his half-empty, walk in closet. He was grateful that his ex's shit was gone, so he could walk in and not fall over shoes. Besides, he was the typical gay man; he liked everything neat and tidy.

Before closing the door, he envisioned Taj standing behind him. Aroused, he closed his eyes letting his hand drift inside his pants.

"Mmm … Taj do you want me, or are ya' just playin' a brotha," he laughed before walking into his bathroom to freshen up.

Taj was ready by seven, waiting for D'Andre to call. After his shower, he talked with Jeff about his date with D'Andre.

"I swear, Taj, don't let anotha night go by without you two talkin' 'bout how ya' feel about each otha! You killin' me wit all this nonsense. You like the brotha', tell him damnit!"

The pep talk with Jeff made Taj feel better about opening up to D'Andre. He hoped that he would come a bit early, so they could chat in private.

Just as he was about to turn on the TV, his phone sang "A Long Walk" by Jill Scott, which was Taj's ring tone for D'Andre.

"Hey D', what's up?"

"Hey Taj I know I'm a bit early, I thought I'd stop by so we …"

Excited that D'Andre seemed to read his mind, he interrupted him. "Sure man, not a problem. I'm ready."

D'Andre chuckled, turning his car off. "Well, I'm downstairs. Can you let me in?"

"Alright D'" Taj thumbed the off button looking around his tiny apartment; making sure things were somewhat in order.

Quickly, he walked to the door, buzzing him in. Taj opened the door and within seconds, D'Andre was standing in front of him.

"Hey Taj. Sorry to call early, and drop in before dinner."

"No, D' it ain't no thing. C'mon in, have a seat."

Taj waved him in, and D'Andre sat on the couch.

Obviously both nervous, they sat in silence for a couple of minutes then Taj took a deep breath and spoke.

"Look D'Andre, when we met on the train, it was real awkward. What started out kind of bad turned out good, but I ..."

D'Andre looked at Taj intently; he knew it was coming. Taj would tell him he thought they were getting too close; that he liked girls and wanted to be just friends. D'Andre looked down at his hands, because his eyes couldn't look into Taj's beautiful ones without showing emotion.

"D', why aren't you looking at me?"

D'Andre looked at Taj again, breathed in deeply, then exhaled. "I'm sorry, Taj, I knew I was wrong to feel something for you. It's cool if you just want to be friends." Suddenly sadness crept into D'Andre as he pondered on what he thought Taj was trying to tell him.

Taj put his hand on D'Andre's knee. "D' what are you sayin'? I don't what to be just friends anymore."

D'Andre gazed back at Taj, then at Taj's hand on his knee. "Taj did you just say ..."

"Yeah D', I like you man. That first day when I bumped you with my bag I liked you. Actually, I did it on purpose to get your attention. I been seein' you walk from your car to the train for about a week or so, before I finally decided to make a move. It's been hard playin' the game your way, dude. A brotha been hurtin', especially since sex gets thrown at me from all directions."

D'Andre could not believe what he was hearing. Wryly, he smiled, putting his hand on top of Taj's.

Taj continued, "When you looked me up and down givin that weak ass excuse about my outfit, I had to use that and Jill (Scott) as an opportunity to talk with ya'. Plus, you know us brotha's can't talk game to each anotha without brotha's and sistah's gettin' all up in tha business. So, I had to give ya' a hard time. Now though, it's all good, D'. You're here, where I want you to be."

D'Andre felt relieved and peered into Taj's gorgeous hazels some more. "Wow, here I was wonderin' if I was barkin' up the wrong tree," he chuckled.

"No D', I've been curious for a long time. And over the last month I've done nothin' but think of you so, I know I'm more than interested. That first day after you bought me coffee I couldn't wait to call you, and now every time we talk, I feel that somethin'. You know that mushy giddy shit when you're fallin' for someone. That's what I feel for you D' and I'm pretty sure you feel it for me, too." Taj took D'Andre's hand into his own kissing it.

Immediately, that sent a shock to D'Andre's groin. He hadn't had sex with anyone since that guy he picked up at the club after his divorce. He felt so cheap and empty after that he decided he would not have sex until he found the right man. Now that Taj was practically throwing himself at him, he didn't know how to react.

"D', what's wrong, baby? Talk to me."

D'Andre smiled at Taj with a tear in his eye. "I do feel that somethin' for ya' Taj, and I'm so happy you feel the same. I've been so lonely lately that I neva saw you tryin' to spit game my way, man. I want you so bad, Taj. I've done nothin' but think about you, too, I've been drivin' my friends mad."

Taj laughed, "Same here man. D'..." he paused taking both D'Andre's hands kissing them again. Taj put them on D'Andre's face reaching over to wipe the tears. Within moments, Taj leaned over to plant kisses on D'Andre's forehead, nose, eyes, and mouth. He parted his lips with his tongue. D'Andre stretched out pulling Taj into him. Taj gently pushed D'Andre back on the couch cushions laying his body on top of him.

They locked lips for a while before D'Andre stopped to look at his phone. He smiled, glancing into Taj's eyes.

"Taj, our reservation was for eight-thirty, it's almost eight. We won't make it at this rate, baby. Ciao Bello is always busy, especially on Friday and Saturday nights."

"For real? My bad," Taj chuckled.

D'Andre grinned taking Taj back in for another embrace. Taj accepted it, rubbing his hand over D'Andre's baldhead. More kisses followed, which incited both of them. Again, D'Andre stopped to gaze at Taj. He just couldn't believe that this young kid he had been lusting after actually wanted him, too. He ran his fingers through Taj's hair, releasing it from the ponytail. Taj shook his head peering into D'Andre's eyes more.

Just as he was about to get lost in Taj's eyes, he thought he should ask Taj if food was on his mind.

"Taj, are you hungry?"

"Not right now, but I got food here that we could fix. I'm actually a pretty good cook," Taj replied while massaging D'Andre's chest through the T-shirt.

"Really? Cool then. I guess when we're hungry ..."

"Actually D', I'm hungry now, but it isn't for food." Taj flashed a wicked look towards D'Andre.

D'Andre reeled Taj in again. Taj started grinding against D'Andre slowly. When their hardened flesh met through the fabrics, both of them were instantly erect. Taj stopped, getting up.

"Baby, c'mon, the couch ain't big enuff." When Taj held out his hand, D'Andre took it.

As he rose, he stared into those eyes again. Taj led him to his bedroom, starting to undress D'Andre. First, his shirt revealing rock hard pecs and abs. Taj loved the sight of that, leaning down a little to kiss his body.

Once he was by his navel, he stayed there circling it, making D'Andre lose his focus. After getting his fill, he unbuckled his pants dragging them downward. He caressed him through his cotton boxer briefs, with his hands and face. D'Andre was so stiff, he knew if he didn't get inside Taj soon he would come.

"Oh Taj ... damn," he whispered.

Taj looked up at him moving his underwear down to his knees. D'Andre started to pant the moment that Taj took him into his mouth. Taj swallowed him fully while stroking his balls gently. He felt his own cock stir using his free hand to release it. D'Andre looked down at Taj before rubbing his head. Taj started moving back and forth on his dick, exciting D'Andre even more.

"Shit, Taj, oh my God."

D'Andre couldn't allow Taj to continue; he had to be inside him.

"Taj, please get up baby. I have to be inside you. Please," D'Andre begged.

Taj licked his lips before planting a soft kiss on D'Andre's.

When they had finished undressing, they lay on Taj's bed with the lube and condoms nearby. D'Andre was "priming" Taj by licking his hole while pushing his lubed fingers inside.

Taj's breaths were quick; he ached for D'Andre to give him what he'd wanted.

"D', now please," he whispered.

D'Andre opened the condom then slipped it on. He knelt over Taj peering into his hazels again. The expression on Taj's face was calm. Taj wrapped his arms around D'Andre's neck.

"Relax baby. Breathe. I'll go slow, ok?"

Taj nodded meeting D'Andre's gaze. He knew it would not feel great at first; still he wanted to look at his facial expressions as D'Andre penetrated him.

Slowly, D'Andre probed his anus with his cock, an inch, and then out, again, he repeated. As D'Andre thrust himself inside, Taj's length got harder.

"Oh my God, D'! Shit. Faster, baby." As he closed his eyes, he dug his fingers into D'Andre's back binding him with his legs.

D'Andre did just as Taj asked rocking him, quicker. Taj's breaths turned into pants, as D'Andre continued to bury himself inside him.

"Oh my God! I can't hold on. Shi …" D'Andre got up tossing the condom aside. Again, he hovered over Taj this time squirting his juices on Taj's stomach. Taj watched, as the last drops came out of D'Andre's dick, thus starting to jerk his own. D'Andre went over to Taj's right side, pushing Taj's hand away. Once he took hold of Taj's shaft, he stroked it hard but slow. His other hand tangled within Taj's hair. All the while, he kissed Taj, lightly nibbling on his lips.

"Mmm, oh D'… " was all he could muster, as D'Andre continued to rub him. With one hand, he traced D'Andre's face while the other pinched his own nipples. As they stared at each other between kisses and nips, Taj started to writhe. D'Andre kneaded a little faster; he knew he was close. Within seconds, Taj painted his own stomach with his jizz.

"Ahh, Shh …" he gasped, as the last bit shot out. Once he was done, D'Andre got back on top of Taj devouring his mouth. For several minutes, they continued making each others' lips numb.

Spent, they were in each another's arms silently with Taj lying on D'Andre's chest. Gently, Taj circled D'Andre's nipples with his fingertips while D'Andre massaged Taj's scalp. Lightly, he kissed Taj's head and continued fingering through his locks. Not much time passed before both of them succumbed to sleep.

# # # # #

Hours later Taj woke up looking at his CD alarm clock; it read two am. When he kissed D'Andre on the lips, D'Andre stirred a bit and smiled with his eyes still closed.

"Mmm …" escaped D'Andre's mouth, he reached out for Taj who settled back on his chest. Again, D'Andre rested his hands within his hair.

Taj lay there thinking about the most amazing sex he'd ever had and how much better it was since it actually meant something.

"Damn brotha, I think I'm in love," he whispered, however not loud enough to disturb D'Andre.

# # # # #

That next morning, D'Andre and Taj decided that they would continue to see each other exclusively, and on the days and weeks that followed, they acted like a married couple.

D'Andre no longer wanted to ride the crowded train. Now that Taj was by his side, he had a better excuse to spend the additional money on parking and gas. Every morning, he would pick Taj up, drive him to school, then leave the car in the garage underneath his building.

Between twelve and one, they had lunch in the park or in restaurants, and after school, Taj would go somewhere to waste an hour or two until D'Andre got off work to meet him in the garage lobby.

Since both wanted no trouble out of anyone, they saved their affections for when they were alone, although this day Taj was feeling frisky.

After they stepped off the elevator to walk to the car, Taj got behind D'Andre bumping him just as he had on the train nearly three months ago. This time, however, he brushed his erection against D'Andre's thigh pushing him against the car door.

D'Andre smiled reaching behind his young lover to grab his backside.

Taj smiled, leaning close into D'Andre's ear, "Sorry, man, my bad," he said, in a deep, seductive voice.

D'Andre immediately turned around kissing his lover's lips. D'Andre whispered, "No problem, man. The pleasure was, is, and always will be, all mine."

PORTLAND AFTERNOON
Jay Starre

Cory's older sister had hooked him up with a ride to Seattle from Eureka in northern California, and after what happened on that eventful trip, he had to admit he was a changed person. He couldn't have thanked her enough.

Dwayne drove a bright red sporty Ford that wasn't hard to miss on the street corner where they were supposed to meet. When Cory got in and faced the driver for the first time, he was slightly startled.

Alicia hadn't told him Dwayne was handsome as hell. Or that he was black.

Of course it shouldn't have mattered, but she knew Cory was gay and might have at least mentioned he was getting a ride all the way to Seattle with a cum-dreamy stud!

After introductions, their conversation fizzled out almost immediately. It was easy to tell Dwayne wasn't a talker. Politeness had Cory shutting up pretty quickly, and he actually fell asleep to the tune of the R&B his hot driver favored.

Cory himself was on his way to a rock concert in Seattle. His own choice of music was progressive rock, along with most of his college buddies. He'd actually never listened to R&B but found it soothing without being actually boring, to his own surprise.

He was in for a few more surprises.

"Hey man, we're going to stop overnight here."

The pleasantly soft baritone woke him. He glanced over at Dwayne, and once again took stock of his awesome looks. Very dark and flawless skin looked even darker when his full lips curled in the left corner and brilliant white teeth showed as he offered a small smile.

"Uh, yep, cool!"

Cory tore his eyes away from that handsome face to realize they were driving through a city. Portland. Alicia had mentioned they'd be stopping there. But, this was a Portland he hadn't realized existed.

In the evening light of early summer, the streets were busy with pedestrians on their way home or out for groceries or maybe just hanging out. They were almost all black.

A black ghetto in Portland? Who knew? Then he chastised himself for thinking he was in a ghetto just because there were lots of blacks around. The buildings looked presentable, a mix of business and residential, it was just that the folks were dark-skinned.

"My bro Terence will put us up. He's a cool dude."

"Awesome. I appreciate it."

Up a few flights of stairs, they found Terence's apartment, a one bedroom pretty typical of a young bachelor. Not particularly clean nor particularly messy, it boasted unmatched furniture and a huge wide-screen television that dominated the living room.

Shaking hands with Terence, he was immediately struck by how different the two friends were. In fact, they were just about as different from each other as each of them was from him. Terence was lanky and so tall he could have been a basketball player. He wore casual athletic top and bottom in vivid emeralds and blues. His hair was thick and curly and slicked back with a shiny pomade. His skin was a creamy chocolate while his features were bold and distinctive, a broad nose, big red lips and huge almond eyes that looked directly into Cory's.

On the other hand, Dwayne was stocky and muscular and a couple inches shy of six foot. He wore expensive jeans and a pale blue short-sleeved button-up shirt. His skin was a deep almost purple black, and his features were as subdued as his dress. A squarish face, perfectly symmetrical wide-set eyes and equally wide mouth were divided by a long straight nose and a dimpled chin. His hair was cut very short against his perfectly round scalp.

"Is this the gay dude Alicia hooked us up with? Nice, man. I'm horny as shit. I hope he ain't shy of taking some big black dick up his pretty white ass."

Cory's hand was still warm from the vigorous shaking Terence had employed as he spoke those words. The tall black was already turning and heading for the fridge a few steps away in the small kitchen just off the living room.

Gawking, Cory flushed bright red as Terence continued. "Let's down a few brews before we get nasty. Are you old enough to drink, Cory my man?"

He turned and winked, guffawing loudly as he opened the fridge and rummaged around in it for beer.

"Never mind him, Cory. The dude's always hot for it. But if you're interested, so are we."

Dwayne's smile was reassuring as he laid a small but firm hand on Cory's shoulder and steered him toward the sofa. Without having uttered more than a polite hello, he found himself sandwiched between two hot black dudes on that sofa, cold beer in hand and watching basketball on Terence's wide-screen HD-TV.

The pair acted as unlike as they looked. Terence lounged on the couch with long thighs spread, hooting and jeering as the game progressed, while Dwayne sat back quietly with one muscular arm draped over the back of the couch and merely smiling now and then as the team he favored lobbed in their baskets.

It was impossible for Cory to pay any attention to the game. Terence's long leg pressed into his and jerked and twitched against him as he hooted and clapped. On his other side, Dwayne's solid thigh pressed into his more casually, while his beefy arm on the back of the couch lightly grazed his own bare shoulders. Wearing only a tank top, khaki shorts, and sandals, he felt nearly naked beside the pair.

His cock strained against the fly of his shorts while his heart beat rapidly in his chest, and he found himself short of breath. Had Terence been serious? Big black dick up his white ass – the thought had his snug hole both clamping and pouting as he squirmed restlessly on the couch between the pair.

"Fuck yeah, man! What a game. I knew my bros would cop a win. So how about it? Before we order in some pizza, let's fuck around. Hey, boy, ever seen a cock this fucking long?"

As he spoke, his big lips opened wide in a huge grin. He actually licked them then smacked them loudly. His hand had descended to his crotch where he'd already shoved down his bright green track pants in the front. Cory's soft grey eyes opened wide as he took in the lengthy dimensions of the cock so abruptly revealed.

"Uh, can't say I have ..." he managed to mutter as his freckled complexion flushed bright pink.

"Wait til you see Dwayne's. It's not so long, but it's a real pipe, man. Show it to him, bro! Don't be shy."

Terence guffawed as he began to pump the foot-long snake into a growing boner. Cory watched with mesmerized awe.

"Don't let him badger you, Cory. He's got shit for brains. But if you like what you see, go for it, man."

Dwayne's soft baritone did little to soothe Cory's trembling nerves. In fact, it only stimulated him. Adding fuel to the fire, the quiet dude unzipped his own fly and pulled out his cock. Tearing his eyes from the growing hard-on in Terence's lap, he looked at the huge piece of meat rearing up out of Dwayne's lap. He choked back a gasp. It really was a pipe! From the crown to the base, it was thick and cylindrical and black as midnight.

Cory could barely breathe and couldn't muster up the courage to speak either, which was totally unlike him. He was usually a real chatter-box, outgoing and confident. Why was he so nervous? He flushed even brighter as he realized what was going on in his own head. If these two had been white dudes, he would have been laughing and joking ... and burying his face in one lap or the other.

He hadn't ever thought of himself as prejudiced, but now he recognized it in himself. Because they were black, maybe they were dangerous. And regardless of the differences in their personalities and looks, they both shared something he did not because of their color. He was an outsider, he imagined.

All at once he thought of himself as naïve and inexperienced, which at twenty-one and still in college and coming from a small hick town in northern California, he was.

So be it. With a gulp of air, he gathered his wits and dove for dick.

He chose Terence's lengthy pole, merely because it looked easier to get in his mouth than the blunt knob down in Dwayne's lap. Opening wide, he wrapped his bowed pink lips around the dripping head and sucked it in.

"The white boy can suck! I bet his other hole sucks just as good. We're in for a fucking sweet ride, man!"

"I believe so," Dwayne replied quietly as he let go of his own cock and moved to begin stripping Cory.

A rough hand on the back of his head pushed his face deeper over that pulsing boner, while gentler hands unbuckled his belt and unsnapped his fly. Cory squirmed around onto his knees as both his shorts and underwear were pulled down and off. At the same time he gurgled around several inches of Terence's long rod.

The taste was sweet! A constant drool of precum oozed from the slit over his tongue. The cock grew stiffer as he massaged it with his lips and sunk deeper over it. It pulsed then it jerked as it only grew lengthier. He was totally into the steamy suck and only half-aware he was being stripped, until those gentle hands behind him settled over his round ass and spread it.

All at once, he realized his position. Naked from the waist down, on his knees with his ass being spread, and his mouth full of cock, this was no time for inhibition! He opened wide and smacked his pretty lips, drooling over another inch of stiff meat as he actually wriggled his white butt and arched his back.

Behind him, Dwayne's steady baritone warned him of what was to come. "Nice, man. You have got one fine white ass. Time for a taste."

He was pushed forward and deeper over Terence's stiff cock as Dwayne's face pushed between his spread cheeks and began kissing his crack.

Unbelievable! He could just picture himself, trapped between two black dudes, black cock in his mouth and black lips in his ass-crack. His ivory pale ass was round and full from his daily jogging and years on a swim team. His face, freckled from the summer sun, was round like that fine butt and dominated by a bowed mouth with bright pink lips and wide-set pale grey eyes. Light brown facial hair framed those features, wispy and short but adding a casual look he believed made him also appear older. His sandy- brown hair was trimmed short but otherwise tousled and untamed.

That chocolate brown cock slid deeper and deeper between his pink lips as he flushed brighter. Lips found his hole and began to suck on it, and even his ass flushed pink as the round cheeks quivered under the hands spreading it.

"Fuck, man! White boy ass and white boy mouth! Love it, fucking love it. Chow down on the chocolate bone, dude. Eat it up. Smack those pretty lips for your big black bro! Yeah, like that!"

Pressing down on the back of Cory's head, Terence kept up a steady chatter while his buddy said little or nothing, his mouth busy slurping over Cory's white ass and pink hole. Again Cory noted how different they were from each other, and wondered why they were friends at all.

But those thoughts fled as the tapered knob in his mouth pressed against his tonsils. In the heat of the moment, he relaxed his throat and let it in. Groaning deep in his chest, he deep-throated almost half that foot-long boner.

Tongue drilled into his snapping asshole. Hot, stiff cock throbbed in his throat. Sweat seemed to break out all over him at once. The fan in the open window to the left blew directly across his bare skin, making him feel like he was a wet, dripping piece of sensitive meat between twin points of pulsating sensation.

"Hey, bro, let's switch it up. As good as the white boy sucks, he ain't gonna get to the bottom of my dick. For some deeper satisfaction, I'm gonna require the use of his fine white ass."Cory came up for air, snorting in a lung-full as the gooey knob slipped out of his throat. With a wet smack out of his pink lips, he rose onto his knees briefly as the pair switched places on the couch.

"Will you look at that cock? Sweet! Not as long as mine or as thick as yours, but hard as hell and with a wicked curve. Maybe I'll take a ride on it later. But for now, bro, time for a piece of that ass," Terence said with a snort and a chuckle.

Cory's cock reared up from his crotch like a curved sword. He was so excited his cock jerked and dribbled as his legs trembled and his heart raced. He didn't want to touch it at all or he might just shoot his load right then and there.

Dwayne offered a crooked smiled and winked as he sat down where Terence had just been. He'd slipped off his shoes, slacks and underwear, and was now dressed in only his short-sleeved shirt. The pale blue of the dress shirt contrasted sharply with his purple-black skin.

In his lap, that impossibly fat dick bobbed between his muscular thighs. The head was a blunt mushroom that seemed to dare Cory to swallow it. He glanced into Dwayne's eyes, soft brown and half-lidded, before he dropped down to bury his face in the handsome stud's lap.

It was a mouthful, to say the least! He gurgled over it just as an open hand landed on his bare butt-cheek with a resounding smack. His body jerked forward, and he swallowed huge crown and a few inches of steamy fat cock as another smack landed on his other butt-cheek.

He heard the sound of squirting lube and imagined it coating that lengthy cock just behind him.

"Lubed up and hot for hole, man. Here comes black dick!"

It came. Fortunately Terence's cock-head was bullet-shaped and actually slipped past his nervous butt-lips easy as pie. He reared back toward the slippery ache and gulped up a few inches of the stiff shank.

"Sweet! But we ain't hardly even started. Let's see how much you can take, man!"

It was wild. Dwayne stroked his hair and his neck as he fed him fat dick. Terence slapped his ass as he fed him chocolate dick. He swallowed more and more of that huge black bone with his mouth as his asshole opened up to deeper and deeper probes of the chocolate one.

His own pink cock twitched and leaked between his spread thighs, stiff and aching. Every inch of dick he swallowed at either end only made his cock jerk and drip more. His butt grew bright pink as Terence kept up a steady slapping, which actually helped open him up to the gut-reaming he was getting from behind.

There seemed to just be more and more of it! Every time he thought that long bone had gone as deep as possible, Terence rooted even deeper. With a steady in-and-out, the tall black plunged farther up Cory's aching hole. His ass-lips were on fire, his prostate throbbing, and those places far up inside where all that stiff meat rubbed were in a constant state of pulsating pleasure.

Dwayne's gentle fingers played with his tousled hair and stroked his cheeks as he buried his face down in his lap. To his own amazement, he managed to swallow all of it, right down to the smooth black nut-sack between his muscular thighs.

Terence kept up his steady chatter. "Fuck yeah, man! So fucking hot! My black balls are right up against your sweet pink butt! Fucking awesome!"

Cory felt those balls slapping against his sweaty crack. Unbelievable! He had a fucking foot of black dick up his butt!

He moaned incoherently between the two monster dicks, stuffed at either end and loving it. He felt orgasm hovering nearby, and would have blown in another few minutes if Terence hadn't decided it was time for a change.

"That white boy cock is about to get a real fuckin' treat! Want to fuck some black butt?"

Cory nodded vigorously over Dwayne's fat dick as the one up his butt slammed home another time before pulling out with a dripping plop. He'd be more than happy to fuck Terence! He'd never fucked a black dude.

But it wasn't exactly how he imagined it. Terence was a real wild card!

Dwayne remained seated on the couch, muscular thighs spread and big arms behind his head. He offered Cory that crooked smile and winked, obviously knowing his buddy well enough to anticipate what was coming.

Cory stood up on shaky legs and peeled off his soaking wet tank top. His pink cock curved out in front of him as he watched Terence do the unexpected. The tall black dude straddled Dwayne, and with a loud whoop, settled down over that big fat dick.

"Lube up that pink dick and shove it in. There's room for more up my hungry black butthole, man!"

Cory's mouth dropped open. A double-fuck? Was it even possible? He stared at Terence's high tight butt, smooth and hairless and creamy-chocolate. It bounced over Dwayne's gigantic shank with effortless ease. The chocolate-brown hole oozed lube, a slippery sheen of it coating Dwayne's darker tool.

With shaking hands, he snatched up the bottle of lube Terence had left on the arm of the couch and squirted a stream over his twitching hard-on.

"Sure you can take it?" he asked in a quavering voice.

"Fuck yeah. Show me what you got, man!"

Terence looked back at him and laughed, no sign of discomfort on his face, even though most of Dwayne's massive dick was buried up his ass.

Cory took a deep breath and stepped in between Dwayne's splayed thighs. Sweaty flesh pressed back as his knees came down on the couch beside Terence's. His curved cock slid between the firm ass-cheeks. Sweat and dripping lube made a slippery glide as he pushed down against the slim head of his cock to aim it at the stuffed hole.

Terence arched his back while reaching behind to grab hold of his own butt to pull it up and open. Cory's cock-head settled on the straining lips of his hole just above Dwayne's buried shank.

He pushed. Terence pushed back. Emitting a huge grunt, he took it.

Cory gasped. So tight! He could feel the chocolate-brown butt-lips strain and squeeze. He could feel the pulsing thickness of Dwayne's rod beside his. He couldn't help himself and thrust upward and forward.

"Hell yeah! Fuck that black butt! Give it to me good, man!"

Leaning forward and wrapping his arms around the squirming black stud, he did as he was told. He rammed in and out, his pale hips slamming against Terence's solid black ass-cheeks.

Terence fucked back just as hard. He heaved and bucked as he rode both cocks. Dwayne reared up off the couch and shoved into his buddy's juicy hole. Squishing and dripping, that hole took it.

It was tight though. Cory felt like he was fucking a steamy vice. And Dwayne's fat pipe rubbed back and forth and up and down against his own, both cocks mashed together up that clamping gut-hole.

"I'm gonna shoot! Fuck!"

Cory couldn't hold back any longer. He was about to pull out when Terence's asshole seized his cock and began to clench and spasm.

"Fuck yeah, man! Me, too!"

Terence's long lean body went rigid. His butt stopped heaving as he held perfectly still and cried out. Then he shot. So did Cory.

His cream flooded Terence's hole, oozing out and over Dwayne's pumping shaft. While the two of them unloaded, Dwayne continued to pump up into that clamping pit, faster and faster.

He didn't say anything, but his crooked smile and half-closed eyes told the story. Cory could feel his fat pipe pulsing beside his as he shot, too.

Terence rose up off the twin cocks spurting up his butt. With a shaky laugh, he turned and faced Cory, who was still coming. He gave the startled college student a big sloppy kiss as his dripping cock oozed against his flat belly.

They didn't bother cleaning up. Lounging on the couch naked, they shared the pizza Terence ordered and watched some more television. As they chatted, Cory realized why the two were friends. They were totally comfortable with each other. Dwayne let Terence rant on with an easy silence then quietly put in his own two cents while his pal took his turn listening.

Envious of their ability to accept each other for what they were, he wondered about his own friendships. He had a lot to learn about acceptance.

They went one more sweaty round before calling it a night, Terence just as wild and Dwayne just as easy-going. Cory got it from both ends again and enjoyed every minute of it.

The next morning, Terence asked him to come by on his way home. "I need some more of that sweet white ass. And some of that cock, too!"

With a totally new outlook on life, he rode the rest of the way to Seattle with Dwayne, comfortably silent, comfortably accepting. When he got home, he'd have to thank his sister.

STEPBROTHERS
Milton Stern

With spring semester over, Adam headed home for the summer before his senior year at State University. His mother had remarried in the last month, and she and her new husband were still on their honeymoon, so Adam knew he was coming home to an empty house.

After a three-hour drive, he was happy to be pulling up in front of the house, and he noticed the hatchback parked in the driveway and figured it must belong to one of his new stepfather's kids, probably checking on the house.

Adam pulled his suitcases out of the trunk and walked up the walkway, let himself in, and walked right up the stairs. After a long drive, he was in no mood to talk to anyone.

He put the suitcases in his room, and the first thing he noticed was how hot it was in the house. If one of his new step siblings was there, why didn't he turn on the AC? Adam shook his head and took off his shirt.

Adam had been lifting weights since he was sixteen. His body was perfectly proportioned and nicely muscled at five-foot-eleven and 185 pounds. He inherited his mother's smooth chocolate brown skin and his father's large round ass, among other large assets.

He walked downstairs to turn on the air conditioning. While adjusting the thermostat, he heard the front door open and someone saying goodbye, followed by a car speeding away. He remembered his stepbrother from the wedding. Louis was a little taller than Adam at six-foot-one, but he was leaner. His nineteen-year-old stepbrother had thick black hair and dark features much like his father's, with black eyes and thick lips that begged to be kissed.

Adam remembered talking to him at the wedding and wondering if it would be incestuous to lay his new stepbrother.

"Hey, Adam," Louis said as he extended his hand. The two of them shook hands.

"Dude, what's with not turning on the AC? It's like a fucking oven in here," Adam said.

Louis shook his head and headed upstairs. That was when Adam remembered that Louis was not much of a talker, and from what he gathered from his mother and Louis's siblings, he was not always playing with a full deck either.

Nutty or not, Adam still wondered if the boy liked to play.

He headed back to his bedroom and unpacked his bags. After putting away the last of his clothes and putting the suitcases in the closet, he headed back downstairs to the kitchen for some water. His mother always kept a large jug of water in the refrigerator, and he decided to forgo a glass and drink it straight from the jug. As he was guzzling the water, Louis walked into the kitchen.

"Adam, the man," he said.

Adam quit guzzling for a second and looked at Louis who had stripped to his boxers. The boy was long and lean, built like a swimmer with broad shoulders and a six pack. This pissed Adam off because he knew Louis never worked out, but he did hold out hope that Louis would end up fat when he hit thirty!

"So, Louis, are you living here now, or are you house sitting?" Adam asked him.

"Wouldn't you like to know, bro," Louis said, and he grabbed a soda and headed back to his room.

Adam rolled his eyes and finished the jug. He filled it with tap water, put it back in the fridge and hoped it was full of bacteria for Louis to enjoy.

Adam headed upstairs, walked into the bathroom, stripped and stepped into the shower. While he was soaping up, he thought of Louis, the weirdo, standing in the kitchen wearing nothing but his boxers, and his dick started to grow. Adam had not come in a few days, so he took hold of his favorite toy and rubbed out a big load, barely taking a couple of minutes to do the deed, and hardly making a sound in the process as he learned to stay quiet while jerking off in the dorm.

He finished his shower and pulled the curtain back, grabbing a towel at the same time. Adam was startled to find Louis there flossing his teeth. The house had two full baths, why was he in this one?

Adam tried his best to conceal his cock, which was still half hard. It was difficult enough to hide when it was soft. However, Louis paid no attention to him, so Adam thought he would take one more stab at conversation.

"So, Louis, are you working or going to school?"

Louis stopped flossing and turned around to look at Adam, who had since wrapped the towel around his waist. Then he faced the mirror again.

"No," Louis said. He finished flossing and went into the guest room, shutting the door behind him.

"What a doofus," Adam said to himself. "I hope the little asshole isn't here all summer."

Adam brushed his teeth then crawled into bed.

At three in the morning, Adam was startled awake by some strange sounds. He thought there were cats fucking outside his window, but he soon realized the sounds were coming from the next room. He heard squeaking, then high pitched moaning, more squeaking, and then Louis's voice saying over and over again, "Good boy, good boy, good boy."

Adam never heard anyone come in. Who the hell was Louis talking to? Then he heard him yell, "AHHH AHHH AHHH," so loudly it shook the walls. Adam buried his head in his pillow to keep from laughing. Once the screaming stopped, he then heard Louis saying, "I am such a good boy, oh yeah, good boy, good boy." Then, there was silence.

Adam was still laughing as he thought about his strange stepbrother masturbating and congratulating himself. Then he got hard again himself, but he was too tired to jerk off, so he rolled over and went back to sleep.

Adam woke up early the next morning and decided to make himself a pot of coffee and work out in the basement gym, provided it was still there. After locating his extra large mug, he filled it with the freshly brewed coffee and headed to the basement.

Since it was still pretty early, Adam decided to work out in just a black cotton jock strap, crew socks and cross trainers. The jock hugged his round butt and displayed his big basket perfectly, and he wished there were someone there to enjoy the view.

Once in the basement, he was happy to see that for the most part his equipment was still where he left it.

He loaded a couple of plates on the bar and secured them with collars. He decided to stretch a bit, and when he bent down to touch his toes he looked through his legs and saw Louis, stark naked and standing right behind him. Adam immediately stood up and turned around.

Louis was standing there with his dick hanging limp but low accompanied by two big, equally low hanging balls, and he was holding a cup of coffee.

"Adam, the man," Louis said. "I took some of your aromatic java." He then turned around and headed back upstairs.

Adam was only pissed because he would now have to brew more coffee.

He slid under the bar and pressed the weights for twelve reps, and he sat up after the set and admired himself in the mirror he had mounted across from the bench. Adam ran his hands over his chest and down his six pack abs. He then flexed both biceps, displaying the high peaks that always earned him attention in the gym at school.

He lay back down and did another twelve reps. With each set, he looked in the mirror and flexed his pecs, bouncing them before doing another double bicep pose.

Adam stood up and removed some of the plates and curled the barbell for ten reps very slowly, keeping his eyes on the vein that ran up his arm. Watching his biceps pump full of blood always turned him on, and his jock was beginning to get tighter.

He put the bar down, and flexed again, doing a crab pose, flaring out his lats and finishing off with another double bicep pose. Adam then did another set of curls.

During his third set, he heard Louis coming down the steps. Adam finished the set and put the bar back. This time Louis was sitting in front of the mirror drinking another cup of coffee, blocking Adam's view of himself. 'Fucking asshole,' he thought, 'Drinks my coffee and interrupts my workout.' However, Adam didn't confront him because Louis was still naked.

"Can I help you, Louis?" he asked.

Silence.

Louis just stared at Adam, studying every inch of him. Adam noticed how Louis was looking at him and didn't know what to make of it.

"Louis, you're sitting in front of the mirror, and I can't watch myself when I work out."

Louis turned and looked at the mirror as if he did not know it was there. He stood up and leaned on an old dresser that was placed in the basement a decade before.

"Louis, are you just going to stand there?" Adam asked him.

Again, silence.

Adam did another set of curls, watching himself in the mirror when he noticed Louis standing behind him. Louis reached around and felt Adam's biceps with each curl of the bar, running his hands over the pumped muscles. Adam continued his set, enjoying the feel of his stepbrother's hands on his muscles, and he started to get hard again.

Adam curled until he was exhausted, then he put the bar back on the rack. As he looked at himself in the mirror, Louis continued to explore his body with his hands.

Louis felt his stepbrother's lats, tracing his fingers up Adam's muscular back, then he squeezed Adam's softball sized shoulders, and as one hand made its way up Adam's neck the other reached around to feel Adam's pumped chest.

As Louis continued exploring his body, Adam's breathing became heavier. He let his stepbrother enjoy every sweaty, pumped inch of him and finally, Louis's hand was inside the black cotton jock strap and going for the prize.

As he released his stepbrother's enormous boner, Louis stepped around and brushed his lips against Adam's. Adam opened his mouth and reached around Louis's head drawing him in and kissing him deep, tasting the coffee the asshole had taken without permission. With his free hand, Adam reached down and grabbed the weirdo's hard dick and was impressed with its length and girth. Adam slid his hand up to the swollen head and slicked it with the precum Louis's big dick generously provided.

Louis had managed to get Adam's jock down around his ankles, and they continued to make out while stroking each other's dicks. Louis's free hand continued to explore Adam's pumped body and found a nipple, giving it a hard pull. Adam moaned, but he did not let go of Louis's mouth. Those full, soft lips were too good to let loose even for a second.

He let go of Louis's head and flexed his right bicep while his stepbrother felt it with his left hand, as they continued to kiss. Louis obviously liked the feel of flexed muscles because his dick would swell and pulse, emitting more precum whenever Adam flexed. This in turn made Adam's thick cock swell up, and he didn't know how much longer he could last.

Their breathing increased, and the stepbrothers were getting closer, but they never unlocked their lips.

Finally, Louis pulled away from Adam's lips and screamed, "AHHH AHHH AHHH," so loud it startled Adam. Then he shot his load covering Adam's belly and chest with pints of cum. The site of his stepbrother's load on his pumped chest made Adam shoot all over Louis, who groaned while Adam was shooting, "You are such a good boy, oh yeah, good boy, good boy." Then, there was silence.

They pulled away from each other, and Adam grabbed a towel to wipe himself off, but Louis stopped him. He bent down and licked his stepbrother's body clean. After he finished his breakfast of cum, he winked at Adam, turned and walked back upstairs without saying a word.

Adam stood there with his half hard cock hanging out and his black cotton jock at his ankles and watched Louis's round butt bounce as he walked upstairs.

"What a fucking nut job," Adam thought. Then he smiled and hoped all his workouts would end like this one.

LASSO AND TLEM
Milton Stern

The day was getting late, but according to the old man at the ranch, the next real town in the Arizona Territory was only a dozen or so miles away. He hoped to find a blacksmith when he arrived as Montgomery, his horse, needed new shoes.

The sun was blazing, more than Lasso ever experienced being raised in Virginia. Sure, the summers were hot, but nothing like this. Lasso didn't know much about temperatures, but he guessed this to be hot enough to cook beans without a fire. He stopped at a pond, one of just a few he had encountered over the last few days, and he hopped off Montgomery, so the poor horse could get a drink and some rest.

Lasso stretched and decided he better fill his canteen and get a drink himself. He leaned over to the pond and filled his canteen then scooped a few swallows of water into his palm to quench his parched throat. He checked out his reflection in the water.

Saying that Lasso was narcissistic would be an understatement. He was damn good-looking, and he knew it, and if you didn't think he was good-looking, just ask him. He was six-foot-six and weighed in at over 240 pounds. His black, wavy hair was shaggy but fell perfectly over his square face with his dark eye brows, deep black eyes, strong jaw and rare for anyone at that time, perfectly straight teeth framed by full lips.

Lasso reached up and patted Montgomery, the only thing he loved more than himself, and his horse neighed appreciatively.

"I'll walk you the rest of the way, old girl."

Lasso stood up, placed his canteen back in the bag hanging behind his saddle, and grabbed Montgomery's reins.

He walked a few miles before stopping to strip off his shirt, revealing his hairy muscular physique, built from years of ranch work and roping cattle.

After about an hour, Lasso spotted what looked to be the beginnings of a town, if one could call it that – just a strip of buildings on a dirt road, maybe ten if that many. He stopped and put his shirt back on before going any further as he didn't want to draw too much attention to himself being so good-looking and all.

As he approached the outskirts of this town, he saw a sign that said, "Welcome to Nemtoh, Arizona, Population 69."

"I guess this is it, Montgomery. Now let's see about getting you some new shoes."

Montgomery answered with an affirmative neigh.

As he walked down the main street – the only street – in Nemtoh, Lasso noticed only a few people, all men actually, walking around. And, all of them, though handsome, every one of them, looked at him with suspicion. He spotted a young blond guy, tall, strapping and looking especially clean for someone in a town like this.

"Excuse me, mister," Lasso called out.

"Yes," the blond answered as he pushed up his hat.

"Is there a blacksmith in this town?"

"What's your name?" the blond asked.

"Name's Lasso, is there a blacksmith?"

"What brings you to Nemtoh?" the blond asked without answering the initial question, and this was beginning to piss Lasso off.

"Look, I'm not here to start trouble. I'm on my way to work at a ranch fifty miles west of here, and my horse needs new shoes."

"What ranch?" the blond asked insistently.

"Jeez, man, what's your problem? Is this some kind of private community? Fuck it! I'll just let my horse suffer until I find the next town." And, Lasso turned his horse around and started to walk back to the main trail.

"Wait a minute, Lasso," the blond called out. "It's just that we're a quiet town, and we like to know who's coming through."

Lasso stopped and turned around. He hesitated before speaking, "So, what are you? The goddamn marshal or something?"

"Actually, I'm the mayor, Mayor Bottumzup."

Lasso smiled and stifled a giggle, "Did you say bottom's up?"

"Bottumzup, and I've heard them all. I don't want to see your horse suffer … the blacksmith is over there," Bottumzup said, pointing to a building across the street. "His name is Tlem."

"Tlem? Thanks," Lasso said as he walked Montgomery over to where the mayor pointed.

"If you need to stay the night, we have a hotel over there," the mayor said pointing to another building with a sign out front that read, "Hothole Hotel – No Women Allowed."

"Thanks," Lasso answered as he continued toward the blacksmith's building then stopped to read the hotel sign again to be sure he saw what he thought he saw. He did. He pushed his cowboy hat up and shook his head, wondering what kind of town he had stumbled upon.

Lasso entered the blacksmith's building slowly and looked around before spotting a very tall, muscular black man, wearing no shirt, a leather apron and those new-fangled dungarees or blue jeans as they called them in California.

"Are you Tlem?" Lasso called out.

The man turned around, and Lasso got a good look at his face, which was very handsome, with a strong jaw and equally full lips like Lasso's, but the blacksmith's muscular torso was devoid of hair, although glistening with sweat, and Lasso felt a stream of precum drip out of his cock and down his left leg.

"Name's Lasso," he said as he reached out to shake the man's hand, "Montgomery here needs a new set of shoes. How long will that take?"

The blacksmith shook Lasso's hand and spoke for the first time, "Kinda backed up, I can have her ready by tomorrow morning."

Lasso pulled out his watch. It was getting pretty late, and he wasn't about to make it to his new job before tomorrow anyway. "Sounds good. I guess I'll stay at that hotel tonight. Should I pay you now or tomorrow?"

"I like to be paid when I'm done," Tlem said then he took Montgomery's reigns and led her to a stall where he had water and hay ready for her to enjoy. "See you in the morning, Lasso."

Lasso took one more long look at the blacksmith before heading over to the Hothole Hotel to make sure the sight was etched into his memory.

For a very small town, the Hothole was quite a fancy hotel. But, Lasso figured that they were the only place to stay in these parts as the railroad hadn't even made it this far. The manager was another handsome Nemtoh citizen, albeit a bit older than the others he saw outside. There were a few patrons at the bar, all looking a little too clean for life in the Arizona Territory, but Lasso didn't mind as he had seen enough filthy men since heading west a few months ago.

"How many nights will you be staying, Mr. Lasso?"

"Just the one. Gotta head out to a job on a ranch tomorrow," Lasso answered.

"Very good, sir. That will be three dollars."

Lasso handed three silver dollars to the manager thinking the price a bit steep, but didn't complain.

"Would you be needing a bath? We can launder your clothes also."

Lasso was puzzled, bath, laundry, who heard of such a thing out here? He pretty much gave up on bathtubs since leaving Virginia using ponds and streams to wash up and launder his clothes. "Yeah, that would be good. Pretty clean town you have here."

"Well, Mr. Lasso, just because this is a small town in the Arizona Territory doesn't mean we have to live like Barbarians," the manager said with a wink.

The manager handed Lasso his room key and told him someone would be up to take him to the washroom within the hour.

Lasso didn't realize how tired he was. No sooner had he entered the room, stripped off all his clothes and climbed onto the bed that he closed his eyes and fell asleep.

He was awakened by the sound of someone in his room. As he opened his eyes, he saw what looked to be a young man, who seemed to be a hotel employee.

"I didn't mean to wake you, sir. I was just returning your laundry."

"How long was I asleep?"

"About three hours, sir. You may take your bath now. The washroom is down the hall on the right, and I have filled your tub with hot water. Here is a towel for you," and the young man handed him the softest towel he ever felt.

Lasso climbed out of the bed and wrapped the towel around him, noticing the young man stealing a peek. He exited the room and walked down the hall and located a room marked 'Wash Room.' He opened the door, and there were two tubs in the room, which was decorated as nicely as the lobby, with a wood stove for heating water and nice curtains over the windows. One tub was occupied, so Lasso closed the door behind him and walked toward the empty tub. As he looked over at the other tub, he saw that Tlem was relaxing in the sudsy water.

Tlem opened his eyes and saw Lasso standing there wearing nothing but a towel.

"You finished with Montgomery already?" Lasso asked.

"Yep, that'll be three dollars."

"No pockets here, I'll pay you after my bath," Lasso told him as he looked over the blacksmith's upper torso and felt his cock start to swell.

"So why do they call you Lasso?" Tlem asked, looking at Lasso as if he were a meal for the tasting.

Lasso removed his towel revealing his slightly swelling uncut cock, whose foreskin barely concealed the large head, which was already reaching nine inches and still had at least two to go. "That's why."

Tlem licked his lips and said, "Impressive."

Lasso climbed into the tub hoping the water would calm him down. "Why do they call you Tlem?"

Tlem looked over at Lasso, then he stood up and revealed a hefty cock that matched Lasso's in length and girth, but was getting harder by the second. Lasso looked at the muscular blacksmith with his large, hard black cock pointing at him and tried to act nonchalant, although he had been hungry for a big piece of meat for days.

"Beautiful, but what does Tlem have to do with that?"

"Three-legged man was my nickname on the plantation. When they granted me my freedom, I chose the name Tlem."

The blacksmith then walked over to Lasso's tub and leaned down next to him, looking him right in the eyes. Without saying another word, he placed his calloused hand behind Lasso's head and pulled him in for a long hard kiss, and Lasso thought he would shoot his load right there as his big dick reached its full eleven inches in seconds.

With his other hand, Tlem reached into the tub and grabbed the hard member and started to stroke it without losing his mouth's grip on Lasso's. The ranch-hand reached under Tlem and grabbed his hard eleven inches and matched him stroke for stroke. They kept this up for quite a while without releasing their mouths, moaning and breathing hard, and slurping …

"I'm gonna blow, if you keep that up," Tlem said, finally releasing Lasso's mouth.

"Me, too," Lasso answered.

With that, Tlem stood up walked around, so he was behind Lasso's head and leaned down so his cock aimed at the ranch-hand's mouth and continued leaning over until Lasso's cock was aiming for his. Both men needed no instruction as they each began to feast on the other's enormous meat, and it was not long before they both fed each other huge loads of ranch-hand and blacksmith cum.

Finally, releasing Lasso's cock, Tlem said, "For that, I'll give you a discount on the shoes."

"That was all I had to do for a discount?" Lasso asked smiling and looking up at this beautiful blacksmith.

"I'll let you have them for free if you do me one other favor."

"What's that?" Lasso asked.

"My horse, York, needs some release, too, and he kinda took a liking to Montgomery. Let him have his fun ..."

"Wait, I can't have a pregnant horse while working on the ranch ..." Lasso protested.

"Let me finish," Tlem interrupted. "I own a ranch just outside of town. You come work for me, and I'll pay you whatever you were supposed to get where you're going."

"Why should I do that?" Lasso asked.

"Because nowhere else in the Arizona territory are you gonna find a town full of men who like doing what we just did, and you can live in my house and do it with me all the time," Tlem said with a wink.

Lasso didn't need any more persuasion and agreed to Tlem's terms, and both he and Montgomery ended up happy in their new home ...

... and if this were a movie, the next scene would have them riding off into the sunset – naked.

THE CENTER
OF ATTENTION
Milton Stern

Billy played center for as long as he played football, beginning with peewee, then middle school, high school, and now, college. For some reason, coaches automatically put him in that position, bent over with a quarterback's hands up his crotch. Was it his size? He was always the tallest – and widest – kid with the ability to run over anyone headed for the quarterback like a steam roller? Or, was it his round muscular butt, which was so tantalizing in that position. He never thought it was his butt. After all, he had a talent for hiking the ball and immediately knocking down at least three defensive linemen before they knew what hit them. Years of playing football in his hometown of Newport News gave him a reputation, and many a lineman would try to challenge Billy, but by the end of the game, the quarterback on Billy's team would never have a scratch on him.

He entered college with a full scholarship. By eighteen, his frame had filled out quite nicely, and now in his senior year at age twenty-one, he was, as one of the cheerleaders called him, 'hunkalicious.' Billy was over six-foot-five, weighing more than 280 pounds, with a chest that measured at least fifty-four inches, biceps that approached twenty inches, a waist that although thirty-eight inches was tight and ripped, quads that measured over thirty-five inches and of course, that big round muscular butt. While many of his teammates were using steroids and other 'enhancements,' Billy had no desire to do anything that wasn't natural. He didn't have to as he was one of the lucky few who could get more muscular just from looking at a dumbbell. To make his teammates more jealous, Billy had inherited the best of both his Russian and Moroccan genes – smooth dark skin, strong facial features, green eyes, thick curly hair and bright white teeth. His hands and feet were huge, and he could palm a football with no problem.

Their first two seasons were highly successful with few losses, so the team was quite surprised when their coach resigned under pressure, and a new coach from a Southern university was brought in. And along with that new coach arrived a new quarterback. The new quarterback was not unexpected as Jerry Garrison had graduated the prior year and was playing pro-ball now. Billy wasn't envious, for he was not looking forward to a pro football career. He was a straight-A pre-med student, and he was actually looking forward to ending his football days. After all, he had been playing center since he was six years old, and all the practices were getting old.

The team entered the locker room silently the day after the announcement of their new coach and quarterback. As they changed into their practice uniforms, there was grumbling about the new coach's reputation, rumors and gossip that Billy didn't care to hear. The advantage to playing center was that all he had to do was remember when to hike the ball, plow forward and hope he hadn't hurt a defensive lineman – too badly.

After changing, they ran out to the field and lined up, awaiting the introductions.

Billy looked to his right and spotted a tall, black man with an almost equally tall, but younger, black man beside him. The older man looked to be in his mid-thirties, around six-foot-three and muscular. Billy guessed he played football in his youth and maintained his athletic physique. He was wearing a tight white polo shirt that accentuated his large chest and bulging biceps and blue coaching shorts that did little to hide his full basket. He was wearing a cap, but Billy could tell the man had a shaved head, and the hat did not hide the fact that he was perhaps the most handsome man he had ever seen with dark smooth skin and a bright smile surrounded by thick sexy lips. The younger of the two looked to be about Billy's age and maybe only an inch shorter if that much. He was muscular but leaner than the older man. His hair was cut short, and he had high cheek bones, a wide sexy mouth and big dark eyes. He was wearing a green practice jersey and matching sweat pants, but they weren't nearly as tight as the coach's, which is why he probably didn't look as muscular at the moment.

The two men approached.

"I'm Coach Clifford Montgomery, and this young man is your new quarterback, Karl Johnston," the older man said with a bit of a Southern twang Billy recognized, for they were from the same part of Virginia that he was. "Assistant Coach Frase will run you through your drills today. Which one of you is Greenberg?"

"I am," Billy answered.

"You come with Karl and me," Coach Montgomery said as he signaled for Billy to follow.

As Billy left his teammates, he shrugged his shoulders but did as he was told and caught up with the new coach and quarterback.

"I think it's important that a center and quarterback get to know each other intimately. You two will have to work closer than anyone else on the team, you understand, Greenberg?" the coach asked.

"Yes, sir," Billy responded.

"Good."

Karl just looked back at Billy and smiled.

They continued walking in silence until they reached the locker room, then went back to the room that was usually used for rehabilitation with its massage tables, whirlpool and other useful equipment. Billy noticed the coach had moved some things around and created a large area in the middle of the room with a section of workout mats. Needless to say, Billy was a little confused. After playing football and the same position for over fifteen years, he was used to new coaches, but never had been brought into a situation with just the coach and quarterback.

"I hear you aren't heading for the pros after college? They say you're going to medical school," Coach Montgomery said.

"Yes, sir, I've always wanted to be a doctor. Playing football was a way of getting scholarship money, and what I didn't spend on undergrad, I can use for medical school," Billy answered, expecting the coach to give him the same spiel he always got about how with his talents he should go pro and all.

"Good for you," the coach said, surprising Billy. "You'll have a longer career as a doctor and be able to walk without pain after thirty as well."

"Wow," Billy responded. "You're the first coach to give me that response."

"Johnston here is also pre-med, and the sexy fucker wants to be a surgeon, so I need for you to protect him, so he doesn't injure those hands," Coach Montgomery informed him. "I am not all that keen on playing pro unless you're too stupid to become something else. All that money and a broken body never make for a good combination."

Karl smiled, while Billy wondered if he actually heard the coach call him a 'sexy fucker.' This wouldn't be too shocking, for coaches and players usually referred to each other with sexual innuendoes and pet names all the time. It was a male-bonding thing, yet there was something about how he said it and the fact that Karl smiled and still had not said a word.

"Damn, a surgeon. Cool. I'm going to become an OBGYN," Billy said directly to Karl.

"All that pussy? Can you handle it?" Karl finally spoke, and what a deep, sexy voice he had, Billy thought as he smiled back at his new quarterback.

"OK, enough of this flirting, love birds, let's get to work," the coach said. He then handed Billy a football. "Greenberg, I want you to practice hiking to Johnston. I don't want any fumbles, none. You hear me?"

They both nodded as Billy bent over to hike the ball. The room was particularly hot, and Billy was dressed in all his pads. He was thankful he had not put on his helmet or he would have passed out.

"Aren't you curious what it's on?" Karl asked.

"Oh yeah," Billy said. "It's just that this is strange for me. I've played center for as long as I can remember, and I never had to practice hiking like this in a room away from everyone."

"You'll find I have new ways of doing everything," Coach Montgomery said. "Before we get started, why don't you get out of those pads; it's hot as fuck in here, and I don't want your parents crying to me when you die of heat exhaustion."

Billy turned to leave the room, when the coach stopped him. "Where the hell are you going?"

"To put on some sweats," Billy said.

"Forget the sweats," the coach said. "Just take off the pads. We're all men here. Hell, you've seen parts of your teammates they've never seen themselves every time you girls shower together."

Billy turned around and took off his practice jersey then his shoulder pads. He was wearing a white T-shirt underneath that was soaked with sweat and clinging to every muscular inch of his torso, but he decided to leave it on. He then took off his shoes and his football pants. Now he was just standing there in a jockstrap that did little to contain his huge basket. His teammates had teased him for years about his big balls and thick swinging dick, so he waited for the usual comments. None came. The coach and new quarterback sort of looked but were all business. Billy was grateful.

"On thirty-two," Karl said as Billy bent over once again. Karl placed the back of his hand against Billy's balls and formed a cup with the other facing up, waiting for the ball, and began, "Twelve, sixteen, thirty-two …" and before he could say hike, Billy had launched the ball between his legs, into Karl's hands and was propelling forward before Karl knew what hit him, dropping the ball.

"They said he was the quickest center ever, Johnston," Coach Montgomery said with a chuckle as Karl picked up the ball. "He's already knocked down three guys, and a fourth is gonna grab that ball … Coach Phillips already warned me about you, Greenberg."

Billy smiled, but he was not the cocky type, so he felt a little sorry for Karl. "Sorry about that. Let's try it again."

"You're gonna take a little getting used to," Karl said as he wiped some sweat off his brow. "This one on three."

He bent over again, and Karl began, "Seven, four, twenty-two, three …" and again he dropped the ball as Billy hiked with lightning speed and lurched forward, but this time the coach was standing right in front of him, so he stopped just short of knocking him over.

"Fuck!" Karl said frustrated.

"Greenberg, bend over," the Coach said. "Watch, Johnston." And the coach took the quarterback's position behind Billy. "You gotta slam the back of your hand up there," and he firmly 'slammed' the back of his right hand against Billy's balls, then formed a cup with the other hand below it waiting for the hike. It wasn't enough to hurt, just enough to send a shiver up Billy's spine. "And hold them there. You should place them in just the right position to lift this big sexy ass off the ground." And with that, he lifted Billy off his feet, leaving the center to use the ball as a support to keep from falling flat on his face. The coach then gently put him back down. "That way, no matter when he hikes the ball, you won't drop it. Now you try."

When the coach removed his hands, Billy actually missed them then he realized his dick was starting to swell a bit, and some precum was leaking out. Now, he wished he had gone to get those sweat pants. He hoped that if he continued to sweat as much as he was now, his jock might be too wet for anyone to notice.

"On twenty-three." Karl resumed his position, this time slamming the back of his hand up Billy's crotch, then forming a cup with the other hand. He then attempted to lift Billy up, but he couldn't, so he just began, "Twelve, twenty, sixteen, twenty-three ..." and this time he held onto the ball, but not before almost dropping it again.

"You're getting it ... again," the Coach said.

Billy quickly assumed the position before they could notice the precum or the fact that his dick was starting to grow.

He really wished he could get his sweats.

"On seventeen this time," Karl said. "Wait a minute; it's too fucking hot in here." Then Karl kicked off his shoes, pulled off his sweat pants and removed his shirt, wearing nothing but a jockstrap himself. Billy could see all this when he looked through his legs. Now he knew he was in trouble, for Karl was a brown-skinned god. He then slammed his hand against Billy's balls, but this time he slid them up and down just a tiny bit. "Damn, your butt is all sweaty," Karl complained.

"Just get to it," Coach Montgomery said.

"Thirteen, four, fifty-six, forty-two, forty-three, sixteen, seventeen ..."

Billy hiked and lurched forward, and when he turned around, Karl had the ball firmly in his hand and a big smile on his face. He looked over at the coach who had taken off his shirt, and he really worried about that wet spot on his jock.

"Again," the coach said.

Billy assumed the position for three more hikes. By now, both Billy and Karl were covered in sweat, and he had finally removed his wet T-shirt. On the fourth try, Billy waited for the familiar 'slam' of Karl's hand, but it didn't come.

Instead, he felt something soft and realized it was Karl's tongue on his ass!

"Oh man, I just couldn't help myself," Karl said between licks. "I couldn't stare at this beautiful butt a minute longer."

Billy looked up and saw the coach's bare feet in front of him. With his hands still on the ball, he looked up, and Coach Montgomery was standing there wearing nothing, not even a jock, and his long thick, dark brown cock was pointing straight out above Billy's head. The coach then squatted down, looked the surprised center in the eyes, and said, "You are one beautiful man." Then, he planted his thick full lips on Billy's, and they made out, swapping spit and encircling each other's tongues. He never took his hands off the ball, and he no longer worried about the wet spot as his jock was one sticky mess with the coach's tongue in his mouth and Karl's all over his ass.

Karl reached up and grabbed the waistband of Billy's jock to pull it off, or at least he tried for the center's dick was so big and hard, it was making it difficult. Karl reached between Billy's thighs and freed the obstruction, giving the sweat and precum coated dick a nice stroking while he removed the jock with the other hand and never letting his tongue leave the hot ass in front of him.

The coach continued to make out with him, and Billy didn't want him to stop, but the coach left the center's mouth for just a second, and replaced his tongue with his long, thick cock. Billy finally let go of the ball and grabbed the backs of Coach Montgomery's thighs.

No one said a word. There were slurps and moans of satisfaction, but nothing needed to be said.

Billy's ass suddenly felt cool as Karl stopped licking it, slid between the center's thighs and flipped over on his back. He then grabbed Billy's butt and pulled him toward him until the center's enormous cock was aiming at his mouth, and Billy did as directed until he felt the warmth of the quarterback's mouth on his dick. But this position didn't quite work, so Karl slid from between his legs, stood and guided Billy over to one of the massage tables. He made Billy lie down on his back. The quarterback then bent over and with easy access gave Billy the wettest, most sensual blowjob of his young life, and it was a good thing he had a wide mouth to accommodate Billy's legendary cock. The coach stood near Billy's head and stuck his cock back into the center's mouth.

Karl was stroking his dick and about to blow, when he announced, "Who wants it?"

"I do," the coach said, and with that he bent over just in time for the quarterback to stroke his cock one more time, aiming it at the coach's mouth. Coach Montgomery then took Karl's dick gladly and swallowed every bit of the young quarterback's tasty load.

"My turn. Take it Greenberg," and the coach blew his huge load into Billy's mouth, which brought him closer to the edge. Billy made sure to get every drop, and the coach did not deny him any.

"Who gets mine?" Billy panted as he let the coach's cock slip from his mouth. Neither the coach nor the quarterback said a word; they just both went down on his throbbing cock, swapping spit between them, and when he shot, one mouth was on it, then the other, and back and forth until he was spent.

The coach looked down at Billy and said, "This is how I like for my center and quarterback to know each other intimately."

DARK AND LONELY
Aiden Lovely

The moment the cold wind whipped around Jamal's muscular body, he longed for the untouched brandy that he wasted. It was watery and stale from how long he nursed it with his lonely eyes, rubbing his thick cock occasionally when watching the others kiss and cuddle at the gay bar. He needed a release – a fun, rough cock pounding. Tonight, he didn't want to get too drunk. It seemed as if he was hitting the bar and staggering back home every night. And as he watched the gentle snowflakes fall, he wondered, "When will these lonely nights end?"

He couldn't say he was sober, but he wasn't as wasted as usual. He was known for passing out on park benches and in dark alleys when he couldn't make it back home. But at times, he didn't want to go home; knowing no one would be waiting for him. And ever since he and his ex-boyfriend parted, Jamal didn't want to admit that he felt he'd never fall in love again. It had only been a month since their break-up and already his ex-boyfriend had started dating again. What was it about Jamal that made him so unlovable? He thought about it over and over again. With his thick eyelashes that aligned his piranha eyes and his cheeky grin he showed when he was happy, even his coworkers at the coffee shop admitted that he was a very attractive – sexy chocolate man. And he was capable of picking up phones numbers from the men and women customers.

In fact, that was where he met his last boyfriend. His ex-boyfriend was a classy gentleman that looked out of place to be in such a little mom and pop owned coffee shop. And, the man was very egotistic, just casually pounding Jamal with his black anaconda in the restroom and then writing his phone number on the receipt, passing it back to Jamal. Never again. Jamal shook his head from left to right. Never again, will he date customers. It wasn't as if he didn't see his ex all the time at the coffee shop. He wasn't sure if his ex-boyfriend was just coming there because he liked the coffee or coming there to bother him; either way it was working.

By the time Jamal realized it, he was already standing in front of a dark alley. The moonlight gleamed off the trash cans and all the city cars could be heard in the distance. He had unconsciously walked himself anywhere but home. Was it really that bad to be alone? He thought. This kind of behavior was pretty much shameful. He never imagined he get this down. But when he was so heartbroken, it was easy to bring him to tears over even a foolish thing. His shadow hung on the brick wall surrounding the alley, and then slowly he sat down between two trash cans, ignoring the odor of the graffitied dumpster. He slipped his fingers in his pants, squeezing his giant cock, getting off on the memories of him and his ex. What was becoming of his life? His eyes began to water as if he had been trying to hold his cries back the entire time. He folded his arms over his knees and bowed his head. His face stiffened, and his eyebrows wrinkled. And, the wetness of his tears raced down his cheeks. He couldn't keep going on like this. Every hour was spent crying. He even cried sparingly at his job with every passing glance. A heart break so bad, he imagined his heart was being squeezed in his chest by every moment. His fettered whimpers filled the entire alley.

And then a warm hand brushed against his dark Caesar haircut. Another soothing stroke followed. It felt so natural; Jamal lifted his sad face without being alarmed at all. The hand was as gentle as snow. As the tears blurred his vision, the image of a tall gorgeous African man stood before him, skin so smooth and dark. Regardless, he was too wooed to reject with his drunken mind. The man was shirtless with tiny beads of snow drizzling down his flesh, tracing his washboard abs. His muscular arms flexed with his every move and his expression was as still as a portrait. His features were deep, chiseled like a Greek god's with his long braids steaming from his scalp like a fountain, hanging pasted his shoulders. Jamal couldn't object. This warmth the man carried was enough to seduce him as the strong gaze laid upon him.

"Excuse me … but your face is far too beautiful to cry." His thick voice held a lascivious tone that Jamal couldn't deny. He blushed and turned away from the stranger. Jamal was speechless.

"Stand up." The man ordered. Jamal was manipulated by that seductive smile. He rose to his feet. The tears ran down his chin. The man's eyes widened. And then, he lifted his hand to wipe the tears that fell from Jamal's eyes.

"At least tell me your name."

In a weak voice Jamal answered, "My name is Jamal." His eyes softened, glued to the man's face. The man smiled and patted Jamal's head, "You can call me Tristan."

"Tristan."Jamal repeated in almost a whisper. He then looked at the littered pavement.

"Let's go to my room." Tristan said, taking him by the hand. Jamal followed him. He longed for the warmth of another hand tugging on his. It wasn't a habit of his to go to hotels with strange, well-hung gentlemen, but at this rate anyone so kind and gentle would do. His cloudy breath rested on his hands, trying to warm them as Tristan wore a long trench coat. He headed for the fancy hotel next to the alley.

Jamal watched him in silence. He looked away every time Tristan's eyes met his.

"I see. We just met and already you can't take your eyes off me." Tristan said. Jamal quickly turned away. Blush covered his face. He sat on the edge of the bed, kicking his legs back and forth. He'd never been in a hotel room so expensive. The walls were a pale blue color similar to a robin's egg and the trimming before the ceiling was a frosty dark shade. Jamal's eyes followed the zigzag pattern on the ceiling. Tristan handed him a glass of wine. Jamal hesitated. His heart had never felt such a strong attraction like this. It pounded so strongly, he imagined he'd faint.

"It's okay. I'll make you feel better." Seeing Tristan's sweet smile, he tried to calm himself and relax his shoulders. His fingers wrapped around the glass. He took a sip. Tristan then skimmed his moist lips down Jamal's nose bridge. Arousing the friction, he railed back, locking his gaze and then he licked his lips as he leaned in and pressed them against Jamal's. A strong feeling surrounded his heart as if it were going to explode. It beat so loudly, he imagined Tristan could hear it. He couldn't take his eyes off the man now. Tristan's fingers cupped his chin. His eyelashes fluttered. His fingertips were heated. His entire body rose in temperature. And then, with their foreheads touching, Tristan kissed Jamal. It was so irrational to say he was in love, so Jamal wouldn't assume something so foolish. But, this pleasure overwhelming his body, he couldn't resist. His flesh flinched at just Tristan's touch. More and more Jamal desired to touch him. Jamal gasped. They only just met and already, he longed for more. Tristan drew himself back. He smirked. He sensed the eagerness. Jamal blushed. He turned away. But Tristan's long slender fingers gently pulled his face toward him.

"You're so eager. It's cute." He leaned in and kissed Jamal once more, taking his breath away. Tristan then pushed himself on top of Jamal's warm body. Jamal's arms tighten around those broad shoulders. Tristan was a sharp man with a member so thick and hard it could only rival lumber. The hot breath flowing into his ear made a moan escape his lips. Tristan's cologne washed over him, and he bit his lip, hoping Tristan would take him that very second.

He could smell the dark man's expensive cologne as the hardness of his member brushed up against Tristan's strong thighs, holding him in a tight embrace from the front. Tristan's strong arms captured Jamal's waist. His jagged breath brushed against Jamal's skin as Jamal parted his lips, allowing Tristan to taste him. His heart was pounding in his chest as he pressed himself against Tristan's chest. Tristan then quickly slipped his hand in Jamal's pants and squeezed the bulge, causing a powerful throbbing in his well-hung member.

"Jamal. You're so impatient," he said in his stylish voice, "You're such naughty guy." Jamal flinched as Tristan's sweet lips nipped at his neck blazing down to his collarbone, unbuttoning his shirt. And then, he licked Jamal's bare chest, his tongue prancing around the nipples. A soft moan escaped Jamal's lips.

And then roughly, Tristan pushed Jamal's face into the pillow. Jamal's heart raced. He didn't think he'd be the receiver with Tristan, but either way, this was going to be fulfilling for both of them.

"I'm more of a bondage fan to be honest. The rougher the better." Tristan said and then grinned. Jamal gulped. Could this be more than what he was asking for? And as much as Jamal hated to admit, just the words alone made his body beg for it. He put his head down. His ass was raised, and he wished Tristan would mount him faster. Tristan hovered over him, grinning. He then took out a pair of handcuffs from his coat pocket.

"W-why do you have those in your pocket?" Jamal said. Tristan clicked his tongue. "Because..." he took a breath, "I use these on all my partners." Without a second thought, he handcuffed Jamal. He liked the restrained Jamal's position.

Tristan's coat layered the floor next to Jamal's clothes. His beautiful, sculptured six-pack abs with a chest as hard as steel was revealed. He slapped Jamal's ass. "You're so impatient. Your cock is so hard already." Jamal blushed. Tristan grinded his thick eleven-inch member against the crack. His fingers then circled Jamal's cock, his fingers quickly sliding up and down the shaft and then with his fingernail, he roughly scrapped against the tip. Jamal flinched, his member twitching and his body hungry for more. A high pitched moan spilled from his lips. Tristan liked this. Pulling down Jamal's pants completely, he dropped them to the floor. His fingers then slid along Jamal's hips, caressing the strong ass of his prey.

"Please fill me up." Jamal softly begged. His breathing was heavy. Tristan enjoyed this kind of control. He trailed his finger down Jamal's backbone and then he plunged it deep inside Jamal. Jamal tried to hold in his groans, but the sensational pain and pleasure was too overwhelming. And then without any warning, Tristan pushed another finger in.

"For a strong black man, you're very sensitive," Tristan said, smiling, watching Jamal's precum make a tiny puddle on the blankets. Jamal buried his face in shame. He didn't even want to catch a glimpse of the expression on Tristan's face, reaping so much pleasure from his greedy, trembling ass. Tristan then placed his hot lips to Jamal's ear, his hot breath tickling the sensitive flesh, "Be a good boy, and maybe I'll let you come."

Jamal closed his eyes and nodded his head. Tristan dabbed his finger in the precum and wiped it against Jamal's innocent anus. Tristan bucked his hips and pressed his dick against the anus. Jamal's body rocked back and forth, begging for it as Tristan pushed all the way inside, his balls pressing near the flesh. Tristan gritted his teeth as Jamal spread his knees farther apart. His hole was being stretched farther than he ever imagined. Tristan thrust slowly at first, letting

Jamal's body get accustomed to his size. His manly hands stroked Jamal's scorching shaft. Jamal's loud voice echoed throughout the room.

"You have such a lovely backside."

Jamal's face was flushed as Tristan smacked his rear once more. These blazing feelings ran through his body like a thunderbolt. But most of all, his dick, being strangled by Tristan's fingers, was throbbing, swollen and dripping, little sprinkles of sperm running down his thick manhood. His balls were a blazing red, the size of baseballs, and his body trembled at every touch.

Jamal's smooth ass, dominated by an enormous cock, stretching his hole big enough to fit a wine bottle. The fat shaft pressed in and out. The curly black hair on Tristan's gigantic balls brushed against Jamal's entrance, the walls of his inside throbbing. His body was on fire as the man pounded harder and harder. His huge cock pummeled Jamal, jerking his body around. Tristan's hot fingers caressed the curves of Jamal's butt, and then his hands grabbed Jamal's swollen cock once again, a trail of sperm rolling down the tip.

Jamal groaned with every thrust, gripping the thin sky blue, cotton made sheet with his teeth. His pleasure filled moans were released in many breathes. And his chest bounced up and down. Tristan's thrusting sped up – powerful blasts. Jamal's hips were rocked, and Tristan's hand squeezed his dick, making Jamal's voice rise to a soprano volume – both of them blasting their jizz simultaneously.

Jamal lay there filled like a twinky. His heart was still racing as Tristan pulled out of him. "That was good." Tristan said and then kissed Jamal's cheek, "We have to do this again sometime." Jamal blushed, "Yeah ... um can you take off these cuffs. My wrists are starting to hurt."

"I don't know. Maybe I should leave a naughty man like you tied up." Tristan teased, running his finger down Jamal's chest and then flicking his nipple. Jamal flinched. And even though he just climaxed, he was ready for a second helping.

"Are you thinking what I'm thinking?" Tristan said, rubbing his hands on his hard cock. Jamal smiled and then pushed his face into the pillow again with his ass raised up. At this rate, he'd never have a lonely night again.

TRANSLATIONS
Roscoe Hudson

I hadn't been in Mannheim forty-eight hours, and I was already being screamed at. The passengers on the *Strassenbahn* looked up from their books, newspapers and grocery lists and stared at me while I fumbled through my pockets and backpack for my *Fahrkarte*, the tiny ticket stub that proved I wasn't a fare jumper. The *Fahrkartenkontrolluer*, a hunky man dressed in a navy blue train conductor's uniform adorned with shiny gold buttons and a matching blue cap, glowered at me, his gunmetal eyes vacant and intractable like those of a hawk. He stood in front of me rigid and silent with his lips tightly pursed in a thin line as he breathed through his nose, his pale white cheeks flared.

"*Keine Fahrten fus freies!*" he demanded.

"I just had it. It's here somewhere."

"*Die Strassenbahn ist nur fur zahlende Passagiere!*"

The *Fahrtenkontrolluer* sighed and turned his head from side to side until he heard his neck crack. His slightly bent Roman nose and chiseled square jaw gave him a classic Teutonic profile. He scanned the faces of the other passengers while I turned my pockets inside out.

My passport and directions to Hans Krieger's apartment were the only items in the pocket of my blazer. Aside from a couple of Euros and the wrapper from a pastry I ate for breakfast, the pockets of my jeans were empty. I wiped sweat from my forehead and continued searching. I had been warned by friends and a few colleagues at the university where I taught that Germans prized efficiency, strictly adhered to rules and had little tolerance for those who made excuses for violating them. Ticketless passengers on public transportation suffered severe penalties.

The transit system in Germany was like nothing we had in Chicago. German rails were immaculate and ran on time. Back home a person couldn't access the El without paying first. Here one could casually board the tram and ride for free without anyone knowing. The driver didn't ask for fare or check tickets. That was the job of a special group of law enforcement who hopped on and off the *Strassenbahn* and asked for tickets with the same diligence as militia men paroling the border between the United States and Mexico demanded verifiable proof of citizenship. I had purchased my ticket just after I left the bakery, and spotting the tram approaching a couple of blocks away, sprinted to the stop. The officer boarded two stops after I got on. Burly and broad, his uniform clung to him like second skin and left little to the imagination. His biceps, deltoids and quadriceps, massive and round, seemed ready to bust out of his clothes with each movement he made. His face was frozen in a scowl that enhanced his authoritative, ultramasculine allure. I felt I was being berated by a Tom of Finland drawing and imagined him shouting at me dressed only in lace-up Jobmaster boots and a metal cock ring. My hard-on bulged in my jeans the entire time he was yelling at me; I placed my backpack in my lap, so neither he nor the other passengers could see. I rifled through my bag while the fantasy played out in my mind.

"*Ich verliere die Geduld. Zeigen Si emir Ihre Karte.*"

"I can't understand you. I bought a ticket. Just give me a minute to find it."

"*Alle Passagiere mussen eine Karte kaufen oder eine Geldstrafe zahlen!*"

I started emptying the contents of my backpack onto the seat next to me: my diary, an English-German dictionary, a gay German travel guide and two novels by Dixon Weatherby, the reclusive ex-patriot black gay author I had come to Germany in hopes of interviewing for my new book. The bag also contained lots of protein bar wrappers and various receipts, but no tram ticket.

"*Stellen Sie Ihre Karte her oder gehen Sie herzlich die Strassenbaun aus.*"

"Look man, I'm not a fare jumper. I just got here. Let me check my backpack again."

He crossed his arms over his chest. Silence settled over the idling tram. The longer it took me to find the ticket the smaller I felt. My horny fantasy faded, and my penis became flaccid again. It was eight o'clock on a drowsy gray October morning, and the irate German officer barking at me had reached his limit. His eyes widened, and a large green vein appeared in his throat like a lightning bolt shocking the sky.

"In *Deutschland* you will speak *Deutsch!*" he roared.

I could feel drops of sweat trickle down my back. "It's in here. I'll find it."

"Produce your ticket now, sir!"

"I will if you give me a chance."

"Your passport, sir."

I gave him my passport, and after he checked it, he whipped out a pad holstered on his belt, scribbled on it, tore off a page and stuffed it into my palm. "You owe the city of Mannheim five hundred Euros. You will please pay by month's end."

He bounded off the tram and walked along the crowded sidewalk, taking long confident strides with his back straight and his chin high. Drenched in sweat and shaking a little, I kept my eyes on his tree trunk thighs and beefy bodybuilder's ass until the *Strassenbahn* turned a corner and he was out of sight.

# # # # #

One of my colleagues in the English department was born and raised in Berlin. When I told him I was going to spend a few weeks in Mannheim trying to persuade Dixon Weatherby to share his life story with me, rather than express doubts that I would ever be able to connect with the stubbornly reclusive writer, he laughed and said, "Mannheim? Don't blink, you'll miss it." He was right. The city has a population of over three hundred thousand, and though many of its imposing granite and limestone Baroque buildings pre-date the seventeenth century, even the gay travel guide I toted in my backpack had little to recommend in the city. The only two places for gays to hang out were a bar called Connexion and a bath house.

After my unsuccessful first attempt to arrange a meeting with Dixon Weatherby, I went back to my cramped studio apartment near the Luisenpark, wrote in my diary and listened to Rosetta Stone, but I couldn't concentrate. Making attempts to study German only made me think of the officer on the tram and how the situation both demeaned and aroused me. Though the officer's caustic behavior enraged me, I couldn't deny how turned on I was by him. If ever a body was made for fucking it was his. I fantasized about him stomping into the studio and pinning me down on the bed, his massive body slamming against me while his long fat dick drilled my asshole. I took the travel-sized bottle of lube from beside my bed, slicked up my palm and let my hand do what the officer couldn't. I tugged and squeezed all nine hard inches of my cock, mixing my precum with the lube, so my dick would be slicker. The more I fantasized about the officer cursing me out in German while he raped my ass from behind, the more furious I stroked my hard-on, tightening, twisting and flicking my dick from root to tip. My butt bounced up and down on the sweat-soaked sheets. I imagined the officer rolled me onto my back and plunged every stiff inch of his love muscle into my quivering ass while I locked my thighs around him tight and held on to his oversized shoulders. My hips bounced off the mattress, my balls jumped towards my pelvis, and a fountain of cum shot into the air, glazing my stomach. I took a nap and woke just as twilight was darkening to night. I dined on schnitzel at a small restaurant around the corner then walked to Connexion.

What the travel guide described as a bar was actually an upscale coffee shop that also served beer and other alcoholic beverages. Furnished with polished mahogany tables and chairs and high stools at the bar, I was more likely to meet a grad student studying Hegel than the brick house muscle daddies I had hoped to find there. Around fifteen men, most of them beanpoles in skinny jeans and pole shirts, sat around smoking and drinking lager. When I, the only black man in the place, walked in, they abandoned their conversations and watched me as I picked up a bar magazine from a rack by the door and took a seat at the bar. A pulsating remix of Lady GaGa songs played through the speakers, and the murmur of casual conversation gradually increased.

The bartender, a scrawny sweet-faced guy with twinkling eyes and a gage in each ear, gave me a quick nod. I ordered a lager, a Konig;

he set a foamy pilsner glass in front of me. I took one sip and scrunched up my face.

The bartender chuckled. "You don't like beer?"

I was grateful he spoke English. "It's not my favorite." I wiped my mouth with the side of my hand.

A husky voice from behind said, "You should try a *radler*. It's sweeter."

I turned and came face to face with the *Fahrkartenkontrolluer* from this morning. He was wearing a red muscle T-shirt, snug jeans that showed off his meaty thighs and butt, white and red Pumas and a leather wristband. His shiny blond hair was short and wavy. Since I saw him earlier that day he had already grown a five o'clock shadow. Even in casual clothes, he appeared menacing, as likely to crack my windpipe as give me a firm handshake.

"A *radler*?" I asked with a sneer, still nursing my anger from the incident on the tram. "Is that another lager?"

"Lager with Sprite." He looked past me to the bartender and said, "*Bilden Sie es zwei.*"

He sat on the stool beside me and propped his elbows on the bar, flexing his football sized biceps.

The bartender mixed the *radlers* and set them in front of us on felt green pads.

As I reached for my glass, the officer gently put his hand on my wrist. "We must have a toast first." He lifted his glass. "*Willkommen nach Deutschland.*"

"*Danke*," I said and took a sip. He was right, the *radler* was sweet.

"Good?" the bartender asked.

I nodded, and the bartender waited on a customer at the other end of the bar.

I thought about ignoring the officer and moving to another part of the bar, but I didn't want him to know how irritated I was. Since he already paid for my drink abandoning him would have been rude, and in spite of our earlier confrontation, I was still attracted to him. He was the hottest man in the bar, and my dick started to get hard again just imagining what he kept in those tight jeans. "So what do you do when you aren't harassing foreigners on the tram?"

He chuckled. I was glad to see he had a sense of humor. "I don't think I was harassing you. I had a job to do; you violated the rules."

I tried to be nice, but I could feel anger bubbling within me. "I wasn't lying. I bought a ticket."

"And, where was that phantom ticket, my friend? Hmm? I never saw it."

He was a smug bastard, but I liked it. The image of him in naked in boots and a cock ring formed in my mind again.

"I am Rolf," he said.

"Vaughn."

His hand was thick and strong, not like my slim artistic hand which he squeezed tight, establishing himself as the alpha male between the two of us. Rolf was being congenial now: the muscles in his face softened and his eyes had lost their steely gaze. He behaved like two completely different men – a burly asshole in the morning and a flirtatious muscle stud at night.

He gulped his *radler* then asked, "What has brought you to Mannheim, Vaughn? Military work?"

"I'm a professor in the U.S., and I came here to locate an expatriate writer. I was on my way to see his former editor when you gave me that undeserved ticket."

"What does this man write?" he asked before he took another drink.

"Fiction. He published three novels back in the 1980s."

Rolf chuckled and wiped the corner of his mouth with his thumb. "I'm sorry. I don't see much point in making up stories."

His laugh faded quickly after he looked at my face.

Marcus Anthony

"I apologize if I have offended you."

"We just can't seem to get off to a good start, can we?" I sipped my *radler* and thought about going back to my apartment.

Rolf scratched his scruffy chin. "He must be a very important writer if you are leaving your work at university."

"Dixon Weatherby. He's a black gay writer. Not as famous as James Baldwin but just as influential."

"I am sure you will find him. There are many gay black men in *Deutschland*, though none quite as handsome as you." He winked at me and took another drink.

The bar had begun to get very crowded and noisy. Rolf patted me on the back and said, "Finish your drink. We will take a walk." The timber of his voice lowered under the weight of furtive plans I could only guess at. He squeezed my thigh, and the tiny lines around his eyes arched.

A few minutes later, Rolf and I were strolling down the dark streets of Mannheim. I zipped up my jacket and walked with my hands deep in my pockets. Rolf's bullet sized nipples grew erect beneath his shirt. We made our way along the dark avenues past closed flower shops, cafes, produce stand and *Apothekes*. The facades of the Gothic buildings looked like ogres grimacing in their sleep. We passed the apartment building where I stayed, and Rolf pointed out places of interest that I should see, but I hardly heard him. My attention was focused on his bodybuilder's physique. He was a walking stack of hefty, robust muscles, and as we walked down the sidewalk an occasional passerby gave him an incredulous wide-eyed stare. Every inch of him was puffed-up, and his crotch was just as humpy as the rest of him. I imagined a flaccid cock the size of a bratwurst coiled inside of those jeans, straining against the rough, unyielding denim, eager for my plump moist lips and wide mouth.

Rolf faced me. The devilish gleam in his eyes was unmistakable. "You are enjoying *Deutschland*?"

"So far, I mean, except for that ticket."

Rolf smirked.

225

"Your English is excellent, not like my German."

"You will learn. I spent time in America as a boy. And, my last boyfriend was American. From Atlanta."

"What was he like?"

"He was in the military. He was closeted. It was not a good situation."

"Was he black?"

"Why do you ask?"

"Just wondering."

"You think all German men like black men?"

"I've heard lots of stories."

Rolf chuckled, staring at the ground while we continued to walk. "You Americans are all the same. You denounce stereotypes, yet when you come to *Deutschland* all you want is to visit concentration camps and guzzle beer." He exhaled a long breath then said, "Yes, he was black."

"So you like black men, huh?"

His eyes lit up, and he gave me a playful smack on the ass. We came to a flight of stairs in a hatch located between two buildings. A sign above the stairs read WC. Rolf said he had to pee. I followed him down the stairs, hoping to get a glimpse of his dick. The dimly lit restroom looked large enough to accommodate a dozen men, but Rolf and I were the only ones there. The restroom's spaciousness was attributed to its lack of urinals; men relieved themselves on a decaying concrete wall with a slim metal cistern affixed to the wall about seven feet from the ground. Water trickled from tiny holes in the cistern and ran down the wall into a two-inch reservoir where the wall met the floor and periodically flushed the piss into the sewer. Three grimy toilet stalls were located to the left of the wall. The whole place stunk of piss, shit and cum.

Rolf and I approached the wall like gunslingers in the old West, each eyeing the other warily to see not only who would make the first move, but also who packed the biggest piece. We unzipped, and our cocks flopped out – his uncut and thick as a cucumber; mine cut and semi-hard. Our piss streams – his amber, mine golden – pattered as they made contact with the wall. He looked over at my cock, raised an eyebrow and nodded approvingly. "Very nice."

"Yours, too." I breathed a little faster and licked my bottom lip. "Real thick."

Once the last drops of pee pittled out of our piss slits, Rolf's face enflamed, coming to life with lust. My cock pointed heavenward and I stroked it. He started tugging on his fat cock too, forcefully yanking the thick foreskin back and forth over the wide bullet head of his dick. When it was fully hard his prick was nearly as long as his forearm. Aside from being the largest cock I had ever seen, it looked as menacing and dangerous as Rolf did. I stopped jerking my own hard dick and stood transfixed by Rolf's manhood. My mouth watered as I thought about the sloppy blowjob I hankered to give him, but I felt phantom pains in my rectum when I imagined his love hammer pounding my hole. As threatening as Rolf appeared, I knew his cock was capable of more violence than both of his powerful hands. It was a cock designed to dole out violent punishments – more like a truncheon than a phallus – yet sheer pleasure, I reasoned, existed on the other side of that violence.

Rolf stared me down and curled his upper lip. "Suck me."

My knees crashed on the damp asphalt and I widened my mouth to accommodate Rolf's stiff member. I grasped his shaft as I laved his dick, taking in only the head at first. Though his penis was hard as steel, the skin was soft and smooth, free of any marks or scars. Light blond hairs covered his balls. I cupped them in my free hand; they were orbic, full and heavy, more like the testicles of livestock than those of a man. Rolf raised his shirt over his head and behind his neck, exposing the globes of his shoulders, his hairy broad chest and flat and hard abdominal muscles. Blue-green veins crossed the landscape of his torso like rivers drawn on a map.

"You like my big cock?" he growled.

Rolf's metallic accent made my anus pucker. I stroked his dick from mid-shaft up to the head, squeezing it just enough to allow his precum to ooze out and pool on my tongue.

He rubbed his big stubby nipples while I kept sucking him off. The squelching sound coming from my mouth competed with the incessant trickling of water out of the cistern. Rolf slowly began to thrust his dick in and out of my mouth before he grunted something to himself in German: *"Saugen Sie mich gutes."* Liberated by the sound of his native language echoing off the crumbling walls, Rolf put both hands on my head, as if grasping a basketball, and rammed his dick into my mouth as far as it could go. I gasped and gagged, fearing I would throw up. Instead, I relaxed the muscles of my throat and inhaled deeply. I glanced up and saw the wrathful face of the man who gave me the ticket earlier that day. Rolf had become the brute again, the barbarian, mercilessly fucking my gaping wet mouth no matter what injury it caused me. My jaw ached and my lips became numb. I was powerless, kneeling at the altar of his pleasure.

Rolf's hips swayed back and forth. He planted his left palm on top of my head, and with his right hand he tweaked one of his nipples. I held on to his ballooning ass, squeezing and pushing it as he forced himself in and out of my mouth. Beads of his sweat drizzled on me as he chugged like a steam engine, pumping my mouth all the way to my tonsils. A frothy mix of saliva and precum lubricated his cock, slid down my chin and made a puddle on the floor.

"Sie mochten meinen Samen essen? Huh, baby? You eat hot German cum, yes?"

Before I even thought of answering, he crammed my mouth with cock again. My entire body quaked as I stroked my own lead dick and anticipated Rolf's gloppy load. He grunted and puffed as his thrusts quickened. Then his glutes clenched; he lifted himself on his toes, and a deluge of briny cum filled my mouth. I kept sucking his dick, determined to draw every drop of semen out of him. I breathed in the must saturating his pubic hair, the fetid restroom, the sharp odor of my own sweat. I jerked my cock until it the skin chafed and the head turned red. I rolled Rolf's cum in my mouth, savoring its salty flavor, its viscid texture, yet I still couldn't come. My lust immured within me, trapped behind impenetrable layers of organs, bones and flesh.

Seeming to sense my difficulty, Rolf bent over and pinched my nipples hard then whispered, "Come for your man, baby. *Ich wunsche Sie ejakulieren."*

They were the words my body had been waiting, the tongue of the Fatherland, the language I couldn't access yet longed to dwell within; the language that, to me, held the sleek, dark aura of a pair of steel-toed boots plodding on pavement, commanding, indifferent, inviolable. It was Daddy's slap across the face and his loving embrace, his admonishment and his approval. Thunder in the night, a rain soaked forest at dawn.

Rolf's thick cock muffled my groans as I bucked and splattered the asphalt with bolts of cum. When I jerked out the last remaining shots, I looked behind Rolf and saw three men standing near the stairs watching us with their hands on their dicks, picking up where I left off.

# # # # #

The next day I decided to visit Hans Krieger again, hoping I would catch him in his office and persuade him to put me in touch with Dixon Weatherby. Weatherby's novels had served as the genesis of my dissertation several years ago. My plan was to utilize his work and that of Baldwin's and other black gay writers in a book on black gay aesthetics in literature. His fiction focused on black gay men who unabashedly pursued their sexual desires with men of all races; they were stories of love and lust, race and identity that unfolded in such varied settings as backwoods speakeasies in the Deep South and posh hotels in the center of majestic European cities. I had already completed much of my work on the book, but I needed Weatherby's insights, the story behind the story, and I wanted to get them while the eighty-five year-old author was still alive and in good health.

Just after breakfast, with my backpack over my shoulder and a hot cup of coffee in hand, once again I raced to the *Strassenbaun* just in time to catch it before it took off. I sipped my coffee and flipped through pages of Dixon Weatherby's first novel when I heard a gruff voice ask, "*Mag ich Ihre Farkarte?*"

Rolf stood before me in his uniform, clean-shaven, stone-faced and humorless. The gold buttons on his blazer shined like tiny suns against his blue uniform.

I looked him up and down and unable to mask the salacious delight I felt, gave my crotch a conspicuous tug. "Hey. You get home all right last night?"

"Ihre Farkarte, bitte." He raised his voice and translated in a sanctimonious tone: "Your ticket, please."

The tram slowed to a stop. Passengers disembarked and vanished among the network of aged stone buildings; new passengers boarded, looking just as washed out and colorless as the sky. Rolf stood out like a blot on a canvas. He frowned, locked his arms over his barrel chest and glared at me, his eyes as gray as Mannheim's persistently gloomy weather.

Every good feeling I had slid off my face. I hung my head for a moment, not sure if I wanted to get off the train or throw my hot coffee in his face. "I should have known," I grumbled under my breath before I reached into my backpack and took out my ticket.

He took a quick look and handed the ticket back to me. "This is expired."

"Say what?" My voice was weighed down with exasperation. "It can't be. I just bought it."

Rolf thrust the ticket in front of my face. Just as he said, it bore yesterday's date in faded red print: the ticket I couldn't find, the emblem of the miscommunication that brought us together.

"You require a new ticket, Sir."

"Are you fucking kidding me, Rolf?"

"Die Strassenbahn ist nur fur zahlende Passagiere."

I crossed my arms and leaned back in my seat, defiant as a child. "Well I guess I don't have a fucking ticket."

He snatched his pad off his belt and scribbled, pressing so hard I could hear the pen traversing the page from edge to edge. He ripped off the ticket and handed it to me then hopped off the tram at the next stop.

# # # # #

In my apartment later than night I searched the Internet for the name and telephone number of someone in the Mannheim transit office I could file a complaint with. In spite of my attraction to him, I thought Rolf should be censured in some way. In addition to getting a second fine on the tram, I was unable to persuade Hans Krieger to put me in contact with Dixon Weatherby. I sat in his ornate living room for over an hour while Krieger, a foppish seventy-year-old man who wore a gray toupee, served me tea and crustless sandwiches as he passed lecherous glances over my body. When he sensed that I wouldn't be going to bed with him, he told me the possibility of meeting Weatherby was out of the question and that I should give up my quest and return to America. On my way home from Herr Krieger's apartment, I got caught in a cold rainstorm and ended up soaked through. I came back to my studio seething, fully prepared to pack my suitcases and catch the next available flight back to Chicago, but first I wanted to exact revenge on Rolf.

I took off my wet clothes, put on T-shirt, boxers and socks, and sat on the edge of my bed assaulting the keys of my laptop as I thought about Rolf and his duplicity. I searched for words and phrases in my English-German dictionary while I typed a long angry e-mail to the director of the transportation department, exposing Rolf as an egomaniac who preyed on Americans. In the midst of my cyber-tirade, I heard pounding on my front door. I got up and looked through the peep hole and saw Rolf, still dressed in his uniform, standing in the hall. He stared right back at me. I flung open the door.

"*Gutenabend*, Vaughn."

"If you're not here to apologize, you need to go, Rolf."

"*Gutenabend* is Good evening in German. *Gutenabend*."

"Look, whatever kind of games you're playing I'm not interested."

"Let me in."

"You need to go."

He stared at me hard and lowered his voice. "You can see I'm cold and wet from the rain. I'd like to talk to you. Let me in."

Once I let him pass and closed the door, he stood in the center of my apartment and with his back turned to me he began to take off his hat and jacket. After he pitched them into a corner he yanked his long sleeved light blue shirt out of his trousers, unbuttoned it and tossed it on the pile as well. The wide span of his nude back enlivened my cold-shrunken penis. I didn't want him to turn around and see my tumescent cock poking through my boxers, but I didn't want him in my apartment either. I fought with my own body; it ignored me.

"Rolf, you need to leave."

"*Stoppen Sie zu sprechen und horen Sie.* Be quiet."

"Having a big dick and a hot body doesn't mean you can fuck around with me. Are you on steroids or something?"

"I can fuck you when I like."

Still facing away from me, he removed his trousers, black briefs and socks and stood completely naked in middle of the apartment. My eyes traveled up and down his gladiator's physique: a plump, ample ass; hamstrings like sides of beef; bulbous calves that rested atop slim ankles. When he turned and faced me his dick was hard. Precum already jeweled the tip.

"*Sie saugen.*"

Rolf's body took up most of the space in my small studio. The precum on his cock began to drip to the hardwood floor.

I hunched my shoulders and tried to conceal my erection with my hands.

"Come suck my cock."

"Look, Rolf, last night was great, and I still think you're hot, but you can't ..."

Rolf's handsome, determined face suddenly metamorphosed into the manic expression of a mad man. The color drained from his face, and deep lines etched into his skin making sharp, dramatic contours beneath his cheekbones and on the sides of his mouth. He lowered his eyelids and clenched his jaw. The muscles of my back tightened and tingled and I braced myself against the front door as Rolf stomped toward me. "*Saugen Sie es!* Stop talking and suck!" He grasped the back of my neck and forced me to the floor. His large hard cock filled me mouth. When I tried to resist, he smacked the back of my head and pushed his dick in farther. A rank yet slightly sweet odor – the mixture of precum, soap, urine, perspiration and the day's labor – saturated Rolf's genitals and soft pubic hair.

I sucked and jerked his Billy club cock with gusto, abandoning all of my rational thoughts, even those of revenge. Rolf stepped back and planted one foot on the edge of my bed. I got down on my hands and knees. Rolf grasped his penis at the base and began to shove it down my throat.

"Pretty cocksucker," he moaned. "Honey brown ass."

I arched my back and stuck my ass out. Two hard smacks stung my butt cheeks before I heard my boxers rip, then the sound of Rolf hocking. A gob of hot spit splashed my anus; another gob followed. His thick hands and pudgy fingers kneaded and probed my eager rump while my ministrations on his engorged cock kept him groaning and mumbling to himself in German.

He stood up straight and demanded, "*Stehen Sie auf und verbiegen Sie vorbei*. Bend over on the bed."

I had my knees on the edge of the bed and my ass in the air instantly, offering Rolf my ass as if it was a bejeweled chalice filled with wine and he was a Roman solider about to go into battle. He slapped my humps a couple more times before he dipped his face between my quivering cheeks and lapped my hole with his tongue. His strong fingers dug into my fleshy mounds as he licked and flicked, slurped and slapped, grabbed and groped. My ass was his playground, and he was as happy as a boy at recess.

He took off my socks, put both hands on the back of my T-shirt and ripped it from my torso. I wiggled my ass in front of him like a bitch in heat. "Get the lube," I said. "Beside the – Aaaaggghhh!"

"My ass, my way."

"Goddamn! Wait ... I' m not ready ..." The language I couldn't access yet longed to dwell within.

"*Süßer, fester Esel!*"

Rolf mounted me, hopped on the bed, planting a foot on either side of my knees, and holding on to my trapezius muscles, so I couldn't break free. He wasted no time thrusting into my ass, filling my cavity with the full measure of his cock, shifting my body to accommodate his pleasure. Tears streaked my face, and I couldn't suppress the shrieks and wails that erupted from deep within me. No man had ever fucked me so hard with so little lubrication. No man had ever fucked me with such a big dick and such a lack of impunity. I guessed the pain there was no way I could have predicted just how excruciating. I thought I would pass out.

Rolf pushed my upper body to the mattress and hoisted my ass higher, then hunkered down over me and held me in a full nelson. As his rhythmic thrusting quickened, his furry chest felt like a large Brillo pad scouring my back. His thighs, just as hairy and thick, collapsed on mine. The stabbing in my anus eventually gave way to pleasure, and my agonizing shrieks and wails became moans of ecstasy.

Rolf panted in my ear. "You get fucked good, baby."

"Wear my ass out."

"*Füllen Sie es auf*, huh?"

"Yeah, baby, fill my ass up."

"Fuck you like a dog. Uggghhh ... Tight ass!"

He rolled me on my back. My asshole had dried up, so he took the lube from the side of the bed, squirted nearly half the bottle in me then submerged his long brawny dick in the river of my ass crack. I held my legs back as far as I could as he began to pummel my asshole, his penis moving like a drill boring and busting the earth for oil. I held on to his round hard ass while his enormous body undulated over mine. He kissed my lips while he continued to fuck me. Sheets of Rolf's sweat soaked my body, and soon a lake of sweat and lube formed in the sheets beneath us.

"You like big white dick?" He grunted and swirled his hips.

"In German." I licked his lips. "*Sprechen Sie auf Deutsch.*" In *Deutschland* you will speak *Deutsch*!

Rolf acknowledged me with a half-smile. His hot breaths puffed in my face before his mouth closed over mine, and his tongue coiled around my tongue.

"*Sie wünschen Geschlecht die ganze Nacht?*" Rolf asked.

"Fuck me all night, baby." The emblem of the miscommunication that brought us together.

"Feste Ass."

The bed squeaked, scooted and rocked: the sound of bridled horses galloping across the German countryside: work boots tromping and scuffing wood floors.

Rolf's mouth hung open and he shut his eyes tight. "Aaaaahhhh! Aaaaahhhh!" Copious amounts of semen flooded my asshole and spilled onto the bed. He kept thrusting into me well after he came; a squishing-squelching sound chorused with the staccato thumping of the bed. He raised his upper body and told me to jerk off. *"Ich wunsche Sie ejakulieren."* He spit on my dick and told me to use it for lube.

I yanked my dick while Rolf's cock kept stretching me out. He grasped my ankles and splayed my legs wide. I looked at his broad torso shiny with sweat and imagined Apollo driving his sun chariot across the morning sky; Hadrion, clad in armor and a centurion helmet, marching off to war, his blood red cape billowing behind him; Hercules slaying the Hydra.

I groaned and a geyser of cum exploded from me. My nut-busting orgasm felt as if it lasted for several minutes, and when I had squeezed out the last drop of cum, Rolf lay down beside me. He kissed my temple and wrapped his arm around me. We slept.

# # # # #

The *Strassenbahn* glides through the rainswept streets of Mannheim during morning rush hour. Though the skies remain overcast and gray, now and again the sun announces itself, not unlike a mischievous child sneaking out of bed to dance and play after his parents have confined him to his room. The citizens of Mannheim are still bundled in their heavy clothes, still stubbornly adherent to their own routines and resigned to the rough unpleasantness of the season.

I take a seat near the door and place my backpack squarely on my lap. I am rereading Dixon Weatherby's first novel. It concerns Eugene MacArthur, a black gay man from Mississippi who narrowly escapes a lynching in 1947 and moves with his female cousin to New York City, where he falls in love with an Italian-American mason named Giancarlo. It is an engrossing novel, and I read it with the same wonder and zeal I did when I first read it my freshman year of college. The book enthralls me so much that I do not notice the *Fahrkartenkontrolluer* standing before me, waiting patiently for my ticket. His looks are handsome in a way that is devastating. His physique is undeniably gorgeous; it is a body not developed naturally but forged over years of discipline and a strict diet and exercise regimen – an archetype of masculine power and strength. I hand him my ticket. He examines it and, satisfied that I paid my fare, returns the ticket to me. "Good book?" he inquires.

"*Ja*," I say.

"What is it about?"

"*Ein Mann, der sich befreit.*"

The officer nods. He appears intrigued. His gray eyes look directly into mine, and for a moment we let the world fall away, existing outside the limits and order of language. We are two men with the same wants and desires, the same need for recognition, respect and comfort. We are not our nations, our languages or the stereotypes that have the power to confine and condemn.

The officer's voice slightly quavers when he asks, "Could we meet for a coffee later today? At Connexion?"

I smile and nod.

"I'd like to learn more about your book. Perhaps you will bring it with you?"

I answer, "*Ich hole Ihnen eine autographierte Kopie. Ich bin auf meiner Weise, den Autor zu treffen.*"

"Ah, so you know the author? Yes, I would very much like an autographed book. Thank you."

"You're welcome."

"At five o'clock?"

I nod and return to my book.

As the officer prepares to disembark the tram, he turns to me and says, "You speak German quite well." Once he steps off the tram, he lifts his hand in a gesture of farewell and maintains eye contact with me until the tram is out of sight.

THUG LOVE
Garland

Sitting back I sighed and gently stroked my hard bulge as I watched the hot young thug slowly strip in front of me. The young guy, skin the color of fresh caramel, was already down to his boxers. They were already nicely tented. Lustfully licking my lips, I unzipped my pants and freed my hard dick, waiting in anticipation to see what the young brother was packin' in between his legs.

He looked right at me and teasingly ran his long braids over his smooth chest and nipples. Turning around, he slowly lowered his boxers revealing his smooth, round bubble ass. It was tight and totally fuckable. I wanted it.

Turning around, I gasped and nearly came. His dick was huge! A large uncut chocolate monster, it pulsated lightly against his navel. His balls were smooth and the biggest set of low hangers I had ever seen. My God! I wanted to drain them.

"Oh yeah," I smiled slightly, rubbing my hard dick in sync with him. I had no clue what his name was and that was fine by me.

"DeLaneo," my boss' voice startled me, making me jump. Quickly I stuffed my dick back in my pants and exited out of the porn site.

"Yes, Mr. Harris?" I asked working hard to keep the guilt out of my voice. This was the fifth time he had almost caught me with my pants down since I started working at the company. I knew it was stupid to look at porn and jerk-off at work, but the fear of getting caught was something I had always thrived on. I loved public fun.

"Come on out here," Mr. Harris said. "There's someone I want to introduce you to."

"Yes sir," I said, grateful that my hard-on had deflated.

"This is a very exciting day for our little record label," Mr. Harris exclaimed smiling wide and showing off his perfect ivory colored teeth. Putting his large mocha colored hand on my shoulder he squeezed it tight. "We've signed someone who could give us the clout to compete with the big boys. The artist we signed has the power to make Hood Records a household name." He was growing more and more excited as he talked.

"Who did you sign?" I asked. "Kanye West?"

"Please," Mr. Harris scoffed.

"Did you finally convince Beyonce to sign with us, Mr. Harris?" I teased. He had been trying to get Beyonce since "The Single Ladies" video had come out. So far the powerful diva had not returned his calls.

"You think you're pretty cute don't you, DeLaneo?" He asked.

"Well I do get my fair share of compliments on my 'fro," I chuckled lightly patting my camel colored hair.

Mr. Harris rolled his eyes and laughed. "That's why I like you DeLaneo. You've got a good sense of humor. That's one thing this town is missing. A sense of humor."

"Yes sir," I answered with a discreet eye roll. Mr. Harris believed all the world's problems could be solved if people had a better sense of humor. "So when do I get to meet the new member of the Hood family?" My curiosity had gotten the better of me.

"Right now," Mr. Harris said leading me into his office.

I couldn't believe who stood before me. King. King was a hot, and I do mean hot, young rapper from Harlem. His lyrics boasted how he was a former OG, had been in and out of jail and the object of every woman's lust and desire. And let me tell you I had done my fair share of lusting after him.

King was tall. Well over six feet. His body rippled with those large muscles you only get in prison and on those glorious prison muscles were dozens and dozens of prison tats. His hair was styled in corn rows and he oozed danger. I had always been drawn to bad boys. And straight boys.

"DeLaneo, this is King," Mr. Harris said. His voice was filled with awe. You'd have thought he was introducing me to God himself. "King, this is DeLaneo. He's one of the best agents we have in the company. He'll be working with you on your debut album and video."

"Nice to meet you," I smiled extending my hand.

King didn't take it. He just stared at me.

"You're young," King finally spoke. I slowly lowered my hand. Uh-oh. This was what I feared. When most of the clients met me, they usually had something to say about my age. "He's young," King repeated facing Mr. Harris.

"DeLaneo may be young, but he's been in this business a long time. His mother was a very famous jazz singer, and his father was an actor. DeLaneo even had a singing career for a while before he became an agent. He's got a business savvy you can't teach. He'll make you millions."

"He's young," was all King said.

"I'm not that young," I spoke up. I hated when clients looked at me and only saw a young boy and not an experienced business man.

"How old are you?" King demanded, sizing me up. "Eighteen? Nineteen? Can you at least order a drink and not use a fake ID?"

"Listen asshole," I responded firmly not caring who he was. "I'm older than I look. Twenty-six. How old are you?"

"Twenty-seven," he responded after a few beats. "I'm sorry. You look younger."

"It's okay," I said. "I'm sorry I called you an asshole. I'm just kinda sensitive about my age."

"Well, no harm. No foul," Mr. Harris said smiling. "I just know you two are gonna be great friends. Welcome to our family, King. I just know you're going to be very happy. DeLaneo, I want you two to get to work right away on King's debut video. *Thug Love*. It's gonna be big. I just know you can put together something that could bring home a

VMA award. I'm seeing lots of girls in skimpy outfits, booty shaking, King shirtless and lots of bling," Mr. Harris spoke eyes wide. I could already tell he was spending all the millions of dollars he hoped the rapper would bring him.

"Yes, Mr. Harris," I said. "We won't let you down. Come on, let's go into my office and talk," I said finding myself getting lost in King's deep brown eyes. He was even hotter in person. It was hard to keep myself from getting hard.

"Okay," I said closing the door of my office. "So let's talk about *Thug Love*."

"Yes let's," King said with a smile. Sitting down in a chair he spread his legs. It was hard not to look at his crotch.

"I … I think Mr. Harris had a good idea. Lots of bling. Flashy cars. Beautiful girls with hardly anything on, and we definitely need you shirtless."

"Oh yeah?" He asked eyebrows rising with amusement.

"That's how we're gonna get the female fans," I said mouth suddenly tasting like cotton.

King laughed. "So all I gotta do is take my shirt off," rising he removed his shirt, and I gasped, "and all the female fans will watch my video?"

"All the gay ones, too," I responded before I could stop myself.

I immediately wished I hadn't said that, but I couldn't believe I was actually staring at his bare chest! My dick was instantly hard, straining against my pants. My eyes greedily drank him in. His skin was a rich dark chocolate. He was completely smooth and had the biggest arms and pecs I had ever seen. Every last inch of his body was decorated in various designs. I wondered what it would feel like to run my tongue over his tattoos and then come on them. His nipples were hard and an even darker mocha color. I don't know how I resisted going up to him and sucking on them.

King laughed. "You okay?"

"Yeah. Yeah. Fine," I stammered quickly. "Just thinking about the video."

"You always get hard when you think about your client's videos?" He asked snickering and staring right at my bulge.

"Um ... Well ... I ..." Quickly I moved behind my desk. I could feel my face burn with a bright magenta. I couldn't believe I was acting so unprofessional. I had never been star struck before. What was wrong with me?

"Hey it's okay," he chuckled. "I'm flattered. You're pretty cute yourself," he said winking.

"E ... Excuse me?" I asked sure I had heard him wrong.

"I said, I think you're pretty cute."

"You ..." I began with a quizzical look.

"Yeah," he nodded with an amused smirk. "I like dick."

I was shocked. I couldn't believe he had just said that. This had to be some kind of weird dream. I was certain I would wake up any moment in my bed.

"But you're King. Your lyrics ..."

"Are just a way to get money," he finished my sentence for me. "DeLaneo, if you're as business savvy as Harris said then you know as well as I do that there ain't no money in Homo Hop."

I was silent for what felt like eons. I couldn't believe it. King. One of the toughest, manliest rappers we had was gay? This had to be some kind of cosmic April Fool's Day joke.

"Are you okay?" He asked.

"Yeah. Yeah," I said quickly shaking the cobwebs out of my head. "I'm just ... a little shocked. Usually my gaydar is spot on, and it didn't even beep when I met you."

King laughed. "Most people can't tell."

"Well in this business that's a good thing. Unfortunately."

"You're telling me," he said with a laugh. "So are you one of my gay fans?" He asked teasingly stroking his chest.

Rolling my eyes, I laughed silently. This guy was a huge flirt, and he was totally turning me on. I still couldn't believe this was real. Nothing like this had ever happened to me. I felt like I had fallen into the trashy erotica I loved.

"Actually ... yes," I finally said with a smile. "I'm one of your gay fans."

"Good."

He smiled, and I had to look away as I giggled embarrassed.

King was my focus the following weeks. The other agents at the label took over my other clients. Mr. Harris was confident *Thug Love* would put us on the map and show Hollywood that we were a force to be reckoned with. This meant lots of long days and one on one meetings with King as we went over every aspect of his video, album promotion and tour. Not that I minded. I really liked him. He was smart and career driven. He had a lot of interesting ideas about the video to make it stand out and was willing to take constructive criticism. He wasn't like some of the arrogant clients I had to deal with who were just in the music business to get rich and laid. He really liked performing and wanted to be the best.

"Oh my God. It's already ten o'clock," I said one Friday night after everyone else had left the office. "I'm sorry I didn't realize it was that late. I should let you go. We can continue this on Monday."

"I hate to stop," King said smiling. "We make a pretty good team. This is gonna be a dope music video."

"Yeah it is," I agreed. "Probably the best one we've ever put out. I think *Thug Love* could definitely take home a ton of awards at the VMAs."

"That would be tight. My first music video winning awards."

"You never know in this business."

We were silent and just smiled at each other for several minutes. Finally, we laughed.

"Well, I'll see you Monday," I finally said tearing my gaze from his and packing up some papers. "Have a good weekend King."

"Hey DeLaneo," King said walking toward me.

"Yeah?"

Not saying anything King wrapped his arms around my waist drew me close to his body and kissed me fully on the lips. His full lips were moist and juicy against mine. They tasted better than I imagined.

"Thank you. For everything," he said before kissing me again.

Sighing, I felt my knees buckle, and I had to clutch his broad shoulders to keep from falling. My own instincts took over, and I kissed him back with a fire I didn't even know I had.

"You're a great kisser," he said running his fingers through my 'fro.

"So are you," I answered, voice barely a whisper. My heart was racing and my stomach knotted with excited anticipation. I had never done anything with a client before. "Take your shirt off," I whispered, surprising myself as I kissed King's neck.

Winking, King removed his shirt. Slowly I ran my hands over his hard pecs. His flat stomach gently quivered when the tips of my fingers made contact with his sensitive flesh. Slowly, I licked his tattoos before biting his nipple and pulling it between my teeth.

"DeLaneo," he moaned, wrapping his arms around me and squeezing me tight, taking my breath away. "Take your clothes off," he said. "I want to see your body. Strip for me."

Grinning, he turned on *Thug Love*. Laughing I let the beat fill my body and began to move my body to the music. Slowly, I raised my shirt giving him just a peek of my caramel colored stomach. Removing the shirt, I carelessly threw it behind me as I flirtatiously tugged on my nipples until they were hard.

Baby, let me take you away

Want to give you a ghetto lay

Feel our bodies move together

Like two street doves

Come on baby

Give in

To our thug love

Turning my back, I unzipped my pants and lowered them. Bending down, I gave him a great view of my ass. Looking over my shoulder, I winked at him and slowly ran my middle finger over my crack before sticking it in my hole. I slowly finger fucked myself as King removed his baggy sweat pants and played with his long thick cock. Removing my finger, I slowly licked it.

"I bet your ass tastes amazing," King said.

"Why don't you come over here and find out," I suggested, adding extra emphasis to the fourth word.

King nearly tripped over his long legs as he rushed over to me. He buried his face so far up my ass, I had to brace myself against my desk. Closing my eyes, I moaned as his tongue greedily lapped at my eager hole. Spitting on my hole, he stuck his finger inside me and vigorously finger fucked me. I'm amazed I didn't come.

"You like that?" He asked.

"Mmmm ..." Was all I could groan out.

Removing his finger, he ate my ass like a starving man. He was moaning and smacking my cheeks. His hand clutched my dick and was furiously jerking me off.

"You're ass does taste amazing," he said kissing me. I loved tasting myself mixed in with his lips. "Suck my dick," he begged.

Getting on my hands and knees, I opened my mouth as wide as it would go and greedily swallowed him. I was amazed I was able to deep throat him. Guess that's one of the benefits of not having a gag reflex. Moaning, I sucked his dick to the hip hop beat as I squeezed his full heavy balls.

Cupping my face in his hands, he thrust his hips in and out of my mouth. I could feel the tip of his dick tickle my tonsils as his salty-sweet precum seeped into my taste buds.

"I want to fuck you," he moaned.

Lying on my back, I placed my ankles on his shoulders. King gently massaged my calves and kissed my toes making me giggle. I had always had super sensitive feet.

He was rubbing his dick, still slippery and glistening with my spit, against my hole. It wasn't long before my hole opened to him like a blossoming rose, and he easily slid his dick inside me.

Sighing, I closed my eyes and savored the feeling of his dick stretching out my ass. I must confess I was shocked I was able to take all of him. I hadn't bottom in months, and King's was the longest cock I had ever taken.

"DeLaneo," he moaned, kissing my neck.

Slowly he began to move his hips back and forth. Before long, he had found his rhythm and was giving me the fucking of my life. My hands were on his chest, tugging on his nipples. King was kissing me and stroking my 'fro as he moaned out my name.

My toes curled, and my eyes rolled back in my head as the orgasm of my life overtook me. I almost passed out; it was so intense. My stomach tightened, and my dick throbbed as load after load of my hot cum shot out of my dick, staining King's tats.

"Oh yeah," he moaned. "That cum feels so good on my chest."

My milky white cum contrasted beautifully with his rich dark skin. A few drops dripped into my navel.

It wasn't long before I felt his own dick throb inside me, and his own cum filled my ass to overflowing. He shot inside me with a low satisfied grunt.

"Oh fuck," he moaned with contentment collapsing on top of me.

He was still rock hard and balls deep inside me as we kissed, smearing my cum into our skin like it was fine oil.

Pulling out of me, we lay next to each other, enjoying the afterglow of what had happened.

"That was great," King breathed out fingers gently massaging my shoulders.

"Yeah. It was," I agreed.

"You ever fucked one of your clients?" He asked.

"No. Never."

"Can't say that anymore, DeLaneo," he laughed.

Smirking, I kissed him, grateful King was a member of Hood Records. I had a feeling me and him were going to have a lot more late night meetings ...

ABOUT
THE AUTHORS

AIDEN LOVELY is a freelance writer. Lovely is also a member of the LG Writing Group. He was born in New Hampshire and dreams of moving to France.

DERRICK DELLA GIORGIA was born in Italy and currently lives between Manhattan and Rome. His work has been published in several anthologies and literary magazines. www.derrickdellagiorgia.com.

DON MIKA is a seasoned writer, who loves to write erotic stories. He resides in North Carolina, where he is currently earning his masters degree. He enjoys feedback from readers, and can be reached at Little_big_mann@yahoo.com.

DONALD WEBB was born in South Africa and currently lives in Victoria, BC. His work has been published in several magazines. He is currently seeking an agent for a completed 74,000word mystery novel. andon402@shaw.ca.

EVAN GILBERT, Southerner-born-and-bred, writes professionally for a major international corporation. In his free time, he writes gay fiction, which is a lot more fun.

GARLAND is a fulltime actor and writer living in Hollywood, California. He is also an accomplished break dancer. Garland is currently working on several novels as well as developing two erotic TV series. www.garlandserotictales.webs.com.

HL CHAMPA has stories published in numerous anthologies. www.heidichampa.blogspot.com.

Published in dozens of gay erotic anthologies, **JAY STARRE** pumps out fiction from his home in Vancouver, Canada. His steamy gay historical novels were also published by STARbooks Press.

LANDON DIXON's writing credits include numerous short stories in dozens of anthologies.

LOGAN ZACHARY is an author of mysteries, short stories, and over forty erotica stories, living in Minneapolis, with his partner, Paul, and his dog, Ripley, who runs the house. www.loganzacharydicklit.com; loganzachary2002@yahoo.com.

MARK JAMES is a writer of gay erotica with several published short stories. www.asstr.org/~Shadowlands.

MICHAEL MANDRAKE is the author of six short published works. www.tabooindeed.blogspot.com.

MILTON STERN is an author of biographies, novels, screenplays, and dozens of short stories, living in Maryland with Esmeralda, his rescue beagle. www.miltonstern.com.

R. TALENT is the bastard seed that STARbooks Press thought they wiped away on the cum towel. He is still driving his big-rig, still playing poker, and still working on his novel.

ROSCOE HUDSON is a creative writer and academic. A prolific author of fiction and poetry, his work investigates the juncture between race, masculinity, class and sex. He counts James Baldwin, Samuel Delany, Toni Morrison, Henry Miller, Anais Nin and Jeff Mann among his influences. He lives in Chicago.

SHANE ALLISON is a prolific editor and writer, who has been published in several anthologies and collections.

ABOUT THE EDITOR

MARCUS ANTHONY resides in Newport News, Virginia, where he works part-time as a personal trainer and bouncer. This is his first anthology for STARbooks Press.

www.ingramcontent.com/pod-product-compliance
Lightning Source LLC
Chambersburg PA
CBHW051633260626
47170CB00004B/1156